PROCLIVITY

PROCLIVITY

*The Lamiaceae Chronicles –
The First Clue*

A Novel

By

Kris Kaiser

ISBN: 0692218998

ISBN 13: 9780692218990

Library of Congress Control Number: 2014908926

Birchbark Publications, Walnut Creek, CA

For Shari, my beloved wife,
who has heard it all before yet
remains by my side.

***

With additional thanks to:
Neil Irish
Arseen Soliman, MD
Brian Black
Michelle Kaiser

1

DAY 143 – Memphis, TN

"Just passed Graceland."

"Never been. You?"

"Shut up! Both of you!" Twig barked from the driver's seat.

"Just sayin. Maybe after?"

"Only a half-click from the target, sir."

"Enough!"

Twig turned the van from Elvis Presley Boulevard onto a leafy side street in the high-end neighborhood.

"Get on point! Sixty seconds!"

There wasn't time for idle banter from his team of six Navy Seals crammed into the small U.S. Postal Service van. This was a mission, not a vacation.

The camouflaged Seal team refocused, checking their weapons in the tight quarters, as Twig slowed the van to a crawl. He scanned the sun-drenched sidewalks for residents walking their dogs, jogging, or simply watching and wondering why his little postal truck wasn't stopping at any mailboxes.

He turned the van through the open gates of a curved driveway that disappeared into the densely wooded grounds of a ten-acre estate.

"Here we go, boys."

In a clearing a brick mansion appeared, a row of thick, white columns across its facade. A driveway spur headed to a set of garages in the rear. He steered the van towards the house, the main driveway making a wide circle around a large fountain out front.

"Ten seconds," Twig said.

He stopped the van close to the steps leading down from the wide porch. Twig casually emerged from the van and straightened his Postal Service jacket. It didn't fit comfortably over the Kevlar vest protecting him.

He reached back inside the van and snatched a long florist's box off the floor. He locked eyes with his soldiers, and they nodded in unison. They all knew the plan and the mission's unique risks.

A midmorning assault in a residential neighborhood on home soil was rarely in play.

Twig carried the box up the steps towards the front door, consciously ignoring a security camera. When he was six paces from the door he lifted the lid from the box, drew out a laser-sighted handgun, and launched himself forward. His first heavy kick on the door splintered the frame. His second broke out the deadbolt and flung the door wide open.

The Seals sprang out of the back of the postal van, guns drawn, and split up. Four men joined Twig, flanking the front door. The other two ran at full speed around to the back of the estate.

Twig burst into the house, followed closely by his team. They set up a covering sweep of the large foyer as Twig found the alarm panel in the expected place. The display was blank. No small lights flickered indicating a silent alarm. When he flipped adjacent light switches for the foyer nothing happened. The house was dark. He checked the alarm panel again. No battery backup had kicked in to keep the alarm system running. It had been manually turned off.

A trap?

Twig gestured to his men to use hand signals only, no talking into headsets. The team methodically spread throughout the ground floor of the home, checking each well-appointed room. A familiar smell followed the men from room to room. They found the empty kitchen spotless, no dirty dishes left in the sink. Their ground-floor sweep encountered no resistance or the source of that smell.

The team carefully retreated to the foyer, and Twig started climbing the large curving staircase. His men followed behind, hugging the walls with their laser sights trained on the second- floor landing. They spread out at the top of the stairs and entered bedrooms, closets, and bathrooms. All were systematically checked and cleared. Nothing.

Twig led them back downstairs in search of the origin of that unpleasant smell. In the hallway by the kitchen, they arrived at a strange door. A number of odd rudimentary measures meant to keep the door locked from the outside had been added. He rotated the three deadbolt locks open and lifted various chains from their tracks. He slowly twisted the doorknob and opened the door, turning away briefly from the strong odor before staring into the blackness. He placed a small flashlight alongside the barrel of his gun as he started down the wooden stairs into the basement.

He heard water dripping. The air was damp. The men immediately behind him pulled out flashlights and sent beams searching the room. The light hitting the misty air obscured what appeared to be finished space. Twig reached the bottom step with a splash, disturbing eighteen inches of cool water covering the floor. He waved his team forward.

Work benches and wall cabinets filled the basement. Scuff marks left from rubber feet on the countertops showed where equipment had once sat. Sprinkler heads dripped water onto floating debris of paper, Styrofoam, and a few empty pill bottles.

A decommissioned lab of some sort.

"Sir! Left, ninety degrees!"

Twig sloshed over to find a Seal pointing his gun at a body face down in the water. An extended right arm on the corpse had three burnt fingers. One ankle was chained to a cast-iron drainpipe. A nearby cot floated on its side underneath the stairs.

He lifted the body's stiff shoulder with his foot. The water-logged face belonged to a man.

"Cut him loose and bag him up! Three minutes, max!" Twig ordered.

"Is it Sizemore?" the Seal asked.

Twig drew back his foot the body flopped into the water.

"Doubt it. Cheating death seems to be Sizemore's specialty."

2

DAY 137 – Swisher, IA

Matt Sizemore flicked his index finger against the butt of the handgun again, spinning it on the tabletop as Bob the cat stared at each revolution. He had never played any variation of Spin the Bottle with a housecat before. He wasn't even sure if the kitten was a boy or a girl.

Just before the revolver came to rest, Bob dropped his paw on the barrel, stopping it. The feline looked up at Matt as if waiting for him to twirl it again.

"Crazy cat," Matt mumbled through a yawn.

He spun the gun again and listened to the large trucks moving across the gravel parking lot outside. Headlights from the big rigs streamed through gaps in the miniblinds as they crunched their way past Matt's small motorhome.

"And remind me not to take your advice on parking spots any more."

Matt slid out of the dinette booth and stood on his sleeping bag that filled the compact floor area. He ran his fingers through his salt-and-pepper hair before bending forward, making a failed attempt to touch his toes. There was just enough room for such a maneuver in the stunted, narrow hallway of the small RV. Everything needed was right there with kitchen, dining room, and living room all rolled into one.

An extra-large dose of sleeping pills the night before still tugged at Matt's eyelids. He opened the tiny refrigerator, pulled out a can of Red Bull, and drained it. He plopped back down on the booth seat, rubbed his eyes, and tried to focus on the open three-ring binder on the table next to Bob and the spinning gun.

It was here somewhere, a clue or reason why he was drawn to this particular truck stop in Iowa, if only he could focus enough to find it. He flipped through pages of scribbled notes, each page recounting remembered pieces of unique recurring dreams--the same mishmash of visions and nightmares that continued to torment his sleep. He knew an event was about to happen nearby, maybe good, sometimes bad.

It had been his mistake at a weak moment, ordering antidepressant meds off a late night TV ad months before. The pills had opened his mind somehow, allowing a flood of broken visions to fill it each night, dreams he tried to capture on paper each morning. He constantly struggled to determine which of the remembered scenarios would present itself next.

One page contained a drawing of six men in a tavern sitting at a round table made from an old wagonwheel. They pushed papers around on a thick Lucite top with old matchcovers imbedded in it. Another page showed a woman spinning a lottery wheel on television. Still another had scratched notes about a canoe swinging back and forth, suspended from the ceiling of an antique shop. The binder recorded forty-odd pages of different descriptions from his dreams.

When Bob meowed loudly, Matt knew what that meant. The kitten wasn't begging for one more spin or to be fed or petted. It was TV. Matt reached for the remote on the booth seat and pushed a button. The small TV hanging from the ceiling above them sprang to life.

"All right, here you go."

Bob walked across the open binder, jumped up on to the back cushion of the booth, and stared up at the TV.

"Not sure what we'll get around here at six in the morning."

Bob watched intently as Matt rolled through channels of snow, finally landing on an infomercial that appeared entertaining enough. The cat glanced his way then quickly turned back to the TV--a silent thank you if there ever was one. Matt had enjoyed taking care of Bob ever since he'd picked up the little hitchhiker in Denver, but he knew it wouldn't last.

Matt opened the flimsy bathroom door and stepped inside, careful to avoid a makeshift litter box. He leaned in closer to the small mirror above the sink. He stroked the scruffy goatee meant as a crude disguise. It had grown in all white, making him look fiftyish and not in line with his thirty-seven actual years. His ex-wife got the credit for that. After he and Lisa had kids, the sprinkling of salt and pepper had spread like a nasty strain of crabgrass.

He yawned into the mirror, briefly fogging it up. He poked at the bags under his tired eyes and knew that this was how it was going to be until the running stopped, until revenge on those responsible was complete.

He stripped off his sweatpants and looked in the small closet stuffed with balled-up clothes for something to wear. He dug out a pair of wrinkled jeans and changed into them. Matt found a faded yellow t-shirt and covered it with a decent long-sleeved shirt that still bore vestiges of fold marks, a surprising sign that it had actually been put away neatly at some point in the past. He shook an old Chicago Cubs baseball cap back into shape before putting it on.

Matt lifted his dangling shirttail, exposing his stomach. He turned towards the cheap mirror glued to the inside of the bathroom door and jiggled what was left of his receding love handles. The fact that he had kept his relatively lean figure during these last few months was a mystery. With the police chasing him, all the greasy fast food, a lack of real sleep, staying thin just didn't make much sense. At least the stress was good for something.

He opened the outside door to check the weather, finding it colder than expected for early May. A frosty morning mist hung in the air. The truck stop hummed with activity now, with many slow-moving big rigs rumbling through the light fog.

There were bright blue and white lights at the truck-stop gas pumps, and a warm pink glow beyond that. Having driven in late the night before, Matt vaguely remembered a restaurant here somewhere, so that must be it. Nothing suspicious jumped out at him as he scanned what he could see of the parking lot. For once, it might be a safe bet to grab a wholesome breakfast out in public.

He closed the door and opened an upper kitchen cabinet, pulling out a set of spiral notebooks. They were the grade-school kind, with ruled lines and colorful covers.

Miley Cyrus's face adorned one with a white file-folder label stuck across her eyes. Scrawled on the label in black Magic Marker was **Day 56-81**. Another notebook labeled with a different set of days had the cartoon faces of Woody and Buzz from the Toy Story movies. He held up another one with the familiar bespectacled face of Harry Potter and studied it. The notebooks reminded him of the first time he'd bought school supplies with his kids on a hot August afternoon back in Austin.

Matt pulled a backpack out of the cabinet and set it upright on the booth seat. He shuffled through the notebooks and found one with Niagara Falls pictured on the cover, the white label referencing a **Day 131** start time. He placed it in the backpack.

He closed the large binder on the table in front of him. Over the beautiful Amazon rainforest picture on the front cover was a big yellow sticker with **DREAMS** written on it. He figured he would look through it at breakfast once he had some coffee coursing through his veins.

From a drawer by the kitchen sink he retrieved a few small glass bottles containing powders of various colors. Four in all, of differing sizes. He tapped each one with his finger to check how much substance was left and, satisfied, put them in a zippered pocket on the backpack.

He reached across the dinette table and grabbed the revolver. There was still some bluing on the muzzle, a leftover sign of light use from his father's desk job during a 1960s Chicago Police Department career. He examined the gun closely and remembered the numerous times as a child he had been told emphatically never to touch it. He smiled at the irony of how much he depended on it now. With a snap of his wrist, Matt flipped the cylinder open--fully loaded and ready to rock and roll. The easy way out would be using it on himself, but he wanted people to pay.

Matt glanced over at the TV. Bob paid no attention to his gunplay. He was lost in the world of infomercials, clearly transfixed by the variety of useless products available to the average human consumer.

Matt rolled the gun up in a ratty sweatshirt and jammed the completed package into the backpack. He tucked in his shirt and swung the strap over his shoulder.

At the door of the motorhome, he paused to study a mesmerized Bob. The infomercial pitched a type of cheap thigh-toning machine demonstrated by a curvaceous blonde model in tight shorts.

Bob was a he, all right.

3

DAY 76 – Rockville, MD

Kevin Sharpe followed the swaying floral dress as it weaved through the sea of color-coded cubicles on the fourth floor of the Food and Drug Administration complex in suburban Washington, D.C. The large blue-and-green flowers danced rhythmically as the young woman's swaying hips led Kevin through the big office. He enjoyed following the attractive movement, easily focused on it while ignoring the chaotic noises vibrating through the wide-open space.

He juggled a bulky cardboard box of personal items along with a heavy computer bag that kept slipping off his shoulder. It was a bad balancing act, slowly getting the best of him. He had to stop for a moment and readjust the load. Kevin reengaged the dress as it turned a corner, and he hurried to catch up.

Beads of sweat began to form on his brow, but he wasn't sure if it was from the box he struggled with or the interesting young blonde taking him on the circuitous route through the maze of cubes.

The floral dress suddenly stopped at an intersection. She turned around to face him and pointed down a row of gray-and-blue cubicles to the left. The blonde was just as enticing from the front.

"Third one down on the right, Mister Sharpe. Number thirteen-seventeen. I'll round up Doctor Kearns for you."

"Thank you. Miss?--"

"Blevins. Becky Blevins."

Becky swirled off in another direction. Kevin enjoyed watching Becky and her dress disappear and then, and only then, did he remind himself to stay focused on the task at hand, his first day at a new job. A job he needed.

Mixing female distractions and work had already caused him enough trouble, practically ruining his career, but it was a hard habit to break. The ladies did respond well to him, and he was never one to miss a decent opportunity.

Was it his fault that he bore a reasonable resemblance to Denzel Washington in his prime?

He took a deep breath and started to look for cubicle number 1317. Moving down the line, he glanced above the cubicle walls to survey the field, an easy task at 6'4". The office landscape overflowed with heads bobbing up and down while employees cruised through the narrow aisles between the banks of cubicles. The perimeter walls of the building were all glass with no enclosed offices to block the welcome sunlight from outside.

Kevin dodged a few people rushing by him in the aisle. A constant hum of conversations filled his ears, and telephones discharged a variety of annoying sounds. Colorful street-type signs hung by wires from the ceiling tiles and pointed in every direction to places unknown.

A short, quick-moving, white-haired man reading papers on the fly bumped directly into Kevin.

"You lost?" the man asked.

"Thirteen-seventeen?"

"Behind you," said the man, returning to his portfolio of papers before zooming on.

Kevin turned around to find the opening into the 8X8' cubicle and stepped inside. Not exactly confining, but it couldn't be considered roomy either. A rectangular desktop protruded from one wall. Two small armless chairs faced the desk. Add one large filing cabinet and a sizable faux-leather chair behind the desk, and that was all that could be reasonably crammed into 1317.

He unloaded the heavy box onto the desktop and put his computer bag on a chair. His undershirt was sticking to his chest. He removed his suit jacket and loosened his tie to get some air.

He sat at the desk and took stock of his new space. A small notepad next to the phone beckoned. He reached into his box and found a pen.

It was a new beginning at the FDA, but the accumulated mental baggage was hard to leave behind. He tapped the pen on the desk a few times, then remembered.

Kevin scribbled "Becky Blevins" on the notepad.

4

DAY 137 - Swisher, IA

Donna Engle smiled as she watched her youthful new side-kick, Nikki Cook, bounce around the diner with her coffeepot serving customers. Donna loved the retro place and the constant flow of people. It was home.

Maybelle's Diner and Truck Stop had turned into more than just a local landmark. Donna had been there from its scant beginnings to a place that was now a regional draw and regular stopping point for truckers navigating eastern Iowa. The diner itself had grown from a small vintage farmhouse into the current glass jewelbox of a building facing the Swisher exit off the I-380 south of Cedar Rapids. The truck stop and related services came along later, as did the mobile-home park on twenty acres in the back.

In the rear corner of the massive gravel parking lot there was even a truckers' church, housed in a retired Greyhound bus surrounded by weeds, with a 30-foot-tall white wooden cross jammed into the roof. A lightning rod had been banded to the top of the cross after the first two versions were consumed by the wrath of God. The big white cross, now with plenty of peeling paint, leaned quite a bit these days and was only marginally secured by wires.

Donna had even helped a few local bar rats write a rambling letter requesting that Swisher become the sister city of Pisa, Italy. Six months later, and in no uncertain terms, they were respectfully denied the affiliation.

Truckers loved Maybelle's. Good food from her original recipes, nice hot showers, and lots of parking. They only had one thing to put up with.

Pink, and lots of it.

Booths, walls, countertops, even light fixtures, all of it was pink. If pink were a smell, the place would reek of it.

On misty mornings Maybelle's glowed like a lighthouse alongside the interstate, a rose-colored beacon piercing the fog. The diner was mildly busy with the usual crowd, leaving enough time for the waitresses to congregate and come up with humorous names for the customers as they passed the time between rushes of activity. All the girls wore the designated uniform, unchanged for the last thirty years, pink-and-white dresses with multiple front pockets.

Nikki returned to Donna's side, and they watched in amazement as the brothers Funderburke devoured their massive omelets. The large twins looked like a tribute band for ZZ Top, and the two waitresses studied their surprising ability to avoid getting food on their sizable beards.

"I don't know how they do it," Donna said.

"Serious forkmanship for sure," Nikki offered.

"Not even a crumb hits the table."

"I'm way messier than that and look, no beard!"

Donna chuckled as she watched Nikki seemingly float down the counter line, stroking her slender chin with one hand and refilling coffee cups for counter patrons with the other. She was glad Nikki was happier now.

Donna had practically adopted Nikki when she turned up on a stormy night, soaking wet and on the run from a nasty relationship with a caveman named Travis Whitacre. She enjoyed mentoring Nikki as the elder-stateswoman at Maybelle's. Donna had made room in her trailer behind the diner for Nikki, and they got along famously from the start despite the age difference. Donna hoped Nikki's plan to make it home, back to her sister in Indiana and the rest of the dysfunctional family she'd left at seventeen, would fade and she would stay.

It wasn't much of a plan, and a few weeks easily turned into months, which was fine with Donna. She liked Nikki and taught her the ropes of working at Maybelle's so she could earn enough to some day make the trip home. That had been nine months ago.

Donna watched Nikki do a lap around the diner. She really took to the Maybelle experience. Nikki even colored her jet-black shoulder-length hair with hot-pink highlights. The streaks of color complemented her pink fingernails, the small flowery tattoos circling each wrist, and the few gold piercings on her eyebrows and earlobes.

Donna surveyed the diner looking for any dishes to clear. At the end of the counter, Nikki leaned on her elbows while talking to a well-dressed businessman. Donna wasn't happy that Nikki occasionally latched onto attractive and seemingly well-to-do male customers who might benefit her in one form or another. She worried that someday Nikki would find that perfect ride and leave abruptly, just as her own daughter had left home many years before.

This particular guy seemed to fit the bill, Donna thought. Reasonably attractive, muscular, and passing through in nice wheels were the minimum requirements. He had on an expensive-looking long overcoat, black dress shoes, and a lavender button-down shirt. She could tell he was tall, because his feet easily touched the floor from his perch on the swivel-top stool. Most everyone else needed to use the brass foot rail running underneath the counter rather than let their feet dangle free.

And he was obviously not from around Swisher. He had a nice even tan. Most locals still hadn't lost their sickly white skin tone carried over from the lengthy Midwestern winter. Donna wondered if he hailed from Florida, or maybe the more mystical Greek Isles.

Donna had nicknamed the tall man Sitting Bull, for he was already perched at the counter when she and Nikki had come on shift at 5 a.m. At least Sitting Bull seemed rather cool to Nikki's effusive personality, and that helped Donna relax a little.

There were other locals and truckers scattered about the diner, including Father Frank from the truckers' church. His rig had broken down at Maybelle's twelve years before, and the mobile-home park became his home base for both trucking and evangelical operations.

Lance was a rotund trucker, all of 5'6" and 300 pounds. He ran transcontinental mail for the postal service and always stopped at Maybelle's. Alone in a booth, Lance sat knitting a bright red-and-white scarf for a Nebraska Cornhusker fan, his chubby fingers moving faster than seemed possible.

Through the big windows, Donna could barely see a figure emerging from a mini-motorhome in a corner of the parking lot. A passing truck's headlights spotlighted the man as he crossed the gravel lot towards the diner, his white goatee reflecting more light than the rest of him. He looked like the scruffy director of a Hollywood movie, shuffling along with his head down, his salty hair just sneaking out from under a baseball cap.

Donna snapped her fingers at Nikki, drawing her attention from Sitting Bull. Nikki looked over for a millisecond and then completed her interview of Sitting Bull. She replaced her empty coffeepot with a fresh one on the way down the counter to Donna.

"What's Sitting Bull's story?" Donna asked.

"Still says he's waiting for a friend."

"Some friend. Been a couple hours, I'd have left by now."

"Seems nice enough, but not much of a talker. Foreign accent of some sort. Good teeth, though."

Nikki yelped as she dodged a swat to the shoulder from Donna.

***

Matt pushed his way through the vestibule doors and shielded his tired eyes from the onslaught of pink.

"Jesus Christ!" he blurted, louder than intended.

"Amen, brother!" Father Frank saluted through a mouthful of eggs, his empty fork pointed towards Heaven.

Matt ignored both the comment and the sign standing in front of him requesting that he wait to be seated. He blindly wobbled over to a large round booth in the front corner of the jewelbox, the best vantage point for viewing the comings and goings around Maybelle's.

Matt slid his backpack in first and pushed it along the pink Naugahyde seat. He climbed in, put his elbows on the table, and pulled the brim of his cap down over his eyes.

Donna finished dropping off the Funderburkes' check and watched as Sitting Bull looked up from his coffee to examine the new arrival in the baseball cap, observing the man's movements via a wall mirror behind the cash register. She approached Nikki as she rang up a customer.

"Maybe he's the one," Donna whispered.

"Who?"

"The one Sitting Bull is waiting for."

Nikki took a quick look but flubbed counting out the change and had to start over.

"Damnit!"

Donna watched Sitting Bull slowly take a sip of coffee and study the new customer, cocking his head ever so slightly to modify the angle of his view in the mirror.

"He seems interested in the guy."

She watched Sitting Bull follow the man's movements in the corner booth with keen interest. Sitting Bull watched the movie director sit up straight and flex his arms towards the ceiling. Once the stretching ended, the man pulled his backpack closer and unzipped the top, reached inside, and retrieved a notebook. He then opened a side pocket and set out four small bottles on the table in a tidy row. Donna thought Sitting Bull stiffened after getting a full view of the man's face. Maybe this really was the person he'd been waiting for.

Sitting Bull pulled a cellphone off his belt with his free hand. Donna saw him hold it under the counter, mostly out of view, as he scrolled though messages and frequently glanced up to keep one eye on the man.

Nikki exchanged her coffeepot for a full one and glimpsed the movie director in the corner booth putting his head down on the table.

"Not a match in my book," Nikki said.

Donna nodded towards Sitting Bull.

"I thought maybe, but guess not. Look."

Sitting Bull calmly stood up, dug a money clip out of his pocket, and placed cash on the counter. He drained the last of the coffee and turned towards the diner's entrance. He purposefully walked a route near the movie director's booth, scanning the table as he made his way towards the exit. Nikki cut in front him on her way to the new customer.

"I can ring--"

Sitting Bull interrupted her.

"No need. Left twenty on counter."

"For coffee?"

"And the company," he said with a smile.

A confused Nikki smiled back, but the fleeting moment of joy faded fast. She realized this big fish was getting away. There was one last chance.

"What do I tell your friend if he shows?"

"Make up a story. How you say--a fabulous story."

Sitting Bull winked at Nikki, turned, and pushed the vestibule door open. Nikki stood speechless as her eyes could only follow him as he disappeared into the misty parking lot.

***

It's her, all right. No doubt about it. The binoculars didn't lie. Travis Whitacre leaned forward on the steering wheel as the headlights of his big Kenworth truck lit up the diner. Nikki stood at the door coffeepot in hand, talking to a well-dressed man in an overcoat. Her familiar figure still made a quality statement from underneath the ugly dress. The hair was different somehow, but he had no doubt it was her. Travis took a deep relaxing breath, thankful that he had finally caught up with her.

He hoped Nikki didn't know about her sister Jill in Indiana. Repeatedly beating the woman had been the only way to extract the truth about where to find Nikki. He'd have to fabricate a story to tell her if she didn't already know.

He leaned back in the driver's seat. He imagined pulling Nikki close to him again, smelling her hair and feeling the touch of her skin, whether she wanted him to or not.

Travis sat up and rolled his rig forward, slowly passing the front door as the man in the overcoat walked out of the diner and put a cellphone to his ear. He walked right by Travis's truck as Nikki intently watched the man leave. She seemed a little too interested in this guy.

The blood in Travis's veins began to boil, and he started to strangle the steering wheel, all the while with his eyes fixed on the well-dressed man walking across the lot.

Smart guy. You just keep moving.

Travis pushed the accelerator and circled the parking lot, ultimately finding a very nice slot between two big rigs facing the sizable windows of Maybelle's.

The perfect place to watch his prey for a while.

5

DAY 137 – Ozark Mountains, AR

Knee-high water rushed by, between, and around the heavyset fisherman's dark-green rubber waders. The swift current was not enough to bother the rotund man as he cast his fly towards a nice-looking eddy pool at the opposite bank of the river.

Ashes dropping from the big man's cigar quickly disappeared in the clear water. The fisherman hoped to land a few sizeable brown trout before noon and put them on ice for dinner before calling the office. There was ample time to prepare a fine meal for his important guest. He hoped the visiting chairman would enjoy fresh Arkansas trout pulled from crystal-clear Ozark mountain waters.

The fisherman's calls to the chairman had not been returned at first, but after he bluntly emphasized the urgency of the matter, the chairman had finally agreed to a meeting. He hoped the special menu would take the edge off the disquieting news he had to share. And if the meeting went very wrong, at least he was on his home turf.

The big man's cellphone rang, disturbing the soothing sounds of the river. The fisherman smiled at the classic 1960s ringtone of "Secret Agent Man" by Johnny Rivers.

It was a call he had to take from his hired gun, a seasoned Croatian mercenary named Sam Asrani.

He pulled open the Velcro tab on his shirt pocket, pulled out the phone, and looked at the screen. He poked the answer button with a fat thumb momentarily freed from gripping the fishing rod.

"So?" he inquired around the slobber of the big cigar.

"It's him," Sam said matter-of-factly.

"You sure this time?"

"Yes. Had closer look."

The fisherman grinned at the answer, looked to the sky, and pulled a long drag on the cigar. This was very good news.

"How is he?"

"Burned out, as you say. Not healthy. Bring him in?"

"No, no, not yet. I can't afford to have him kill himself like the rest of them."

"You not pay me enough to stay chasing this guy cross country."

"Don't worry about the money. There's plenty more if you can find out how he's doing it."

"He got vials with him. Little bottles. Powders of some kind."

"Interesting," the fisherman said looking down at the water. "Must be ingesting a compound."

"He look tired, maybe dead soon. Sure you don't want me grab him now and take to Amanda?"

The fisherman cringed as a nice looking trout casually weaved its way between his legs and headed upriver behind him.

"No, damnit, just stick with him and see if you can find out exactly what he's doing. Keep him alive at all costs. You've received the device?"

"Yeah, going on his vehicle as soon as we done here."

"Then we're done."

The fisherman hung up and quickly dropped the cell-phone back in his breast pocket. He reeled in his lure and turned upriver to follow that bold trout. Dinner wouldn't be as bad as he'd imagined.

The chairman would be encouraged by the news that the last one was still alive.

6

DAY 76 – Rockville, MD

Doctor Wade Kearns leaned on his cane in the opening of 1317 and tapped on the metal cubicle frame just as Kevin reluctantly crumpled the note with Becky's name on it into a tight ball.

"Settling in already, I see."

"It's a new day, right?"

Kevin calmly arched a perfect toss into a corner waste-basket. Wade hobbled in and shook Kevin's hand.

"Good to see you, Sharpe."

"Glad to be here, sir."

"I would imagine so."

Kevin was happy to see his former FBI instructor still wearing one of his signature Disney bowties decorated with miniature Mickey Mouse figures all tumbling about. The solid-white temples stood out as they always had, but the gray had moved aggressively into the uncharted terri-tory on the crown of his head.

The lack of direct eye contact spoke volumes about Wade's unease, but Kevin was grateful for the opportunity nonetheless and hoped to prove himself again. He knew Wade was taking a big risk after what had happened during his stint at the FBI, and there would be repercussions if this new job didn't work out.

"I hope this is okay for now. I'll try to land a better spot for you if I can," Wade said.

"No problem. This is fine as long as there's a bathroom within a half-hour walk."

Wade smiled at Kevin's accurate assessment and loosened up. He patted Kevin on the shoulder.

"For you, it might take ten minutes, one way. I've got the longer commute with this hip."

"I believe it. Not getting any better, eh?"

"Nope. I've given up on it. Starting the countdown to surgery. I'm thankful to have one of those motorized chairs in my office for long trips around the campus. Only run over a few folks so far."

"Here, Wade, let's get you off that thing."

Kevin moved one of the chairs out of the way for his friend and then sat behind his new desk. Wade slowly worked himself into position to sit. He lowered himself into the chair with a heavy sigh before smiling at his former student.

"Thanks again for bringing me over from Langley. I won't let you down," Kevin said, "What happened over there won't happen again."

"I'm counting on that. I'm a bit out on a limb here."

"I know."

"The press sure raked you over the coals, so it took some doing internally. Anyway, if this works out, you'll probably end up helping me a lot more than vice-versa."

"That bad?"

"The situation here--it's even worse than we discussed on the phone. My staff is just slammed with all the salmonella outbreaks, product recalls, and shoddy food-manufacturing issues to follow up on. Too many companies are cutting corners to stay alive, given the economy, and it has created havoc around here. Not enough bodies to investigate all the crap going on out there. On top of that, the director keeps reassigning my agents to whatever hot case gets the most negative press."

"Sounds like a perfect storm."

"I could go on and on. Meanwhile, the pile of files on my office floor covering counterfeit prescription drug cases just keeps growing. That's where I need your help."

Kevin remembered the first time he'd met Wade, when he was guest lecturer at the FBI training center in Georgia. Wade had admired his ability to analyze large data sets and pull out the relevant information important to a case. Unlike Wade's other students, Kevin didn't get bogged down in massive amounts of data.

They had largely kept in touch over recent years, and Kevin always wondered if they would work together at some point. He just wished the circumstances in joining Wade at the FDA's Office of Criminal Investigations had been better.

"I'm up for it, Wade. Keeps me off the streets. When do we start?"

Wade struggled to his feet.

"Get yourself organized here, and let Becky know if you need anything. I'm down in thirteen fifty-one. Come down when you're ready, and I'll give you the lay of the land. And then we'll grab some lunch."

"I'm buying, so don't get any crazy ideas," Kevin said.

"No surf and turf?"

"Not at my new pay grade."

Wade stopped at the doorway and clung to the cubicle frame for support. He raised his cane, pointing it towards the window line at the end of the row of cubes.

"Go down to the end here, turn left, and I'm the fifth one on the right."

Kevin instinctively raised his hand to his former teacher and cleared his throat. The sound stopped Wade just as he started to limp down the aisle. Wade turned and acknowledged the raised hand with a nod.

"Yes, Mister Sharpe?" Wade asked in feigned seriousness.

Kevin lowered his hand and squeezed his knees together.

"Exactly where are the restrooms?"

7

DAY 137 - Swisher, IA

Matt dozed at the corner booth with his forehead laid over crossed arms on the open notebook. Pen still in hand, he had managed to only write **Day 137** at the top of a fresh page. His sluggish mind tried to recall any specific dreams from the night before. His eyes occasionally flickered open, and he tried to process the small 1950s pattern of pink and brown squares on the laminate tabletop touching the end of his nose.

With no warning, a flirtatious female voice broke his limited concentration.

"Can I buy ya a drink, mister?"

Nikki stood over him, offering the coffeepot in one hand, her free hand firmly fixed on her hip. He had been propositioned a few times before, but not this early in the morning. Without lifting his head Matt raised a wavering finger and coughed to clear some sticky phlegm before answering.

"Coffee. Strong."

Nikki rolled her eyes and swished her pot around.

"I was joking, dummy."

Dummy?

Curious about the source of the interruption, he pushed himself upright and rubbed his eyes. Nikki filled his empty coffee cup.

"You looked kinda drunk when you came in. It was funny to watch."

"That so?"

Matt attempted to focus on the waitress. She quickly slid into the booth seat across from him and jumped right into her expert analysis.

"Too much partying, eh? I tell the guys to stay out of Mike's Roadhouse, that place is plenty wild. They play the music way too loud in there for me, and believe me, I like it loud. Did you think it was too much? I bet the bartenders there are getting hard of hearing, so they just keep turning it up and up and up!"

"Christ! Talk fast enough?"

Matt reached for his coffee, slid it closer, and dumped a couple of sugar packets into the cup.

"Just wondering if that's where you got drunk last night."

"I didn't get—"

"Hope it wasn't Smelly McCool's, that place is a real dive. Only trouble comes out of a night spent at that place. Don't ask me how I know."

Matt drained the coffee and enjoyed the warm burn in his throat followed by the sugary finish. He put the cup down, and she quickly refilled it.

Nikki sat back and crossed her arms, content that she was on the right track. A wide smile spread across her face.

The smile was the best part of her, Matt thought. He wasn't a fan of the eyebrow piercings and the flowery tattoos circling each wrist. She would be prettier without all that stuff. No way he'd let his daughter do that to herself. He fumbled for a couple more sugar packets.

"Listen, I've never been here before, I don't know those places, and I'm not hung over," he said in self-defense.

Nikki slowly leaned forward, her big brown eyes fixed on his bloodshot ones.

"Drugs?" she whispered.

All he wanted was a nice quiet breakfast, and now he was the one being grilled.

"It was a few too many sleeping pills, okay?"

"Mister, that's worse than drinking. Might even kill ya."

"It hasn't yet."

Nikki wondered what the deal was with this guy. He was a little bit of a mess, and she wondered if he had slept in his clothes. He certainly appeared to have major issues of some sort, the kind of stuff she should likely avoid. That had never stopped her before, but if her Travis experience was any guide, she needed to improve her decision-making skills where men were concerned.

She studied his bloodshot greenish-gray eyes. They glistened like small Christmas ornaments hanging from a worn-out tree.

Matt stared at her staring at him.

What's her problem?

She obviously worked here, and he wanted service. He waited another moment, then picked up his pen and pulled the notebook closer. She needed a push.

"Just tired AND hungry," he deadpanned.

Nikki continued to stare blankly at him.

Enough was enough, Matt thought. He'd snap her out of it.

"This place have a goddamn menu?" he growled.

It worked. Her blank stare turned sour, just as if she'd bit into a lemon.

"Yeah, sure."

Nikki climbed up onto her knees and twisted on the pink Naugahyde seat, deftly stretching over the seatback to snatch a leftover menu from the next booth. As she did, the soft contours of her young body were subtly on display. She turned back to Matt and before handing him the menu swiped it across the front of her dress, knocking off some crumbs but also smearing it with leftover raspberry jam. Nikki reluctantly handed the sticky menu to him.

"Sorry."

"Thanks. I think."

She gestured to the badge on her pink dress.

"Me Nikki, by the way."

Matt opened the big menu and buried his face inside, ignoring her invitation to respond in kind.

"Just gimme a minute."

Nikki shrugged at being cut off and climbed out of the booth. She twirled an index finger around her ear as she approached Donna.

"What's his name gonna be?" Donna asked.

"No-brainer. Got to be Chief Crazy Horse."

***

Travis easily followed Nikki's movements inside the diner with his binoculars. He'd never liked how open she was in talking to strangers, but he had benefited from meeting her in the same way. She wasn't the drop-dead, prettiest girl delivering drinks to gamblers at the big riverboat casino in Tunica, Mississippi, when they met a couple of years before, but she was terminally cute with a quirky personality to match.

He remembered how she hadn't been scared of him right out of the box. Travis knew his size intimidated women, and for that matter most men as well. They also didn't like his massive arms full of spidery tattoos with no seeming rhyme or reason to the actual design. Most people just stared, probably wondering about his sanity before simply moving out of his way.

Nikki had been different from the start. She treated him like any other regular Joe. Her attention made him feel normal, less like the loner outcast he'd become. A real relationship had been a new and welcome experience.

But over time he worried more and more that it would end, that she would leave. His specific thoughts on what she could and couldn't do hadn't gone over well with Nikki, and she hadn't taken too well to his brand of discipline--the kind of discipline where the back of a hand came first and apologies came later.

And now here she was talking with yet another guy in a booth at this funky diner and getting way too chummy for his liking.

***

Matt rearranged his bottles on the table in anticipation of his order of scrambled eggs, sausage, and toast. He opened one container and sprinkled some ground cinnamon into his coffee and stirred it in. As he watched the rust-colored powder disappear, he thought how ironic it was that what he'd learned from his ex-wife about herbal remedies was keeping him alive, even though at times in the past he was sure she had wished him ill will.

Lisa had been into it all, from aromatherapy to homeopathic cleansing. He blew it off at first as crap science, but much of it seemed to work for her. And now he was using that same knowledge to keep his own sanity.

Matt sipped the coffee and enjoyed the added flavor. He liked cinnamon. It was easily attainable and boosted his mental capacity every morning, helping him recover from downing sleeping pills the night before.

He looked around the diner, his eyes finally adjusting to the brightness. He felt good that he had leveled the playing field with the mixture of herbal medications. He could function, and that's all he needed right now. His little collection of compounds on the table was doing its job.

He watched the annoying young waitress as she picked up his order at the kitchen window and headed in his direction. He cleared the space in front of him, sliding the notebook to the side. She set the plate down and winked at him.

"So, it is drugs after all," Nikki said.

She picked up and rotated one of the bottles to see the label.

"Natural herbs, thank you very much," he said.

"Does this actually say wort?" she asked.

"St. John's Wort. Helps the mind."

"Really?"

"Yes. Please put that down."

Nikki complied but quickly lifted two others.

"I can understand cinnamon. I think I've heard that's good for you. Don't know what this one is."

"Astralagus from China. Immune-system booster."

"I bet that helps with hangovers."

"Let me have them back, please," Matt retorted.

Rebuffed, she slowly returned the bottles to the table.

"Just curious, mister."

As Nikki spun away to leave him her black hair flung wildly, revealing a small tattoo on the back of her neck just above the collar of her dress. It was the head of a snake, black and gray with bright yellow eyes, its tail ending somewhere further south.

In the flash of that split-second moment, the parting of the jet-black hair, the image of the snakehead above the white collar, twinkling shards of glass flying around her head, the visual of it all instantaneously washed through Matt's brain like an electrical tsunami sweeping over a beach. The small hairs on his arms and the back of his neck danced to attention. A quick jab of pain shot behind his right eye.

He had seen this very image in his fitful dreams many times, always accompanied by a distinct feeling of dread. Matt's body jerked in his seat, as if jolted by a live wire. He bumped the table, rattling the silverware and sloshing his coffee.

Nikki turned at the sound to face him. Matt stood up and pointed at her with a trembling finger. He tried to speak but couldn't draw a breath.

Not again!

Those two words coursed through his brain, then two words shot loudly out of his mouth.

"SHATTERED GLASS!"

His exclamation got everyone's attention in the diner.

"What?" asked a confused Nikki.

"THERE'S FLYING GLASS! ALL AROUND YOU!"

Donna dropped her hot coffeepot hard on the counter, just short of cracking it. Nikki turned away from him.

"You're crazy, mister."

"NO! I can show you!"

Matt started to get up then abruptly stopped and returned to his booth. Nikki flashed a dismissive wave and retreated towards Donna.

"No thanks," Nikki said.

Matt yanked the Amazon rainforest **DREAMS** binder out of his backpack and onto the table. He whipped the binder open and aggressively flipped through the pages.

"It's here! You need to see this! Your life might depend on it!"

Nikki stopped. He was frightening her, but somehow she couldn't overcome the pull of a moth drawn to a flame. She wanted to see. She had to see.

She took a step towards the booth then paused, looking back to Donna. Matt's searching stopped. He pounded his forefinger at the open page.

"Here! This is it! This is why I'm here!"

Donna waved Nikki off from moving closer, fear evident in her flailing arms. Nikki disobeyed and slowly shuffled towards the corner booth.

8

DAY 13 – Austin, TX

Matt teetered on the railroad bridge, his balance compromised by a severe lack of sleep and the thin rail underfoot. He grabbed the cold and rusty bridge rail for support. It was going to take some energy to scale the five-foot side of the graffiti-laden bridge high above the river.

He wiped his runny nose on the sleeve of his sweater, swung his leg up, and hooked one foot over the steel top of the side wall. One last shimmy and he arrived flat on his stomach, straddling the rusted edge of the iron bridge. Tired from the effort, he let his legs dangle loose on each side. He looked at his trembling hands, all red and scratched, then folded them under his head to get some rest for a moment.

The morning sun was rising above the horizon now, and the reflections off the downtown Austin office buildings began to warm one side of his body, even though he could still see his breath. Matt turned his head away and looked down at the slow-moving water sixty feet below.

He was here for a reason.

Christmas had not been kind to him. His kids had been scared of him when he tried to deliver a few poorly wrapped presents to the house. He saw it in their eyes, not happy to see him. He looked like death warmed over, complete with greasy hair and bags under his eyes. The kids didn't recognize their dad anymore and didn't understand what had happened. They had been through a lot too, he reminded himself. He wasn't the only one adjusting to a new situation.

As he peered down at the river fear suddenly flowed through his sluggish mind--fear that the fall might not be high enough to do the trick.

Would Lisa tell the kids he committed suicide, or would she make up some other story?

It seemed the only way out. Constant and intense nightmares battered his brain each night. He couldn't fall asleep without being immediately bombarded by unsettling visions and disturbing dreams. The inside of his eyelids became movie screens showing random clips of faceless people, sometimes doing horrible things. There were places he didn't recognize, situations he didn't understand. It was all driving him crazy, driving him to this--this bridge over the river. He was winding down, his ability to think clearly fading fast. Matt struggled to remember the past, the chronological sequence of events.

How had this all happened?

Two lousy weeks ago, he'd taken the pills he ordered from late-night TV. After just a couple of doses, they came--the vivid dreams, the tormenting nightmares that robbed him of much-needed sleep. So much for trying to clear up a mild case of depression stemming from the divorce.

Matt's swelling fear of failure on the bridge generated a new and desperate resolution. He would still do the ultimate deed, but just not here. Too much risk of a complete fiasco. He had absolutely no desire to fail, to be merely injured in the fall. There was another way, a more peaceful way back at his apartment.

He squirmed on the edge of the bridge, preparing to dismount. But then he felt a slight shudder. Maybe it was just his freaked-out nerves jostling him, but it was a distinct vibration as if someone had hit the bridge with a sledge-hammer. He started to slide off and down onto the tracks when another vibration shook the bridge, a much stronger one with no hint of letting up. Matt looked up the tracks and saw an oscillating headlight rounding a curve on the far bank.

The freight train arrived on the bridge before he could even react, his mind unable to give his muscles direction. He did the only thing left to do and clung tight to the bridge, squeezing his thighs as hard as he could against the cold metal. The vibrations increased exponentially now, forcing him to clench his teeth hard to keep them from chattering. The locomotive horn blew a loud warning as it approached. It was nearly on him now. His body shook. Matt closed his eyes and hoped he wouldn't get sucked into the spinning wheels. This was one way he did not want to die.

It seemed an eternity for the freight train to finally pass. His body continued to tremble for a while, even after the bridge had settled. He spat small pieces of rust out of his mouth. He slowly dropped down onto the rails and brushed the debris off his clothes before carefully retracing his steps away from the bridge and down to the riverside park. He staggered back up the Shoal Creek Trail from the river, passing a few morning joggers and bikers who tossed curious looks at his rust-stained clothes.

Matt labored as he climbed stairs from the trail leading up to West Sixth Street. He turned left past the Whole Foods store, oblivious to the smell of fresh bread wafting out the sliding doors as customers entered. A few blocks more and he slowly made the final ascent to his second-floor apartment in an old brick building above Pinky's Pizza Parlor.

The upstairs apartment had been a gift, a helpful gesture from Matt's former best friend and business partner who owned the building. The one-room studio didn't look lived in, even though he had called it home for six months. A number of boxes remained packed and randomly stacked against one wall. They had just been sitting there for the last month, since the divorce was finalized. It still felt hard to move on.

The place had come furnished with crap in his opinion. The hide-a-bed sofa was definitely past its prime. The tan walls had once been white, thanks to a former tenant with a serious smoking habit. A small TV sat on a wooden chair facing the hide-a-bed. Three other chairs, two of them upright, surrounded a square card table covered in papers.

Matt stumbled over to the table and picked up a scribbled drawing to examine it, trying to focus. Giving up, he tossed the sheet of paper on the floor and grabbed at another page of childlike writings. He could hardly read it. It was the best he could muster in his usual middle-of-the-night stupor.

Frustrated, he sat down on the hide-a-bed and picked up a medicine bottle from the side table to stare at its label. Matt silently cursed the plastic bottle.

This was the culprit, the last straw. The drug called Cecilimate. It had opened up a terrifying window in his mind that wouldn't close. He flung it across the room, bouncing it off the wall.

A second medicine bottle on the side table contained generic sleeping pills he'd bought a week ago to try to stem the tide. Normal adult doses hadn't helped. The nightly plethora of dreams and visions continued. Matt picked up the bottle and shook it. The sleeping pills rattled around inside.

All in all, there seemed to be plenty left for the job at hand.

9

DAY 137 – Swisher, IA

As Sam Asrani slammed the door of his SUV the big Croatian swore at the cellphone in his hand, the verbal equivalent of excrement in his native tongue.

"*Govno!*"

He was frustrated with the fisherman and tired of chasing this Matt Sizemore guy around the country when he could be in Miami, relaxing at his South Beach condo during the day and trolling for action all night.

At least following the guy would be easier now with the tracking device. With Sizemore out of his motorhome for the first time in a week, the foggy morning was Sam's best chance to install it without being detected. He pulled the unit out of his coat pocket and walked to the rear of the motorhome.

He fingered the small device as he looked over the RV for possible attachment points. It needed to be high off the ground for maximum signal strength. He stood next to the rear roof ladder and looked up to the top of the motorhome. He had to decide fast. The fog would be his friend for only so long.

Sam spied the location he required. The ladder itself! Each aluminum step was made from a square tube with each side about an inch high. And the ends of the tube protruding through the side rails of the ladder weren't soldered shut. The tube opening provided a perfect place to hide the device.

He flipped a tiny switch with a fingernail then quickly climbed up the ladder and inserted the tracking device into the second rung from the top. A nudge with his index finger pushed the unit in far enough so it wouldn't attract attention. Sam jumped down and checked his handiwork. The thin wire antenna could barely be seen hanging out the end of the tube.

He casually rounded the motorhome and walked towards his SUV parked a few vehicles away. Muffled sounds turned his attention to Maybelle's. Clearly something had happened inside. Sam saw the man named Sizemore yelling at the same poor waitress he had flirted with earlier. It was a fragile situation with this Sizemore guy, but she had no way of knowing that.

A heavy door of a semi-truck cab slammed hard nearby, and Sam instinctively flinched at the sound, quickly searching in his overcoat for a nonexistent firearm. He noticed a large man with tattooed arms and clenched fists storming towards the diner.

Sam ran the last few yards back to his SUV and opened the door. He quickly leaned in, reached over to the passenger seat, and picked up a pack of cigarettes, a brushed-metal lighter with a Grateful Dead logo, and his silenced Glock semi-automatic pistol.

***

Nikki stood still at the edge of the corner booth. The man pointed to the drawing he'd made of her tattooed neck and her wild black-and-pink hair, surrounded by hundreds of little checkmarks he said were shards of flying glass. She leaned closer to see the snakehead tattoo close up, and there was no mistaking the likeness.

"It's you," he said. "I drew this weeks ago."

Nikki tried to comprehend the drawing of her and the scribbles off to the side.

How can he possibly know this?

"I-- I don't understand. How--"

"I don't even know. These dreams just come to me, and I try to write them down."

Nikki shook her head in disbelief and slowly backed away from the table.

"Are you--following me?"

Before Matt could answer, Travis pushed his way through the vestibule door hard enough to rattle the frame. A few long strides, and Travis was on top of Nikki before she could react. She recognized the familiar vise grip of his massive hand on her upper arm before she even saw his face.

"We need to have a little talk, dearest. Outside."

Travis started pulling her towards the door. Nikki screamed and tried to fight back against his powerful grip.

"NO! Travis, stop!"

She grabbed the edge of a booth behind her, temporarily halting his tugging. Nikki's eyes pleaded for help. A stunned Matt lunged across the booth for his backpack.

"Hey, let her go!" Donna yelled as she charged around the counter.

Travis quickly lifted a switchblade off his belt and flipped it open in one continuous motion. Donna stopped in her tracks at seeing the shiny blade.

"Smart lady. Very smart. Now back off!"

"Travis!" Nikki grimaced. "Please!"

Father Frank stood up. Matt found his prize.

"Let her go!" Matt demanded.

Travis ignored him and pulled with more force. He could yank her arm off if he wanted to.

"Come on, sweetie, we've got some catching up to do."

"TRAVIS!" Nikki gasped. Her hold on the booth slipped with each tug.

"LET HER GO!"

"I'd listen to the man if I were you!" implored Father Frank.

Travis cocked his head to see Matt's gun squarely pointed at him from across the aisle. Customers scattered. He smiled at Matt, his mostly yellowish teeth a contrast to one gold incisor. Travis paused for a moment then looked at the floor. He softly shook his head. A hearty chuckle migrated out from his massive lungs. He stood up straight and released some pressure on Nikki's arm, yet still held on to her.

"I said, let her go," a focused Matt reminded him.

Travis stared straight into Nikki's panicked eyes.

Maybe not today for us, but he can't have you either if I can help it.

Travis slowly released the vise grip on her arm and turned to Matt, closing the switchblade and returning it to his belt. He then opened his own arms wide, acquiescing to Matt's demand. Nikki rubbed her imprinted arm as Donna ran over and directed her away. Matt motioned to Travis with the barrel of the .38.

"That's better. Door's over there."

"You a cop, my friend?" Travis asked.

"Beat it. Now."

Travis moved sideways towards the vestibule door, continuing to face Matt.

"Don't look like a cop to me."

"I'm sure you've seen your share."

"Yeah, that, my friend, is true. Some were face down, though. Does that count?"

Travis grinned as he pushed on the door.

"Keep going. Move it," Matt coaxed.

Travis pointed a stiff finger at Matt.

"Plan on me being the last thing you'll ever see."

After the door closed behind Travis the silence in Maybelle's was deafening. Matt watched Travis through the window as he strutted off into the misty parking lot, repeatedly pounding a fist into his hand. Customers fled the diner.

Matt slumped back into his seat. His hands trembled as he carefully set the gun on the table. He looked again out the window, scanning the dim parking lot for any sign of Travis.

Donna cradled Nikki as she brought her over to the booth and sat her down across from Matt. Nikki picked up a napkin and dried her eyes. Donna came around to Matt, leaned over, and hugged him. He stiffened at her effort.

"Thank you, thank you, so much."

Matt realized breakfast was officially over, and his stay in Swisher was going to be even shorter than he'd thought. Maybe he had saved Nikki the snakehead girl and could now move on.

"Call the police. Someone somewhere must be looking for that asshole," he said.

"I'll do it. They'll be here quick," Donna said.

Donna released him and dashed back to the counter. Matt surveyed the cold breakfast plate for anything worth a bite. He had to get moving before the cops arrived and questioned him. He looked up at a trembling Nikki sitting across the table.

"Nice boyfriend."

"I hate him. I wish I'd never met him."

"It's all right. He's gone now, and I'm mostly awake."

"He's not gone," Nikki stuttered. "I know him. He's relentless. I don't know what to do—"

Matt casually began to put his notebooks in order, making a stack next to the open backpack.

"The police will find him."

Nikki dabbed an eye with the napkin. This man was leaving too. Another one getting away.

"I doubt it," she sighed. "I can't stay here—"

Nikki looked out at the parking lot, hoping she wouldn't see Travis. She blew her nose again before turning to Matt.

"Thank you—for what you did."

Matt stopped packing up and stared right at her.

"I'm sorry if I scared you before, with the drawing."

"Can't understand—how do you know me?"

"Have you cut yourself recently on broken glass? Anything like that?"

"No."

"So, no broken mirrors, or maybe a shattered water glass?"

"Been a while since I broke anything."

Matt finished stuffing the backpack.

"Then it hasn't happened yet," Matt said.

"What?"

"Look, just be careful."

"I don't—" Nikki said as the tears began to flow again.

"Watch yourself around glass. It's important. Trust me."

"I—I don't know your name."

Matt had a variety of options to answer her question. He bent a thumb towards his own chest.

"Me George."

Nikki managed a weak smile.

"George Kaplan of the Chicago Kaplans," added Matt.

"Thank you, George."

"You're welcome, Nikki."

Despite the red eyes and the mascara-streaked tears on her cheeks, Matt enjoyed her smile one last time.

***

Donna hung up the phone behind the counter and looked out over the nearly empty diner. The police couldn't get here soon enough. She peered through the windows praying Travis wouldn't return before the police arrived.

Unfortunately her prayer went unanswered.

It was becoming brighter outside now, the last vestiges of the morning mist lifting. Trucks moved slowly in the parking lot, and most still needed their headlights to navigate cleanly.

It was a pair of headlights that caught Donna's attention. They were getting bigger, moving faster, and heading straight for the front corner booth occupied by Nikki and the man with the gun. Donna screamed.

"NIKKI!"

***

Travis chuckled out loud as he clamped down on the accelerator. If he hit the diner just right he could take the corner clean off and just keep going.

That would teach that cop a lesson.

He braced himself for impact, shielding his eyes with his right arm and steering with his left. He caught one last seemingly slow-motion glimpse of movement inside the diner, feeble attempts to evade the chrome grille of his big Kenworth.

Travis heard two popping sounds just before his driver's side window shattered. He felt a searing burn in his left shoulder, followed by a stinging sensation in his neck. He instinctively reached for the source of the pain, letting the steering wheel go. The Kenworth jerked right and off target, bounding over a raised planter bed and connecting with only the last set of big windows at the exposed corner of Maybelle's.

***

Donna watched in horror as the big truck shattered the large windows, sending shimmering slivers of glass into the air. Matt pushed Nikki hard out of the corner booth, tumbling her onto the floor and away from the impending carnage. Matt didn't make it out of the booth in time.

The Kenworth's big bumper jammed the side of the booth hard, spinning and splintering it into pieces towards the middle of the room. Matt was instantly ejected and thrown airborne, twirling into a bank of booths the next aisle over. The impact flung silverware, ceiling tiles, and light fixtures through the air in all directions. The truck crunched its way through the corner of the diner and back out into the parking lot, the cab finally cementing itself into the side of a 40 foot trailer full of suddenly vocal chickens.

Donna rushed down the counter, eyeing the last place she saw Nikki.

"NIKKI!"

She yanked at pieces of debris, frantically tossing them to the side. The roof groaned overhead, its corner support cleanly severed by Travis's truck. Donna pulled back some broken ceiling tiles and found Nikki, the back of her pink dress spotted with red dots courtesy of flying glass shards.

"Oh God! Nikki!"

Donna carefully rolled her onto her side. A few decent scratches on one side of her face made Donna gasp. Nikki slowly came to while Donna took inventory of her injuries, checking her limbs and looking for any serious puncture wounds. She was relieved to find the blood droplets coming from only superficial cuts.

The roof shifted again, and Donna looked up to see a large crack develop, creating a triangular section above the damaged corner that gravity began folding down into the restaurant. She looked around the diner and saw movement under a pile of pink booth cushions. Donna quickly helped Nikki out of danger.

"It's okay, honey, I've got you."

"What the--?" Nikki stammered.

Donna cradled Nikki as she moved her behind the counter, setting her on the floor, and carefully leaning her against the lower storage cabinets.

"Don't move," Donna told her. Nikki nodded.

Donna heard a soft groan and waved to Father Frank as she climbed over a damaged booth towards the sound.

"Help me over here!"

10

DAY 33 – Berkeley, CA

Doctor Jacob Shelby attempted to sit quietly in the ornate lobby of the private law offices of Garrett, Garrett, and Moore located just off campus. The lawyer assigned by the University of California to defend him sat across the room and looked over a not-so-recent copy of *TIME* magazine. He couldn't remember the lawyer's name exactly, Michael something or other.

Jacob squirmed in the imposing leather chair and tried to relax. The available magazines all contained mostly bad news anyway, and he already had enough of that to deal with lately. He preferred to stare out the picture window and up at the eucalyptus-covered hills behind the campus as he tried to visualize a pristine Costa Rican beach.

The deposition scheduled for one o'clock was already going to start late. It was practically two. Jacob thought the whole thing was ridiculous. The Berkeley police already had his statement, and the federal government's lawyers had been all over him as well. It was frustrating, all these multiple interrogations and questions in recent months over the simple suicide of one of his graduate-student assistants.

So what if the kid's mother was suing the school? She thought there was some sinister connection, which there wasn't, and he had even been out of town when the kid did it. He wanted to go up on the roof and just yell "Duh! It was a goddamn suicide!" as loud as he could.

Jacob didn't know exactly why Brad had killed himself, but he had his suspicions. It was the kid's own fault. Brad must have tried the compound—the one Jacob and his brother Jonathan were testing on primates at his Berkeley lab. It was the only explanation.

The kid had been a good worker at the lab, and Jacob never noticed anything really odd about the boy. He had trusted him, and if he was at fault for anything, it was for trusting him too much, giving him too much access to his research lab and the animals housed at the federal facility tied to the university.

The primates had reacted oddly to the drug, dancing around and grasping at straws in the air, apparently seeing visions or acting out their own monkey dreams before going completely mad. It was the same hallucinogen that Brad ultimately decided to try on his own, that his mother had watched derail her son's life. And now the lawsuit and the possibility of the Feds pulling his research funding loomed over Jacob's head, just when he and his brother could have stumbled on something interesting with the new compound.

He stood up and paced on the big Oriental rug in the middle of the room.

"This is crazy. What are they doing?"

"Just making us wait. Pretty typical," Michael the law-yer said while continuing to read.

"So I have to wait hours just to answer a couple ques-tions that will take a total of five minutes?"

"It'll take longer than that."

"Why? There's nothing to say. Sure, the kid worked for me, and then he just up and jumped off a bridge. End of story."

Michael calmly closed the magazine and looked up at Jacob.

"You know what this is about, Jacob. A fat settlement for Brad McConnell's family at the university's expense. Their counsel will waste time messing with you, baiting you with typical leading questions, and this waiting game is just part of getting you all stirred up."

"Well, it's working."

"You have to stay calm and not give them any ammuni-tion. Let me do the talking."

"This is so pointless."

"It's not pointless, there's serious coin at stake here."

"My career is likely shot anyway. You think I'll have easy access to any federal grant money in the future after all this hoopla?"

"You've been cleared of any wrongdoing by the school."

"The stigma's there, though, and it's not about to fade away. People will still wonder. All those late nights at the lab. Was it a gay lovers' quarrel? What exactly led to Brad's decision to end his own life? Crap like that."

"You've got to calm down."

Jacob's pacing escalated.

"How do you think this has played out with my wife? She's wondering the same thing. Know a good divorce lawyer?"

"Jacob, come on."

He stopped pacing and faced Michael.

"You know what, I'm done. Let them say what they want about me, I've had enough."

He turned and started to walk towards the door. Michael jumped out of his chair and rushed over to stop him, putting a hand on his chest.

"You can't just leave. We have to do this."

Jacob grabbed the hand and flung it away.

"I'm not going to sit there and let them accuse me again of pulling out chunks of hair from the kid's head or having some illicit affair with him. He killed himself, plain and simple."

He reached for the door handle to leave.

"Wait a minute! You just can't—"

The stare from Jacob said it all.

Don't stop me or else.

"Tell the chancellor, once and for all, to go screw himself. I'm done."

Jacob slammed the door in Michael's face, stormed down the hallway to the elevator lobby, and pushed the call button. He waited for a total of two seconds before opting for the stairs. Michael opened the law-office door and yelled down the hall.

"Jacob! Jesus Christ! Come back here!"

All Michael heard in return was the slamming of the stairwell door.

✳✳✳

It was three flights down to the lobby of the office building, with the underground garage another level below that. Jacob dug in his pocket for car keys as he crossed the main lobby and passed by the elevator to the garage, again opting for the adjacent stairwell to lower level P1. A few drinks at his favorite Irish pub on College Avenue would set him right before heading home to an unsympathetic wife.

He needed a trusted friend to talk to. He needed his brother Jonathan. But he couldn't call him, or email, or anything. His brother had disappeared four months ago with no trace and no trail. It had not been a good year.

Jacob bounded down the stairs and pushed through the metal door into the parking garage. He started left a few steps then stopped, remembering he'd parked on the right. He pivoted and stepped directly into a rapidly approaching right cross from Sam Asrani.

The vicious blow easily knocked the scientist off his feet backwards, crumpling him to the ground between two parked cars. A dazed Jacob crawled up onto all fours as blood liberally flowed out of his split lip onto the concrete floor.

Sam casually followed Jacob as he tried to crawl away. He grabbed him by the back of his collar and yanked him upright. Sam spun him around and grabbed the scientist's throat with a massive hand, choking off any possible scream, and pinning his head back against the side window of an SUV. Jacob flinched upon seeing the passing flash of the knife blade, but his attacker held on tight as he twisted the hunting knife deep into Jacob's chest. Sam stared into Jacob's disbelieving eyes as he let him slide down the side of the SUV and onto the oil-stained pavement.

He dragged the dead man to the back of the parking space and sat him up against the concrete-block wall. Sam took a picture of Jacob with his cellphone as the victim gurgled for the last time.

He had started to rummage through Jacob's pockets when the light above the garage elevator flickered on, followed by the bell announcing the doors were about to open. Sam dashed back across the parking aisle, hiding between two cars. He lay flat on his stomach, cheek to the pavement, and watched from underneath the nearest car as two feet stepped off the elevator.

***

Michael's eyes searched the garage for his client.

"Jacob? Come on!"

He took a few more steps into the garage.

"Damnit, Jacob! Now is not the time!"

Michael pulled his cellphone off his belt and turned towards the elevator while dialing.

The phone never made it to his ear. It succumbed to gravity, falling out of his suddenly limp hand.

Michael stared at Jacob, slumped against the wall behind two cars, his eyes blank and his white dress shirt soaked in blood.

11

DAY 93 – Rockville, MD

Kevin didn't last very long in cubicle 1317. The drug-complaint files to be reviewed crowded him out before Wade Kearns had found him a larger work space. The stacks of files on his desk had slowly morphed onto the floor to become a full-blown "carpet" filing system.

He was happy with the new conference room given to him, an interim space-saving option that had involved sweet-talking Becky into letting him reserve it for a few days. That had easily turned into weeks, and the senior agents in the office weren't happy about the special treatment Wade allowed him. Worst of all, Becky didn't smile in his direction any more.

Kevin guessed Becky might be a little jealous of his new assistant Erin Owens, a junior analyst on loan from the Office of the Administrative Law Judge. Erin was not in Becky's class physically, but she was nice and certainly smart enough to help him through the morass of drug-related complaint files. At twenty-eight she already wore strong reading glasses that weren't very stylish, hiding her otherwise pleasant girl-next-door features. The lenses were so large that Kevin could see the full reflection of her laptop screen from the other end of the long conference table.

Kevin and Erin sat at opposite ends, going through their own personal stacks of case files. They worked as a team, keeping the table clear except for the current files being examined. Once a file was reviewed and pertinent details had been entered into a common spreadsheet on the network, the file was sorted based upon the severity and type of complaint. Yellow Post-It notes on the perimeter walls of the conference room every foot or so delineated each type of file piled on the floor below.

Kevin got up from the table holding a file and walked over to a group on the floor.

"Here's another one. Suicide. Stepped in front of a train."

"Not there. Next pile over," Erin said, correcting his placement.

"That's eleven now."

Kevin was surprised by the depth of Wade's backlog of files to review. They varied from simple complaints on potency of over-the-counter medications and treatments to more serious issues of injury or death caused by prescription-drug side effects. All these issues were mixed together with other complaints about vitamins sold over the internet and unrealistic expectations of diet pills hawked in women's magazines.

Kevin told Wade about the suicides they'd found last week, when there were only three that seemed connected. Now there were eleven, and he still had more files to categorize. Eight of the suicides related to the purchase of something called Cecilimate sold by a company in Cincinnati. The pills had been touted as a holistic antidepressant by a pitch-man calling himself Dr. Cecil Ross on late-night cable TV. There was no record of the compound ever being reviewed by the FDA. Wade even had the local FBI office check out the company's address, and they were long gone. Nothing was left, and miraculously, no fingerprints were found. And while there were a few people called Dr. Cecil Ross around the country, none of them remotely resembled the pitchman from the video provided by the TV station.

Kevin was about to sit back down at his end of the table when Erin raised her hand and snapped her fingers.

"You should look at this."

"Another one?"

Kevin walked down to her and stood next to her chair. Erin slid the file around so he could see it.

"Maybe. It's a suicide, but it just smells funny. This guy was an intern working with a government scientist on new drugs."

"Really?"

"But not in one of the cities where the drug was sold on TV."

Kevin picked up the open folder and paced along the side of the long conference table. He read the basic facts out loud.

"Graduate student, twenty-three, Lawrence Berkeley National Laboratory in California. Jumped off an interstate overpass into rush-hour traffic. Bet that was a mess."

"Thanks for the visual."

"Timing is off though, six months earlier than the others. What's the connection?"

"It's the mother's letter."

Kevin flipped the divider over inside the brown folder. The FDA complaint form and a transmittal letter from the student's mother lay side by side. The mother basically wanted the FDA's help in investigating the federally funded lab in California. She believed her son had been exposed to a toxic substance at work that changed his behavior and somehow caused him to jump to his death.

"What about it?"

"The hair. She says he'd been pulling wads of hair out of his head in the days before he jumped. Wasn't sleeping much. Having bad dreams. Chasing visions around the house. All of those Cecilimate files say the same thing. People acting odd, not normal, and pulling hair out of their heads before--you know."

Kevin sensed she was on to something with this file. Even though the event didn't occur in one of the four cities where Cecilimate was sold, the mathematical probability of a connection existed. The kid worked at a developmental drug lab, no less. All the Cecilimate complaint files contained evidence of the victims' yanking clumps of hair out of their heads, some so strongly that a piece of scalp came with it.

"Pull up your list of the Cecilimate files, and let's double-check against other files with suicides. Wade needs to hear about these pronto."

"Got it."

Kevin quickly moved to the conference-room door. He stopped before exiting.

"Nice work, Owens."

"Thanks," she said softly.

Kevin pushed through the door and into the hallway fronting the glass-paneled wall of the conference room. As he rounded the corner on his way to see Wade, he paused and leaned back to peek into the conference room. Erin sat quietly, staring forward, but only for a brief moment.

Kevin grinned as he watched Erin stand up and pump her fist in the air a few times.

12

DAY 137 – Cedar Rapids, IA

Donna surveyed the waiting room at Memorial Hospital's emergency entrance. Although it was busy, there were enough empty seats that she and Father Frank could sit one on either side of Nikki with few encroaching neighbors. The randomly placed bandages on parts of Nikki's face and arm were courtesy of the flying glass back at Maybelle's. Nikki appeared fairly calm as she clutched Donna's arms and pulled them tight around her waist. But Donna could tell she wasn't calm. Her eyes dashed from side to side exploring the hallways. After all, Travis was in the building too.

"So we're all clear on this?" Donna whispered to both of them.

"You're sure?" asked Father Frank.

Nikki nodded.

"We all agreed on this, Frank, after what he did. We owe him one."

"I'll go along. Just uncomfortable with it."

A nurse at the reception desk stood and pointed towards Donna, directing a trio of police officers over to them. Two of the men were sheriff's deputies from Swisher that Donna recognized as frequent customers at the diner. One of them had an on-and-off crush on her. The third one, a plain-clothes officer, flashed a Cedar Rapids badge as they approached.

"Okay then, here they come," Donna whispered.

The officers arrived, and one Swisher officer smiled at Donna right away. Sergeant Pete Thurman dropped to one knee in front of her.

"She okay?" he asked.

"She'll be fine. Just cuts and scratches," Donna said while giving Nikki a good squeeze.

"Good, very good. I worried after seeing the damage to the place. Glad you're okay."

"Smashed Maybelle's up pretty good," injected Father Frank.

"You might know Officer Brent Hays here with me, and this is Tony Charles, a detective with Cedar Rapids," said Pete.

"Yes. Thank you, I know Brent."

"Any of you know the truck driver?" asked Detective Charles.

Nikki lifted her head and stared at the detective.

"Travis. He's going to jail, right?"

"So, you do know this guy?"

"Former boyfriend of hers," Donna said.

"Former asshole boyfriend," Nikki clarified.

"Last name for him?" asked Detective Charles as he jotted down the information in a small notebook.

"Whitacre. Travis Whitacre," Nikki said.

"So what exactly happened out there?"

Nikki collected herself and glanced at Donna, who gave her a slight nod.

"I broke up with Travis months ago, ditching him in Reno. I couldn't take it any more. He started hitting me, like all the time."

"Married to him?"

"No."

"So he tracked you here, to Swisher?"

"I guess. I don't know how he found me, but he just stormed in and grabbed me."

"She's been living with me for a while," added Donna, "And he just showed up out of nowhere."

Nikki looked up at the ceiling with wet eyes.

"How did he find me?" she asked an unseen divinity.

"He was literally pulling her out the door," Donna said.

"Okay. So, Whitacre comes in, grabs you, and then what?" asked the detective.

"I tried to fight back, I did, but then this customer stood up and confronted Travis and he let my arm go."

"That's Trotter," Officer Pete said.

"Who's Trotter?" Donna asked.

"The guy that stepped in," Pete responded. "We're seeing him next."

Nikki's stomach churned. This man Trotter had told her his name was George Kaplan.

"So Whitacre here just left after this guy said something?" a confused Detective Charles asked.

"He thought the guy was a cop, so Travis backed off," Nikki said.

"Did Trotter wave a gun at him?" asked Detective Charles.

Nikki paused, unsure what to say. Donna took charge.

"No, never saw a gun," Donna said.

"One of the cooks in the back said he caught a glimpse of a gun," the detective said while flipping through his notes.

"He must have seen the knife from way back there. The man waved a knife at Travis."

Detective Charles turned to Officer Pete.

"Do we have a knife from Trotter?"

"No, sir."

Donna clarified herself.

"It was silverware. He was having breakfast. There was no gun."

"Is that true, Father Frank?" asked Pete.

"I didn't see a gun," Father Frank said.

"We'll search the restaurant once it's safe," said Detective Charles, "but someone sure as hell shot Travis Whitacre twice before he drove his truck into Maybelle's."

Donna and Nikki looked at each other in stunned disbelief.

Had they made a mistake covering up for this guy Trotter?

"Shots? I didn't hear any shots," said a surprised Donna.

"Me neither," added Nikki.

"This Whitacre guy told paramedics he was peppered with bullets right before he drove into the diner. We've confirmed that on the truck cab. There's no glass left in the diner wall, so we can't tell if the shots came from inside."

"There was no shooting from inside, I can tell you that," said Father Frank.

"You don't own a gun, do you, Father?" asked the detective.

"No sir, I do not!" Father Frank exclaimed.

"Calm down, Frank," Pete said, "I'll vouch for him."

"Fine. Had to ask."

Father Frank stood up, twisted his face at the detective, and marched away from the group. He turned at the hospital reception desk and pushed his way out the entry doors into the sunlight.

Nikki brought the group's attention back with a question.

"Is Travis going to die?" she asked.

"I'm afraid not, Miss," Detective Charles said, "We have him under guard upstairs, so there's no need to worry about him. But the shooter now, he's still out there."

13

DAY 14 – Austin, TX

The fire-engine siren grew louder and more distinct in Matt's ear. The sound irritated him, and he thought there should be no such irritating sounds in Heaven. He briefly opened a crusty eye, slowly focusing in on the vintage light fixture on the ceiling above his head. His clouded mind finally realized where he was. The siren was real.

He had not left for Heaven after all.

His mouth was dry, and his tongue stuck to the roof of his mouth. He hadn't moved on the hide-a-bed since taking the nine remaining sleeping pills the day before.

Matt struggled to roll onto his side and groaned as the siren sped by the building.

Something was wet.

He rolled back and realized he had urinated in the bed. He pushed himself upright inch by inch, his sore muscles quivering as they reacquainted themselves with action. He sat on the side of the hide-a-bed and dropped his head into his hands.

Then the pounding started. But it wasn't a headache. His cranium wasn't throbbing. He actually felt kind of okay, almost rested, which was surprising. He tried a few deep breaths, and his lungs responded with a bubbling wheeze that made Matt cough. He needed water.

Another set of poundings jarred him.

Was someone working on the building?

But it wasn't coming from outside. Someone was thumping hard on the door. He turned and looked at the door just as the pounding stopped. Matt heard a key being slipped into the lock, and he watched the doorknob slowly turn.

A bearded yet mostly bald Kyle Mobley stepped into the room and nervously surveyed the mess in the small apartment. Matt struggled to raise an arm and wave to his former best friend and current landlord. Kyle was the last man he wanted to see, but there was no choice this morning. He could hardly move.

"Hey," Matt gurgled.

Kyle pocketed his key chain and walked around the bed, noticing the wrinkled wet sheets as he made it over to Matt and knelt down in front of him.

"How you doing, man?"

Matt had to think about it for a second. He didn't feel as bad as usual. It was the closest thing to normal he had felt since the whole ordeal started. His head didn't ache, and the ringing in his ears had subsided. He didn't remember having any dreams or visions.

"Better, actually. Not that you care."

"Jesus, man. This is serious! I still care, and Lisa does too."

"I'm sure she doesn't, not any more. You of all people would know that."

"Come on, Matt. Enough on Lisa."

Matt coughed again and ran fingers through his short matted hair. He wasn't going to tell Kyle about his railroad-bridge encounter and the sleeping pills. The less he knew the better. Kyle changed the subject.

"You been in bed all day?"

"Looks that way."

"That's good, right?" Kyle said as he stood up.

He walked over to the window and raised the mini-blinds. Matt shielded his eyes.

"Yeah, no bad dreams this time."

Kyle looked out the window, scanning the street.

"Eaten anything today?" Kyle asked as he turned back to Matt.

"Not that I remember. What time is it?"

"Around six."

"Too early."

"Six p.m., buddy. But looks like that's morning to you."

Kyle sat down close to Matt on the bed, careful to avoid the mess.

"Can an old friend take you out for something to eat?" Kyle asked.

Just the mention of food got Matt's stomach awake and asking for fodder. He thought about the offer from the guy that stole his wife.

Better to play nice and keep an enemy close.

"If I can get up on my feet."

"Great. Let me help."

Kyle stood in front of Matt as he tried to stand up on wobbly legs. He would have fallen back on the hide-a-bed had Kyle not been there to catch him.

"Okay, one more time," said Kyle. "Ready. One, two, three!"

Matt made it to his feet and waited for a moment to get his bearings. He was still woozy from the sleeping pills. Kyle held onto him.

"I think I'm good."

"You sure?"

"Yeah, I got this."

Kyle let Matt shuffle towards the bathroom door on his own, following closely behind in case he stumbled. Matt made it to the door frame and held on to it for a second, his back still to Kyle.

"You sure?" Kyle asked.

"Yeah, just got to get my blood flowing."

"Well, unfortunately you look like crap. Clean yourself up and put some clothes on. I'm gonna grab a smoke. Yell out the window when you're ready, and I'll come up and get you."

"Got it."

Kyle checked his watch and then left the apartment. Matt could hear him in the adjacent stairwell. He grabbed the sink faucet and waited, listening as Kyle took a few steps, then stopped for some reason before continuing down the stairs the rest of the way.

Matt turned his attention to cleaning up. He gargled a glass of water to get the accumulated slime out of his mouth and then spat it into the sink. He found his toothbrush and leaned a forearm on the edge of the sink for support. As he brushed his teeth, he let the froth fall freely into the running water. He splashed cold water in his face multiple times and ran some wet fingers through his hair.

He dropped his stained boxers on the floor and gingerly stepped out of them. Matt washed off his groin and legs and found a small towel to dry off. He then sauntered, naked, back into the main room and tried to remember where any clean clothes might be hiding.

He felt pretty good, considering. Best he had felt in a week. He was hungry, and the growling from those environs was picking up the pace. He looked around the studio for clean underwear and, unable to find a pair, started poking around in a couple of unopened cardboard boxes. Matt lucked out and found a new pair of white boxer shorts with big red hearts stamped all over. A gag gift from coworkers at his old mortgage company, something he never intended to wear. They would have to do.

He found a grey sweatshirt with a splattered tomato-sauce stain from a pizza incident. He picked up a pair of jeans off the floor, but they were the ones covered with rust streaks from the bridge. He dropped them and spied another pair hanging on the back of a chair over at the table.

Matt rounded the table near the window to get at the jeans. He stood in front of the window and stepped into them while holding onto the windowsill. It was pretty busy on West Sixth, rush hour traffic whizzed by.

As he zipped up the jeans he saw Kyle across the street leaning up against a car, a cigarette dangling from fingers held by his side. He was talking to someone in the driver's seat of a very familiar car.

Who was that?

He watched Kyle take a long drag and turn to blow the smoke away, revealing Matt's ex-wife Lisa behind the wheel, her hand draped over Kyle's arm. Matt stood still and tried to focus. He didn't see the kids in the back seat.

How nice to see the happy couple at his time of despair. A friendly reminder of what went wrong, of how partners in the mortgage company spent their ill-gotten gains before the financial meltdown tore though the economy. Matt had bought single-family homes in Las Vegas. Kyle had purchased apartment buildings in downtown Austin. One loser. One winner. In the end, it was more than about money or the lack thereof. Things had been rough with Lisa for a while.

So what was Lisa doing here now? Kyle didn't mention her.

Matt's brain started to kick into gear as he absorbed the full scene on the street below. There was a van parked a couple cars behind Lisa and a police car behind that. On the sidewalk a black man in hospital blues walked out from behind the van and stopped at Lisa's passenger window. He could see her lean over to talk to him. The policeman got out of his cruiser and stood behind the van, leaning up against it, and putting his foot up on his patrol car's bumper to tie his shoe.

Something was seriously amiss.

He tried to connect the dots in his muddled mind. They were up to something, and the full realization suddenly hit him.

They were committing him!

Matt backed away from the window. It made total sense. Get him to come outside quietly and then take him away.

Damnit, Kyle!

His adrenalin kicked into gear. All his senses were instantly enhanced. Matt scurried around the room bumping into furniture and found a pair of mismatched socks. He jammed on a pair of well-worn tennis shoes.

This was it. He could either get out of there quickly or be destined for a slow, drugged-up death as a ward of the state.

Matt pulled a backpack out of a box and rushed over to the table and slid all the papers and notes he had made into it. He found the Cecilimate bottle on the floor by the radiator and put it in his pocket. His eyes darted around the crummy studio apartment. Any random pieces of clothing within reach were crammed into the backpack.

He stumbled over to the window for another look and saw Kyle stamp out his cigarette and start to walk back across the street. Matt bounded towards the door and stopped. He picked up a creased photo of Lisa and the kids off the arm of the hide-a-bed and found his wallet on the floor. A few more steps, and he stood alone in the hallway.

Matt heard Kyle's methodical footsteps echoing in the stairwell. He turned and hobbled quickly to the back of the building and down the fire escape to the alley below.

It was fight or flight time. No help would be coming from Lisa or any friends in Austin. He didn't want to spend the rest of his life, however short it might be, cooped up in a rubber room.

Matt's mind raced as he rounded the corner out of the alley. A seething headache grew by the second. Yet surprisingly he felt alive and powerful, his heart truly pulsing for the first time in weeks. He had slept at last.

Could he keep it up, keep the nightmares away?

Thoughts of suicide faded from his mind as a portrait of revenge welled up inside him and took the forefront. Revenge delivered against a Dr. Cecil Ross and his evil pills. How nice it would feel to shove some of them down the doctor's own throat.

It was only possible as long as he remained free.

14

DAY 134 – Chicago, IL

Ex-con Randy Knox immediately returned any phone call received from Sam Asrani. This morning was no exception, and with good reason. It usually meant a lot of money for dubious work somewhere far away from his luxury apartment in downtown Chicago.

He used to think of Sam as his big brother after they met in Iraq while working private security assignments for Blackwater. They had been good friends for a time, at least as close as two trained assassins could be. After Iraq, the relationship had soured, as he often competed with Sam on the open market for security work or other sinister assignments. Sam knew what to expect from Randy, and this morning's call was just another subcontract job that paid well.

Randy stood in the small galley kitchen and stirred some cream into a second cup of coffee. He was dressed for a run and was ready to go except for the untied laces of his running shoes. The laces tickled the hardwood floor as he walked across the modern living room. He pushed open a sliding door onto the open balcony of the high-rise building, thirty-two floors above Lake Shore Drive.

He carefully centered the mug of coffee on the metal railing, sat down, and tied his shoes with double knots. He retrieved the mug and leaned back in the chair to take in the quality view on the sunny morning.

Randy had accepted the job on the return phone call with Sam not ten minutes earlier. This time the proposed task was much closer to home than usual, only a four-hour drive east, around the south end of Lake Michigan.

Sam's instructions were simple enough. He needed help with a task and was currently tied up near Denver. Plan on a few days of covert surveillance activities and be armed as usual. Drive to a village called Cannonsburg, about twelve miles outside Grand Rapids, Michigan. Be at a tavern called The Honey Creek Inn at 7 p.m. and wait for his call.

Maybe this time it wasn't going to be a high-risk, high-paying international gig, but he never questioned Sam's reasons for doing anything, just his own. He was tired of this line of work, and a simple job this time out sounded just fine.

Randy stood up and drained the coffee. He looked over the railing and down at Oak Street Beach. There was just enough time for a three-mile run along the lakefront before heading out on the assignment.

The day was shaping up to be very nice and especially clear with no rain in the forecast, but taking his beloved Porsche Boxster was unfortunately out of the question. He'd have to go get his big Suburban out of a rented garage six blocks away. It had plenty of room for his needed equipment and various unsavory supplies.

It was also big enough to conveniently transport a body or two when called for.

15

DAY 137 – Cedar Rapids, IA

Matt slowly sat up on the examining table, every degree of incline causing him to clench his teeth tighter due to the pain. Drawn curtains surrounded him. He heard voices nearby. He didn't remember much after the impact of the big truck, maybe half a second of spinning in the air and not knowing which end was up.

He looked himself over. He couldn't remember being transported to the hospital, getting his left shoulder wrapped or his arm immobilized. The shoulder hurt like hell. He could feel pieces of his newly broken collarbone grinding against each other when he tried to move or adjust himself in the slightest way. An intravenous drip was inserted in his right arm. Matt contemplated yanking it out with his teeth. He had to get out of there.

There was suddenly activity at the examining room next door, shoes dancing back and forth below the curtain line. Muffled voices calmed the patient down in between the electronic beats of various monitoring machines.

Matt felt his jeans pockets. His keys were still there and his wallet was intact. He scanned the floor for his backpack but didn't see it.

His father's gun and his notebooks, gone.

A beach-ball-shaped nurse, all of 5'4", entered quickly through a crack in the curtain and was surprised to see Matt sitting up. Her short black hair was in distinct contrast to the sky-blue and yellow-polka-dot smock covered with colorful pins and badges.

"Hey, you should lie back down," she said. "Doctor's orders until he comes back to see you."

"I feel much better," Matt said unconvincingly given the grimace on his face. "When can I go?"

"We'll see about that when Doctor Marks gets here."

She pushed her palm on Matt's good shoulder with ever- increasing pressure to get him to lie back down. He resisted her at first, but doing so brought tears to his eyes from the pain.

"Come on now, Mister Trotter, please."

Matt finally gave up and reclined. A sigh of relief exited his lips as the pain subsided.

"Now just rest here for a bit."

The round nurse checked the fluid level in his IV bag. She stepped towards the curtain opening and turned.

"The police have some questions for you, and I imagine the doctor will release you after that."

Matt watched her pass through the curtain. He tried to see around her and into the hallway before the curtain quickly closed.

***

The portly Cedar Rapids police officer stood up and stretched his tight back muscles. The small folding chair in the third-floor hallway outside Travis's hospital room was tolerable for only short periods of time. He figured he'd pace the hallway again. It was better than sitting in the nasty chair. Before moving off down the hall, he opened the hospital-room door to look in on his prisoner.

The large man with the tattoos lay motionless on his back. Probably knocked out from pain-killers, the officer guessed. He walked up next to the bed and looked down on his charge. This guy wasn't going anywhere. He had taken a slug to the left shoulder, and another bullet had grazed his neck. The guy had probably lost a lot of blood along the way.

The officer surveyed the crazy tattoos on his arms and massive upper body and wondered if whoever shot this guy might have had a very good reason.

***

Nikki pulled Donna into the hospital elevator just before the doors closed.

"I need to see for myself."

"Why?"

"You don't know Travis."

Nikki tapped the button for the third floor.

"We know he's been shot by someone," said Donna, "and the police are guarding him."

"He's dangerous, Donna. Ex-special forces kind of dangerous."

"Really?"

"Really. You saw what he was like."

The elevator arrived and the doors opened. Nikki slowly stepped forward and carefully looked both ways down the hallway. There was no sign of a police officer. A folding chair sat empty by a door down the hallway to the right.

"This way," Nikki said.

She gripped Donna's hand and led her cautiously down the hallway. She kept them both close to the wall as they approached the open door by the chair.

***

Travis opened one eye, watching the back of the officer as he shuffled towards the hallway. He wasn't yet strong enough to have taken down the overweight cop, but the time would come. He closed his eye and rested.

He had been in worse shape in Afghanistan, twice actually, and had survived to fight another day. The shoulder wound was the biggest problem for an escape, as he'd likely need the use of his arm to overcome the guard. Travis knew he should wait, recover, and get some strength back, but his anger was growing and time was short. He needed to break out and find whoever the hell shot him, and he still had a score to settle with Nikki and her new boyfriend.

Travis quietly listened as soft voices echoed in his room. The cop was talking to a couple of women at his door. Nurses maybe--wait, but no, one of the voices was familiar.

It was Nikki!

***

Nikki peeked around the officer to look at Travis lying in bed. He seemed asleep, but then he sat up abruptly and gazed at her. She could see the fury in his stare. She gasped, startling the officer.

As the officer reacted and turned to look into the room, Travis quickly fell back in bed—a response worthy of an acting award. Wondering what the one girl had seen, the officer turned back to the women.

All he saw was the back of their pink dresses as a stairwell door closed behind them at the opposite end of the hallway.

***

Nikki raced down the drab stairwell pulling Donna behind her. The pace was too quick for Donna, and she stumbled a few steps above the landing between floors and careened out of control. Nikki stopped, but it was too late to catch her friend. Donna barely stayed on her feet and banged her shoulder into the wall.

"Slow down, honey," Donna said while rubbing her arm.

"I gotta get outa here, Dee! Away from Travis!"

"We will. We'll take a trip while Maybelle's is shut down."

"I mean leave, Donna. Out of state!"

"You mean for good?"

Donna realized what was happening. Nikki quickly paced back and forth in the small square space. Their escalating voices reverberated off the hard surfaces of the stairwell.

"What do you want me to do? Sit around here until Travis escapes and comes after me again? He'll kill me!"

"You can't leave," Donna said softly.

Nikki wiped a tear from her cheek and reached for Donna's hand.

"Then come with me."

Donna took her hand and followed her down the stairs.

16

DAY 102 – Rockville, MD

Erin's stomach growled loud enough for her to hear the gastro-chorus clearly, even with the earbuds of her headset firmly in place. She'd had a productive morning, making calls about the Brad McConnell suicide in California, and time had gotten away from her. She had already contacted the local police and the university and tracked down a few of McConnell's friends. For a rookie, she was pretty good at this investigator routine and enjoyed announcing herself as such. A lot more interesting than the boring legal research stuff she had been doing only a month ago.

She had already written down notes about McConnell's boss at the Lawrence Berkeley lab on campus, a Dr. Jacob Shelby, who had died in a robbery or carjacking attempt just over two months before. He was the closest link to the details of whatever specific science experiments Brad McConnell was involved with at the lab. With the loss of this valuable source, now she'd have to chase down other connected people to fill in the blanks.

She was on a roll and wanted to place one last call before seriously contemplating food. She adjusted the microphone on her wireless headset as the phone rang on the other end of the line.

"Hello?" said a shaky woman's voice.

Erin quickly glanced down at her notes.

"Yes. Hi. Is Charlotte Ransford at home?"

"Speaking. And who is this?"

"Erin Owens, ma'am. I'm an investigator with the Food and Drug Administration in Washington, D.C."

"It's really—it's just hard right now—to talk about all this."

"I'm very sorry about your recent loss, ma'am. I'm actually calling for some help about your brother's research at the lab."

"I don't know how I could possibly help. I shared everything I know before."

"I'm sorry to trouble you, and I promise not to keep you, but this is about Brad McConnell, the grad student who worked for Jacob at the Lawrence Berkeley lab. With Jacob having passed I thought you might be able to help me with a couple of lingering questions."

"Jacob?"

"Yes, ma'am. Your brother."

"Is this the FDA, or the FBI?"

"The FDA, ma'am."

"You're not calling about Jonathan?"

"No. I'm afraid not."

"I don't understand. Jonathan works—"

The woman's voice tailed off, and Erin could hear sniffling over the line.

"Ma'am?"

"I'm sorry, he—he worked for you people in Arkansas."

"The FDA?"

"Yes."

"And he is?" Erin inquired.

The woman at the other end of the line broke down, soft sobs between heavy breaths.

"My other brother. Lost. Missing. I don't know. Nine months ago. And now Jacob, murdered."

Erin sat stunned, listening to the woman's pain-filled voice and trying to process the news.

"Ma'am?" she finally asked.

Uncontrolled sobbing filled the line before it suddenly clicked off, dead.

"Mrs. Ransford? Hello?"

***

Kevin's commandeered conference room resembled a downtown cityscape model. Piles of complaint files were stacked on the floor and on a couple of chairs. The table itself was mostly clear, although some intrusions had occurred onto the otherwise flat space.

Doctor Wade Kearns sat at the head of the table with Kevin standing behind him and pointing over his boss's shoulder to a map of the United States spread out in front of them.

"Four cities, smaller ones in general," Kevin said.

"And all on the same day?"

"Yes. Middle of the night commercial on local TV stations, shown only once, right before the holidays."

"Interesting. How many victims?"

"No way to tell exactly how many people responded to the ads. No records were left behind in Cincinnati. We're working on phone records. We've got twenty-eight complaint files so far that fit the profile, and all come from these four cities except one. Twenty-two fatalities, all suicides in some form."

"Jesus," Wade said.

"The other six are in hospitals, psychiatric or otherwise. All are comatose, unresponsive."

"Any hope of decent intel from those?"

"Unlikely. They're basically being kept alive from a medical standpoint."

Wade looked closer at the map where the four cities were circled with a yellow highlighter and shook his head.

"Kevin, I've seen these scam artists roll out fake pharmaceutical products before, but they don't do this," Wade said as he waved his arm over the map. "They usually go after the numbers, big cities, mass markets. Not this. I mean, Spokane?"

"Austin and Albany are state capitals, but I don't see a connection there, or to Chattanooga," Kevin added.

"What about the other one? The exception."

Kevin paced the room behind Wade as he described the Brad McConnell case.

"Grad student at Berkeley in California. Worked part-time at the Lawrence Berkeley National Laboratory. Fits the profile. Seeing visions, having bad dreams. Pulled clumps of hair out of his head before committing suicide. Jumped off a freeway overpass. Mother filed a complaint suggesting he was exposed to a compound or chemicals at work. Erin is tracking down information on the research at the lab to see if that concern is viable."

"Could just be a random anomaly."

"Maybe. The case certainly doesn't fit the timeline of the other cases. All the others happened within weeks of each other after the ad for Cecilimate appeared on TV. This one is earlier by six months."

"The numbers seem to show it's unrelated," Wade said.

"Or the exact opposite. Maybe this one case is at the root of all this mess, the source location. That's why we're active on this path right now. We need more information on what experiments Brad McConnell was involved in."

***

Erin grabbed her notes and bounded out of her cubicle. She just had to find Kevin and tell him about what she had turned up about Jacob Shelby and his brother Jonathan, another FDA employee no less.

There were obstacles in her way, other people busily chasing down their own investigations as emissaries of the FDA. Erin raced down the narrow aisles, dodging the oncoming human traffic as best she could.

Kevin's cubicle was vacant, and she dashed over to Wade's and found it empty too. Erin came upon the glass wall of the conference room in time to see Wade stand up from his chair at the end of the table and lean on his cane. She quickly pushed through the door and slammed it shut behind her, firmly getting the attention of both men.

"Speak of the devil," Kevin said.

"You've got to hear this," Erin wheezed.

She plopped down at the conference table. Kevin motioned to Wade to sit and he complied, slowly lowering himself back into his chair. Kevin rounded the end of the table and sat across from Erin.

"This about McConnell?" Kevin asked.

"Yeah, but there's more," Erin said as she gulped in some more air.

"Take your time, Owens," Wade interjected.

Erin nodded and took a few deep breaths to help her settle down. The dash to the conference room had been more of a workout than she was used to, and that wasn't saying much. She leaned forward and spread her notes on the table.

"We know Brad McConnell worked for a Doctor Jacob Shelby at the Berkeley lab for over a year before he died. McConnell managed the vivarium where they kept the animals and mice used in drug trials. Shelby had been primarily working on developing drugs to control epilepsy until recently. The McConnell family commenced litigation with the university over Brad's death."

"What does this Doctor Shelby have to say?" Wade asked.

"The doctor was killed in a robbery attempt in a parking garage about two months ago."

Erin slid a printed article from the local Berkeley newspaper about the killing. Kevin looked it over, then spun it around so Wade could see it.

"Unfortunate," Kevin said.

"I tried Shelby's wife but haven't heard back. I left messages for a few of his colleagues. His sister lives near

Berkeley, and I called her to see if she knew anything. This is where it gets weird," Erin said, pausing to catch her breath.

"And?"

"She thought I was calling about her brother Jonathan Shelby, an FDA employee who disappeared nine months ago."

"FDA? Here?" Kevin asked.

"Arkansas. Pine Bluff."

"That's the National Center for Toxicological Research," Wade offered.

"Disappeared or run off with his secretary?" Kevin asked.

"No trace. Family man. No bank accounts accessed, no credit cards used. Car never turned up. FBI even looked at it."

"And a scientist just like his brother?"

"Yes. He specialized in toxic pharmacology, testing new drugs for interaction problems with existing medications," Erin said.

Kevin leaned back in his chair and stared at the bland ceiling.

"Brothers in the same field would talk shop. We need to know what they talked about. Can we get internal email records for this Jonathan?"

"I can make that happen," Wade said.

"We also need police reports on these two men and Jacob's autopsy results. Could be random, but I doubt it."

"I don't like this," Wade said as he struggled to his feet.

"I'm with you, Wade. We're onto something. This sounds like it's rapidly becoming a four-bagger. Nice work, Erin."

"What's a four-bagger?" she asked.

Kevin leaned forward onto the table and crossed his arms to answer the question.

"Sorry, just a little FBI slang. A baseball reference. Some criminals aren't that smart, or their plans basically stink and they only, say, hit a single before being caught. A one-bagger. A few more crooks are smarter still, or just a little lucky, and get to second base before tripping up and landing in jail. Others make it to third base. They're pretty smart, but they make just one, one very small mistake that costs them. A four-bagger is the guy who has thought his plan out and worked hard to make sure all his bases are covered. Obviously the hardest ones to catch. This one smells like that. The Cincinnati office they used was clean, way too clean for any amateur."

"I know some folks at Pine Bluff," Wade said, "Do you know who his superior was?"

"A Doctor Neil Hoffman, sir. Associate director."

"A plan of some sort related to these brothers must have gone sideways. A criminal plan at that," Wade said.

"Maybe McConnell knew too much, and Jacob Shelby killed him to cover his tracks," Kevin wondered out loud. "And then someone removed Jacob."

"I'll call Hoffman personally and also get you the access to those emails."

"Give Erin the access," Kevin said. "This is her find." Erin avoided direct eye contact with Kevin and looked down at the table, gathering up her notes.

"Thanks, but this is scaring me a little bit."

"And with good reason," Wade said firmly. "If this problem drug is remotely internal to the FDA in any way, we need to be very careful. These case facts must stay between us until I can collect more intel. Clear?"

"Perfectly," Kevin responded.

"Good work, you two," Wade said.

He shuffled past Kevin, patting him on the shoulder on his way to the conference room door.

***

It took some time for Wade to make it back to his cubicle on the window line with the panoramic view. He hobbled up to the glass and stared at the rolling Maryland hills in the distance.

He would do exactly what he told Kevin and Erin he would do in securing access to internal FDA emails and police reports. And he might sniff around and see what, if anything, the FBI knew.

But if he was going to actually talk to anyone about this case, it wasn't going to be Dr. Neil Hoffman.

17

DAY 15 – Austin, TX

The first night since his escape from the apartment was cold and wet. Sitting still made the shivering worse and drew unwanted attention, so Matt kept moving all night long. His eyes continuously scanned the streetscape. He knew they'd be looking for him, Lisa and Kyle, and with the help of the police. He spent the night dodging the cold rain showers by jumping in and out of doorways just north of downtown. He sorely needed a safe place to rest, stay warm, and try to think straight.

In the morning Matt found a place to hunker down. A hole in a chain-link fence let him into a utility company's maintenance yard under the elevated portion of the I-35 freeway. He checked a number of the blue work trucks, and all but one were locked. The rear double doors of one box truck had been left unlocked, admitting Matt to a mobile warehouse of electrical parts. Metal racks on each side of the interior were loaded with cardboard boxes full of small fittings. There was a small vent lid in the roof of the truck with a crank handle next to it. He looked around at the sparse accommodations. If he was careful, he could build a small fire and spend New Year's Eve warm and dry.

Matt emptied his backpack and put the wad of clothes and papers in an empty box on the top shelf of the rack. It was a risk to leave the stuff, but it was a holiday weekend after all, and he needed the room in the backpack. The mini-storage unit he and Lisa had rented was only about twelve blocks away near Three Points. He had just enough time to get up there and pull some items out of storage to pawn for cash before the place closed.

***

The lean long-haired clerk holding down the fort at Ace Mini-Storage was all of eighteen years old, the son of the on-site managers. The boy looked out of the window at Matt standing outside the wire fence. Matt hoped the kid would recognize him from his prior visits since he didn't have the access card.

What was that kid's name?

The teenager took a closer, confused look and Matt waved in response. He figured the kid was thinking he looked like just another vagrant living on the streets. If he only knew how right he was.

A tall man appeared next to the boy and looked out at Matt. After a second or two, the man nodded, and the boy reached under the counter. A buzzer sounded near Matt, and he stepped back as the tall wire gate groaned and started to roll open. Matt walked towards the front door of the small house that doubled as the office and manager's residence. The man opened the door and pointed at him.

"Sizemore, right?" the man said.

"That's me."

"All by yourself today, Mister Sizemore?"

"Yup, working on the house a bit while the wife and kids are at a birthday party, of all things."

Matt walked inside as the man held the door open, watching as the gate started to close.

"Do you want to pull your car in?"

"Actually, I took the bus today. Car's in the shop."

"Ah."

"You can guess where my access card and padlock key are."

"I see. Well, we can fix that. What's your space number?"

"Two-fifty-three."

The man nodded and disappeared around the corner into another room. The boy slumped onto a stool behind the counter and picked up a handheld video game. How the kid could actually see the game through all the hair dangling in front of his eyes was a mystery. The man returned holding a key and handed it to Matt.

"Jesse here has a birthday next week. Always a problem when birthdays are close to Christmas. Can't imagine having one on New Year's Eve."

"Happy birthday," Matt said.

Jesse barely nodded and didn't look up from the game.

"Just bring that key back when you're done."

"Will do. I'll try not to come empty-handed next time."

Matt shook the man's hand and stepped outside. He looked over the rows of red and grey metal buildings. Two-fifty-three was about halfway down the second row. The painted numerals on each locker were badly faded, and he double-checked before trying the key in the padlock.

Opening the roll-up door took some effort after removing the lock. The door squealed like mad for the first couple of feet, metal pinching metal in the ungreased track. Matt pulled up hard on the third try, and it finally slid up smoothly the rest of the way overhead.

The storage locker wasn't jammed full like most. It was organized, the way he liked it. There were boxes piled up against the three walls, a few pieces of furniture and kids' bikes standing in the middle. A narrow walkway around the furniture pile made access to the boxes possible.

He needed a few specific items. It was just a matter of finding them--items small enough to carry, yet valuable enough to sell or pawn. He passed up boxes marked for old college textbooks and kids' clothes that had been outgrown. The big target was a baseball-card collection he and his dad had started in the '60s. He could get some good money for that.

Matt dug through the piles of boxes, turning some around to read the scrawled writing on the cardboard. He came to a corner and looked at one tall flat box standing alone, labeled in his ex-wife's hand.

It was Lisa's wedding dress. He paused for a moment and looked around the storage locker, noting her distinctive handwriting on many boxes. He sat on one of the small bikes and rang the bell on the handlebars. The small storage locker practically chronicled their life together, a journey that didn't end up going quite as planned.

He rocked back and forth on the bike, his head down, contemplating all the history piled in this one place. The good times were stored here, before the failed businesses and the open arms of Kyle came between them. A reluctant tear rolled down to the tip of his nose, and he watched it drop onto the concrete floor. Maybe the bridge wasn't such a bad idea after all.

Matt stepped off the bike and moved more boxes around. He found the one marked **YAZ**, the middle name his dad had given him as a tribute to Carl Yastrzemski, his dad's favorite baseball player back in the day, a gutsy Boston Red Sox outfielder who made it to the Hall of Fame in Cooperstown.

The trading cards were in this box, along with his old leather mitt and other baseball equipment. He pulled it open and found the flimsy shoebox full of old baseball cards wrapped in twine. He put the shoebox in his backpack.

His father's service revolver was next, and he found the small gray metal case tucked behind a filing cabinet. It was the size of a small briefcase, complete with a tiny padlock and a beefy handle to carry it.

There was just enough room in the backpack for the metal case and the baseball cards. Matt zipped up the sides as far as they would go. He took one last look around the storage locker before pulling the overheard door closed and returning the remnants of his life to the dark.

18

DAY 137 – Cedar Rapids, IA

Matt parted the curtains and stepped into the neighboring examining room. The old woman was asleep on
her side just as he hoped. He reached over to her bedside table and pulled a tissue out of a flowery box and
dabbed at the bloody spot on his arm where he'd ripped
out the IV moments earlier. He carefully walked around
the bed to the other side and pushed open the next set
of curtains.

A teenage boy lay partially awake on the table, his leg
immobilized with a light-blue inflatable cast. The familiar scene tickled Matt's brain, searching for the connection before a short, sharp pain shot behind his eye. The
boy's sedated eyes followed him.

"Don't mind me," Matt said quietly.

He moved around the boy's bed and opened the next
set of curtains before turning back to the boy.

"Dirt bike?" Matt offered, already knowing the answer.

The boy nodded.

"You'll be okay, up and riding again soon," Matt said as
he disappeared through the curtains.

The last examining room was empty but had been recently occupied. Personal possessions were still scattered on the rolling tray table, and the bed was unmade. A dark-red windbreaker jacket hung off the side of the chair, and he walked over to it. He might only have a minute before the patient would be brought back from tests and the family members returned.

Matt winced as he carefully pulled on the jacket. It was too big, but that was good. He had room to zip it up and keep his arm and sling inside the jacket. He slowly zipped it up high and tucked the dangling sleeve in an outside pocket. He slowly opened the curtains and saw a window on his left.

He stepped to the window and gave it the once over. No latches or operable hardware were present. He ran his fingers around the inside frame and confirmed it. Sealed shut. Outside he could see the circular driveway leading up to the main entrance of the hospital. There were office buildings on the next block. He was in the downtown area of Cedar Rapids, he guessed, maybe half an hour north of Swisher and his motorhome.

Matt turned around and looked alongside the examining rooms towards the exit door. A small bathroom was situated on his left, and beyond that, a series of cabinets running the length of the wall back towards the corridor. The four examining rooms were on his right. Now or never. Matt took a few steps towards the exit before he heard voices coming closer.

***

Doctor Russell Marks led the officers down the hospital hallway towards the examining rooms. The beach-ball nurse trailed behind the group.

"He's apparently awake and sitting up, so this should be fine," Dr. Marks said.

He opened the door to the examining room for the group and followed after the nurse. Detective Charles pulled out his notepad and flipped through it as he walked in. The officers stopped once inside, allowing the nurse to hold the curtain open at the first examining room.

"What are his injuries again?" asked the detective without looking up.

"Broken collarbone is the primary—uh, where is the patient?" Dr. Marks asked.

The nurse looked around the curtain to find an empty bed and the torn IV line dripping fluid onto the floor.

"He was here a few minutes ago," she said.

The policemen and Detective Charles poked their heads through the curtain to look around. The nurse frowned as she pushed open the curtain to the adjacent examining room and found only the old woman asleep. She continued down the line, opening each examining room's curtain in succession. The doctor and the officers followed her. The old woman was there, while the boy next to her dozed, waiting to be casted up with plaster. The nurse opened the last examining room and found the patient back from the x-ray department. She was asleep too, curled up on her side with the sheets pulled up high so that only the top of her grayish hair showed.

The nurse closed the curtains and shrugged.

"He's not here."

Doctor Marks opened the bathroom door and found nothing.

"You're sure he was here a few minutes ago?" he asked her.

"Yes, he wanted to be discharged. I told him you wanted to see him first, and that the police were here too."

Detective Charles rolled his eyes and turned to the Swisher officers.

"Looks like we might have a runner. Scan the hallways and get hospital security involved."

"Crap," said Officer Hays.

Both officers pivoted and exited quickly, splitting directions once they reached the hallway.

"Is this man dangerous?" asked Dr. Marks.

Detective Charles thought for a second, wondering what the heck was going on.

If Trotter was just a victim, why would he run?

Someone certainly had shot the truck driver Whitacre, and Trotter was acting more and more like a suspect.

"I would say yes until proven otherwise."

***

Officer Pete Thurman jogged down the hallway and into the main lobby, all the while with his right hand draped over his unclasped holster. He circled the reception desk and took off down another corridor. Thurman turned left at a junction and almost ran over Nikki and Donna.

"Have you seen Trotter?" he asked with a heavy breath.

"Nope. I'm hoping we can see him," Nikki said.

"That'll be tough, he's gone."

***

The voices faded, and quiet returned to the examining rooms. Matt wanted to jump up out of the hospital bed and throw the sheets off, but the shoulder pain prevented him from moving that fast. He drew a deep breath and decided to count to twenty before getting up. He closed his eyes and focused on pushing the pain into the background. Then he slowly rose and carefully poked his head out from behind the curtains of the last examining room.

Matt quietly approached the door to the hallway and quickly glanced in both directions. Activity filled the corridor, but no faces jumped out at him of anyone he could place, no one who might recognize him. He opted right, the direction away from the busy front entrance of the hospital. A rear exit would do just fine.

He walked confidently down the hallway. He did his best to smile through the pain at a passing nurse carrying a tray. As he approached an intersection, a police officer chugged across his path, hand on his holster, and disappeared down the crossing corridor. Matt kept moving straight ahead and made his way through the intersection as fast as he could, thankful to find a door marked **Service Staff Only** near the end of the hallway.

The door opened to the hospital's laundry, and his entrance drew a few curious looks. Matt quickly weaved his way between the large baskets of linens being pushed around by a few sweaty employees.

A rear door with a small square window in it was his salvation. He could see blue sky outside. He pushed the door open and stood on a loading dock. A small metal staircase led him down onto the concrete driveway, and he squeezed in between two large dumpsters to catch his breath, think for a minute, and let the pain in his shoulder subside.

The driveway from the loading dock emptied onto a commercial street behind the hospital, one lined with old industrial buildings with steel roll-up doors and intermixed with vacant retail shops with apartments rising above.

Matt crossed the street and walked briskly down the block. He felt exposed given the traffic volume, and he was too out in the open for his liking. A quick turn down a side street brought him into a rundown residential area. A few blocks in, he stumbled upon a small corner market and deli set up in an old house. It had clearly been there for years. The place had vines covering most of the exterior walls, the exception being where they had been cut back to show the faded name of the store painted on the wall.

***

The Cedar Hill Market's proprietor matched the place. His clothes mirrored the overall environment, too much stuff packed inside too little space. His sleeveless white t-shirt was stretched tight, matting down most of the dark curly hair on his chest. Matt nodded at the man as he passed three tall refrigerators with glass doors crowding the entryway. He felt the heated air bathing his ankles as he walked in front of them.

Matt weaved his way back and forth through the narrow aisles. He'd have to buy something and then ask for the favor.

A chest freezer in the back caught his eye, and looking down through the glass top he focused in on a Drumstick ice-cream cone, his favorite from childhood, with the peanut pieces on top. Matt slid the glass open, snatched one, and unwrapped the paper. There was no telling how old it was but it actually tasted good. He took another one out and walked back to the front of the store.

He laid the unopened cone on the counter and pushed the one in his mouth deeper in and held it there while he dug into his pocket. The man watched him struggle to retrieve his wallet. Matt tried to smile and almost crushed the cone in the process, and dropped a few peanut pieces on the counter. He found a ten spot, put it down on the counter, and took the cone out of his mouth.

"These two."

"Nothing else?" the hairy man said while ringing up the sale.

Matt looked around the crowded store.

"Pay phone around here? I need a cab."

The man reached under the counter and Matt froze, worried about what would be coming out. A cellphone appeared in the man's hand.

"Brother drive cab. I call him," the man said.

Matt gave him the thumbs up as he took another bite of the ice-cream cone. The man dialed and started talking in what sounded like Greek or maybe Turkish. Matt walked over to the doorway and peered outside to see if anyone followed him.

***

In front of the hospital Sam Asrani sat in his SUV, a folded newspaper mostly covering the Glock on the passenger seat. Still no one from the crash at the diner had emerged from the emergency room after being taken in hours ago. He had thought about going in, but the police had showed up, and he didn't want to be recognized by the young waitress still inside.

It was after 3 p.m. now, and he had been putting off calling in about what had happened back at Maybelle's. He checked the screen of the small receiver display. No movement of the blue dot of the tracking device since the last time he'd checked. Sizemore's motorhome was still at the diner. He'd have to go inside the hospital at some point and try to find out what the prognosis was on Sizemore and if his shots had killed the driver of the truck.

Sam lifted his sunglasses up onto his head and picked up a small pair of binoculars. He scanned the front of the hospital starting at the entry and slid his view down the bank of windows on the side of the building. Upon returning his gaze to the front door, he locked in on an officer walking out the entryway, a hand on his holster, and looking both ways. The cop turned and ran off around the side of the hospital.

Something was going on.

Sam dropped the binoculars on the seat, reached for the police scanner, and turned it on. He then pulled his cellphone off his belt. Better update the fisherman while he still had the chance.

"What now?" asked Neil Hoffman.

"Someone else after him."

"What?"

"A truck driver tried to kill him. I stop him."

"Is he safe?"

"Injured and in hospital. Police running around and situation is heating up. I get his status when I can."

"Goddamnit," Hoffman growled, "keep me informed. I've got the chairman showing up in a couple of hours."

The line went dead before Sam could reply, and that was fine with him.

The less yelling out of the fisherman, the better.

He picked up the binoculars and scanned the front of the hospital again, just in time to see the two waitresses from the diner coming out of the front door with the young one pulling the other one across the parking lot.

19

DAY 102 – College Park, MD

Doctor Wade Kearns turned into his driveway and punched the button on the garage-door opener. He had just an hour to spare before his wife arrived home from dinner out with her sister. The commute from Rockville had been a mess, as usual, and he needed to hurry to complete the evening's task in time.

Moving his home closer to his office at the FDA had always been out of the question. His wife loved the little house they'd bought twenty-five years before, when Wade taught at the University of Maryland.

One thing Wade hated about the place was that the garage wasn't connected to the house. It made life a little difficult now that he had problems with his hip and down-right dangerous in the winter months when he had to navigate the rickety back steps. Today it was just a frustrating inconvenience as rain showers pelted him on his way to the back door. He hobbled up the steps and into the kitchen.

Wade opened the refrigerator and grabbed two beer bottles, putting one in each front pocket of his raincoat before heading down the narrow hall to his small home office at the back of the house.

After unloading the beer bottles on his desk, he hung the coat up and finally sat down on a swivel chair topped with an extra pillow in a flowery pillowcase. He was supposed to avoid alcohol while taking the pain medication, but difficult times sometimes required deviations from doctor's orders. He twisted off the cap of the beer and knocked back a good gulp before setting it down.

He then reached into his pocket and pulled out a set of keys. A small bronze one fit the bottom drawer of his desk. He opened the drawer and removed a pile of paid bills. He lifted out the false bottom and found the seldom-used secure satellite phone. He turned it on and checked the battery life.

Wade needed one more swig of beer before dialing the number for his fellow scientist Dr. Solomon Carr, chairman of the supposedly non-existent government agency dubbed Otter One. He thought the agency's nickname was a goofy choice, but it had stuck with the staff from the beginning. It was short for the Office of Terminal Resonance or O.T.R., the government-supplied name for the emerging scientific team placed deep inside the FDA to explore the human brain's connectivity to past and future events.

Otter One tested previous independent research that had danced around the global issue of how little of the brain's power human beings actually use. Wade often wondered how a mother senses her child is in danger when thousands of miles separate them. Was it base instinct or a potentially tangible connectivity? How does an Australian child, no older than four, have the ability to recount an exact battle sequence from the Napoleonic Wars in French? Is a déjà vu experience a seemingly unconnected dream to one's own life or an actual glimpse at a past or future event?

Otter One existed to pursue the truth in secret, catch any new drugs passing through FDA examination to exploit it, learn how to control its power and, most importantly, be able to weaponize that knowledge in order to vanquish any foe.

How helpful it would be to know what an opposing military force planned to do before they made a move. The ability to see the future was the Holy Grail, yet grasping the full spectrum--distant past to present and beyond--was the Great Understanding, the universal continuum that earthbound society could only toy with around the edges until the formation of Otter One.

A soft pulsating buzz filled Wade's ear. Solomon finally answered.

"Doctor Kearns, this is a surprise. Are you well?" Solomon asked his old friend.

"Nothing a complete hip replacement won't cure," Wade responded after finishing a sip of beer.

"Still a bother, then."

"Quite."

"Is this about needing some time away?"

"No, Solomon. Something a little more serious has come up."

"I see."

"We're seeing a pattern of unusual deaths reported to my office at the FDA, and the number of cases is growing daily. Some scam drug was sold on late-night TV, on one night only, in four smaller cities. Pills called Cecilimate and pitched by a Doctor Cecil Ross."

"Never heard of him."

"A local actor paid in cash. The FBI interviewed him."

"Go on."

"Company is gone, offices cleaned out professionally."

"Doesn't yet sound worthy of our involvement, Wade."

"This will change your mind. There were two actual scientists we've traced the drug back to. One dead, one missing. Brothers, Jonathan and Jacob Shelby. Respected researchers, one at Berkeley, the other an FDA employee working on toxic pharmacology at Pine Bluff."

"An experimental compound then?"

"It appears so, yes."

"How legitimate do you think this is?"

"Very promising, given the reports. Similar side effects leading up to the deaths. Vivid dreams. Visions that aren't understood. All cases lead to suicide attempts after extreme overstimulation of the visual cortex. Most are successful."

"Have you secured any of the drug in question?"

"Not yet, but we're working on that."

"Who else knows about this?" Solomon asked.

"A couple of my FDA agents are working on the complaints coming in. They know nothing beyond the caseload right now, but they're smart and resourceful."

"We need some of the drug as soon as possible."

"Yes, I agree. But unfortunately there is one more problem. A big one. There's a link back to Neil Hoffman in Pine Bluff. He was Jonathan Shelby's boss."

Wade waited a few seconds for a reply which didn't come.

"Solomon?"

"That asshole's been calling me, asking for a meeting. A dinner at his cabin somewhere. It appears I'll need to actually go."

"I haven't talked to Hoffman yet, but my agents are after more data, emails and phone records," Wade said.

"Of course, of course. They are doing their job. Just slow-play your investigation until I find out what he's up to. Do not let your agents get in front of this."

"I'll do what I can."

"Reassign them if you have to. I don't want have to deal with them, too. Send me a report on what you've found to date, and keep me in the loop on new developments. And get me some of that drug."

"Yes sir. I will."

"Wade?"

"Yes sir?"

"Good work, and thank you."

Wade switched the power off and returned the phone to the hidden compartment in the desk. He drained the remaining backwash of the first beer, unscrewed the cap on the second, and leaned back in his chair. He knew there would be more routine drinking in the challenging days ahead.

He closed his eyes and held the cold bottle against his forehead, swiping the cool condensation back and forth across his brow. He worried about Kevin and Erin and hoped they wouldn't get in the way of Solomon and his mandate. He could only hope that restricting the information flow would slow them down, at least until the he could resolve the Hoffman issue.

Proclivity

He glanced at his watch and sat up straight. A few large gulps finished the bottle of beer. Wade worked himself out of the chair, collected the other empty beer bottle, and headed back to the kitchen to dispose of the evidence and brush his teeth before his wife returned home.

20

DAY 134 – Cannonsburg, MI

As far as Randy Knox could tell from driving through, there were no actual cannons on display in Cannonsburg, Michigan. The place was basically a rural crossroads on the banks of a big creek. A few turn-of-the-century buildings had been meticulously fixed up, and the restored Victorian building called The Honey Creek Inn stood front and center in the small village of one stop sign surrounded by farmland.

A newer gas-station-and-combination-grocery-store called The Grist Mill sat on the main corner which, for some unknown reason, had a full-sized bronze statue of a giraffe out in front.

The drive from Chicago around the southern tip of Lake Michigan had been smooth, and he had arrived early by design. Casing an unfamiliar location ahead of time usually paid dividends later. He could check escape routes and gauge any immediate risks.

He circled his SUV through the few residential streets dotted with small houses set on manicured lawns. Cannonsburg appeared very quiet and peaceful, and he wondered what possible reason could bring Sam to require his kind of help in a place such as this.

The parking lot of The Honey Creek Inn had been restored as well, back to its original 19th-century condition of mud and dirt. Randy parked the big Suburban under a tree and decided to walk the parking lot while smoking a cigarette. He peeked around the rear of the building, checking for exit points. Two waitresses stood near a rear door, smoking and sharing a can of soda. He walked around to the front and found the strangest car he had ever seen parked at the curb.

It was a vintage Volkswagen bug, neon yellow with a colorful Honey Creek Inn logo hand-painted on the driver's side door. The roof of the car was disturbing. It was covered with light-brown shag carpeting that had seen its share of the effects of Midwestern weather. A frayed ponytail of tattered rope had been sewn onto the scraggly carpet above the back window. Streaks on the small rear window were evidence that the ponytail acted like a bad rear windshield wiper when the car was in motion.

Long mutton-chop sideburns of the same nasty shag carpet were glued to the VW's sides behind the doors, contributing to the funky look. Randy shook his head in disbelief while finishing his smoke. He flicked the butt into a planter bed and headed up the steps into the establishment.

Inside the noisy tavern, the floor was covered with peanut shells. A beat-up wooden bar stretched the length of one side of the old shotgun building, a line of dark wooden booths with tall backs covered the opposite wall. The interior had a beadboard wainscot that went six feet off the floor, the balance of wall space above that covered with pictures, beer signs, and local paraphernalia including numerous racks of deer antlers.

Randy found a vacant barstool and contemplated his beverage options from a long line of bottles on a narrow shelf behind the bar. He watched as the tall, balding bartender with a sizable handlebar moustache finished a conversation at the other end of the bar with a booming laugh. The bartender noticed him and made his way down the bar, scooping up a bowl of peanuts along the way.

"Welcome, sir. What can I getcha?" the engaging man said. He deftly spun a square cardboard beer coaster in front of Randy and set the peanuts down nearby. The moustache accentuated his already wide smile.

"Not sure. You've got a lot of choices up there."

"We've got all the big boys, plus a number of local brews."

The bartender dropped his index finger on the spinning coaster, stopping it, and turned the colorful logo of a bird towards Randy.

"Ever had hard cider?"

"Once. In England."

"Well, you might like a pint of this Goldfinch hard cider. Locally produced from Michigan apples just down the road here."

"Sure, why not."

"Coming right up. Need a menu?"

"Not yet. Maybe in a bit."

"Gotcha."

The flamboyant bartender slid a few steps to the left and pulled on a carved-wood tap handle in the shape of a songbird. As he filled the glass with the liquid gold, Randy watched as the bartender greeted and waved at numerous customers, both coming and going. He acknowledged almost everyone by name. One arriving patron even saluted him as "Mister Mayor." The bartender returned and placed the full pint on the colorful coaster.

"Here you go. Enjoy!"

"Did I hear you're the mayor of this town?"

"Only by default. I own most of the village," the bartender said.

He quickly moved off down the bar to help a new customer waving him over. This character seemed to be quite the local celebrity.

Randy took a swig of the cider and liked it. He cracked open a peanut and surveyed the memorabilia high on the wall above the bar. He spun around on his stool and looked up at the other walls. The place was getting busier by the minute.

The bartender owns the town?

The mayor rushed by Randy.

"Harry's the name. Just yell when you're hungry. Great burgers if you're in the mood."

Randy nodded and then tossed a peanut in the air which bounced off his lip as he attempted to catch it in his mouth. More fodder for the floor.

He caught the next peanut cleanly just as his cellphone started vibrating on his belt. He slid it out of the holster and looked at the screen. Sam would know he'd be there already. He poked the green button.

"Yo."

"Early as always," Sam Asrani said.

"Sitting at the bar. Place is hopping. So what's the deal?"

"I need you to hang there for next few days and keep an eye on someone. A snatch might be needed."

"Terminate or hold?" Randy asked quietly.

"Depends. I know in a couple days."

"Target?"

"In front of you," Sam said.

A confused Randy leaned forward and looked up and down the bar. Harry the bartender noticed his searching eyes and grabbed a menu.

"Who?"

"The bartender with the moustache."

Randy sat back stunned and speechless as Harry approached and handed him the menu.

"Here ya go."

He accepted the menu from the mayor and held his hand over the cellphone.

"Thanks, just a minute or two."

"Righty-O," Harry said as he swirled away.

"What about him?" Randy asked.

"Name is Harrison Carr. Bit of a nut job. Not married. Owns the bar."

"Told me he owns the town. Everyone seems to know him. A local celeb."

"No matter."

It didn't make sense to Randy, this guy and this place. He was used to dealing with people who usually deserved what Sam had planned for them. This Harrison Carr person didn't seem to fit the bill. Randy decided to ask a question he probably shouldn't.

"You sure about this?"

"I pay you to do everything but ask questions."

"I know, but—"

"Listen, the bartender is just, how you say, leverage, and only if needed. There's an important relative in his family that my employer has interest in."

"Okay, okay. I get it now."

"He work there most of the time but follow him around. Get his pattern down. Show up there again on the evening of the twenty-first. I call you at eleven p.m. No moves before then. Clear?"

"Crystal."

"Good."

The connection clicked off, and Randy wondered if he was doing his last job for Sam. He drained the pint of cider and raised the empty glass for Harry to see. The mayor finished a joke with another patron and then slid down the bar to him.

"Yes sir?"

Randy stood up from the stool and pulled a cigarette pack out of his shirt pocket.

"Another round and I'll take the mushroom burger, medium, with fries."

"Cheese?"

"Swiss."

"Good choice, my man."

Randy motioned to the front door as he snagged a couple of Honey Creek Inn matchbooks from a glass bowl on the bar. He pointed at the entrance.

"Grabbing a smoke."

Harry the mayor nodded and turned to enter the order in the computer terminal.

Randy pushed his way through the thickening crowd to the front door. He turned and saw Harry draw the glass of cider and place it on the bar. He watched him for a second, this colorful man and de facto mayor of Cannonsburg, Michigan, as he shared a laugh and high-fived an elderly woman sitting at the bar. Harry certainly was a piece of work, but in a good way. He hoped Harry would somehow be spared any painful plans Sam had for him.

Randy stepped outside and lit a cigarette on the front steps. He looked up and surveyed the center of the small village in the fading daylight. The surrounding trees swayed with the light evening breeze. The giraffe still stood guard over the one main intersection in town, and the ugly VW still sat prominently at the curb in front of him.

He stared down at the silly excuse for a car while taking a few drags on the cigarette. He compared the printed tavern logo on the matchbook in his palm to the older, hand-painted logo on the door of the Volkswagen.

Randy thought about Harry the bartender and local icon and admired his rather carefree existence. Something he didn't enjoy in his own life. Too much of his adult life had been entrenched with powerful underworld forces operating just below the surface of society. A wrong move at any time on his part likely meant the end of the road. He felt burned out. Maybe he wouldn't answer Sam's calls any more. Checking out completely was the ultimate plan, and he wondered if the right time to disappear was now.

He sat down on the steps in front of the VW bug and contemplated his ultimate fate, and Harry's, while puffing on his cigarette.

Proclivity

Then it suddenly hit him, and he snorted out a smoky laugh. The reason behind the funky decoration on the Volkswagen finally became self-evident. It made total sense.

Harry Carr drives a hairy car.

21

DAY 137 – Swisher, IA

Matt winced as he stepped out of the yellow cab at the gas station across the street from Maybelle's Diner and Truck Stop. The happy cab driver waved as he punched the accelerator and forced his way back into the traffic flow. Matt had paid the cabbie forty bucks for the $22 ride. There was no time to wait for the guy to count out change.

Matt found shade under the canopy of the gas pumps and looked over at the damaged diner. Yellow police tape surrounded the collapsed corner of the diner, and a couple of carpenters were boarding up remaining windows that had been broken during the impact.

A Swisher police cruiser appeared from behind the diner, slowing as it drove across the gravel. Matt watched the police car turn and face the gas station. He moved behind a gas pump to shield himself from view. The patrol car rolled out of the driveway and turned down the street. He observed the car make a left into a Burger King parking lot just down the block. This was his chance.

Matt walked briskly across the four-lane street, dodged a couple of cars, and tried to jog the last few steps before the pain caught up with him. He circled around the back

side of Maybelle's, away from the two carpenters position-
ing sheets of plywood into place. He passed through the
truck-stop gas pumps that were still open for business and
walked by the entrance to the mobile-home park. Matt
sneaked up on the back door of the diner, weaving between
Dumpsters, one of which smelled of day-old food scraps.
He tried to turn the dented doorknob, but it was locked.

He moved to the other side of the door and down
the short wall to the corner of the building. He peeked
around the corner. No boarding-up activity had started on
this side yet. Police tape surrounded the big Kenworth that
remained wedged into the side of the chicken truck. A few
chicken feathers still danced across the gravel parking lot
in the soft breeze.

In the distance his motorhome was still there and
behind that, the leaning white cross of Father Frank's
trucker church. Poor Bob had to be plenty hungry by now.

He stepped around the corner and stayed close to the
wall as he moved towards the damaged end of the building. A few windows had dangerous pieces of glass hanging from the top of their metal frames. He ducked under
the police tape and looked for a window opening to crawl
through. None of the entry options seemed truly safe.
Jagged glass remained in most of the window frames.

A nailgun fired up on the other wall of the diner as
the carpenters attached more plywood. Matt picked up a
splintered 2X4 off the ground and listened to the repeat-
ing pops of the nailgun, trying to time the pattern of the
sound of the nozzle hitting plywood. He waited, then
poked the wood at the broken glass of a window, breaking
off pieces when the nailgun fired. He paused, hoping the

sound had been masked, and then he began again at the sound of the quick 'pop, pop, pop' of the nailgun.

Matt cleared a section of the window ledge to sit on, held the frame with his good arm, then pivoted and swung his legs up and over. His feet landed with a crunch on broken glass, and he stood still. The jolt of the landing made his collarbone shift, and with it came a stinging shot of pain.

The damaged corner of the diner had fallen in and, ironically, dropped pink tufts of ceiling insulation over the already pink-suffused debris. He slowly stepped around inside Maybelle's trying to get his bearings on where his particular booth might have ended up. He heard a circular saw cut through more plywood outside. He had to find his backpack and get the hell out of Swisher, sooner rather than later.

Matt slowly picked his way through the pile of tables and overturned booths. He nearly twisted his ankle stepping around a chair but caught himself. The offending scrap of ceiling tile on the floor rocked like a seesaw. He kicked it away and found his father's gun underneath. He unzipped his windbreaker, picked up the gun, and tucked it into his sling. He had to be getting close to the backpack.

The written record of everything that had happened to him had to be found. He needed it. It had to be here. Then he saw part of the backpack shoulder straps, sticking out from under an overturned pink booth. Matt groaned as he slowly knelt down, reached around the end of the booth cushion, and pulled the backpack free with his one good arm.

As he turned to leave, he caught a glimpse of his Cubs baseball cap in a pile of insulation. He frowned as tried to brush off all the pink fibers.

***

Donna kicked up gravel and dust as she pulled her pickup truck off the street and into Maybelle's parking lot at a faster speed than she ever had before. She and Nikki drove around the end of the diner just in time to see Matt take the last few steps to his motorhome with the backpack.

"Hurry! He's leaving!" implored Nikki.

Donna gunned the truck past the motorhome and Father Frank's bus and into the mobile-home park entrance. She stopped hard in the narrow concrete driveway in front of her fifth-wheel trailer. Nikki was halfway out the door before the pickup came to a stop. Donna followed and opened the trailer door with a key as Nikki impatiently bounced up and down next to her.

Nikki raced inside and pulled a duffle bag from behind the couch in the small living room and tossed it onto the floor. Donna walked in behind her but didn't move with the same frenzy as Nikki. She simply put her purse on the counter as Nikki raced past her to the back of the trailer. Donna calmly opened the refrigerator and pulled a half-empty bottle of white wine out of the door. She let the door swing closed and sat in the small dinette booth across from the sink.

Clothes flew past Donna from the back of the trailer as she took a swig of the cheap chardonnay. She could hear Nikki rummaging in the bathroom for her things. It had all happened so fast—the crash at the diner, the events at hospital. She'd thought she was ready for this day to come and had even thought about it many times. But here it was, so fast, and all the preparation didn't make it hurt any less.

A flash of Nikki clad in only bra and panties went by as she dove onto the floor. She crammed jeans on her legs as fast as she could fight them on. She pulled on a couple layers of t-shirts and jammed the rest of the pile into the duffle bag. Nikki looked up from her knees at Donna.

"Come on!"

"I can't," Donna said quietly.

She tipped the bottle high for another drink.

"I can't just leave."

Nikki rushed over to Donna and hugged her, setting both of them sobbing. Nikki released her quickly.

"I have to go, Donna. Travis, he'll—"

Donna reached for Nikki's cheeks and held her face for a moment.

"I know. Don't want you to, but I get it."

"I'll come back. I will. I promise."

"When they put Travis away, come back home."

Nikki nodded and quickly spun away from Donna, grabbing her purse off the counter and the duffle bag off the floor. She was out the door in an instant and didn't look back.

Donna watched the door slam closed and then slowly stood up. She drained the rest of the white wine, holding it high above her head until the last drop fell. She put the empty bottle in the sink and opened the door of the fridge again. She tasted salty tears at the corners of her mouth, a flavor another full bottle of chardonnay would help remove.

***

Nikki struggled to run with the duffle bag, the weight of it throwing off her stride. She tried to hug the heavy bag to her chest, but that didn't help her move any faster. She finally made it out of the mobile-home park and onto the gravel parking lot. Nikki saw the couple of bullet holes in the door of Travis' truck as she ran alongside the police tape. She rounded the end of the truck trailer to find only an empty spot where the man's motorhome had once sat.

Nikki squeezed the duffle bag tight and bit hard on the end of it.

"Damnit!"

She flung the duffle bag to the ground and kicked the gravel around it for a moment before grabbing it up again and running off towards the diner.

Nikki received a couple of strange looks from the carpenters cutting plywood pieces as she ran past them. She came to the street and frantically looked both ways. Nothing. Just cars and more cars. Her mind raced.

Then her gaze finally fell on a one-armed man who had just dropped the gas-pump nozzle while trying to fuel his motorhome across the street.

***

Matt stared down at the nozzle on the ground and knew he had some pain coming if he tried to pick the damn thing up. Then, as if by magic, a small hand with tattooed wrist appeared out of nowhere, lifted the nozzle, and put it in the open fill pipe. Matt followed the motion and found Nikki, her big brown eyes and wide smile standing there, a duffle bag at her feet. He immediately guessed what she wanted.

"Oh no," Matt said as he turned away from her, "no stowaways."

"I have to get out of here! You saw what Travis can do!"

"Not my problem any more."

"But I can help you, like this," she said pointing to the nozzle, "and I can drive."

"I can't, Nikki, you can't go where I'm going."

"Why? Where's that?"

"Not gonna happen," Matt said as he paced at the back of the motorhome.

Nikki followed him, not letting him escape her.

"But you'll know if he's after me. You can see it before it happens!"

"It's not like that."

"What about the broken glass? What about that?"

"Lucky guess," Matt said, avoiding eye contact.

"That's bullshit and you know it!"

"Sorry, kid."

"You're so full of it!" Nikki sobbed.

She feebly swatted at Matt. He tried to turn his injured shoulder away from the onslaught. Nikki gave up the fight and plopped herself down on her duffle bag and silently stared across the street at Maybelle's.

After a few moments with only the sound of pumping gas filling the void, Matt inched closer.

"I have money. I can give you some money," he offered.

"Why can't I go with you? Where are you going?"

"To hell, and then I don't know."

"Take me part-way then."

"No. It's safer for you this way."

"I'll be quiet. You won't even know I'm there!"

Matt struggled to overcome the pull of her desperation. He had to stand firm.

"No, I can't--I can't help you any more."

Nikki stared down the busy street trying to figure out what she could possibly say to get him to agree to take her along. The big Burger King sign down the street made her stomach growl, reminding her she hadn't eaten all day.

"I'm sorry. You've just got to find another ride," Matt said as he turned to open the door of his motorhome.

Nikki and Matt watched as a police car pulled out of the Burger King parking lot and turned down the street towards them. Their eyes followed the police car as it slowed and turned into Maybelle's parking lot, pulling up next to the workmen juggling pieces of plywood. The cop handed bags of burgers and sodas to the carpenters.

Nikki stood up and put her hands on her hips.

"I'll leave, then," Nikki said firmly.

"Lemme give you some cash first."

Matt started to step inside the motorhome as Nikki turned towards him.

"I'll just go over there and tell that cop that you escaped from the hospital, that Trotter isn't your real name, and that you have a nice big gun in there. That sound good to you?"

The nozzle clicked off, indicating a full tank of gas.

Matt stepped back down to the pavement and looked at her. She was smarter than he thought. There was no easy way out of this, at least not now.

Nikki casually returned the nozzle to the pump and twisted the motorhome's gas cap back on. She picked up her bag and smiled at Matt.

"Guess that's one thing you didn't see coming."

Matt reached in his pocket and pulled out the keys. He looked down at them for a moment and then tossed them to Nikki.

"I'm pretty sure you're a lousy driver."

22

DAY 137 – Above Arkansas

The sleek black business jet sliced through a thin cloud layer at 10,000 feet and banked to the right. From his leather window seat in the plush private cabin of the jet, Solomon Carr glanced up from his laptop computer and slid his reading glasses down to the tip of his bulbous pock-marked nose. As the wing dipped further earthward, the verdant Arkansas countryside came up to meet his aging eyes.

The landscape wasn't unlike the Otter One home base 800 miles north in Michigan, a similar patchwork of farm fields, lakes, and rolling woodlands. The only ordered patterns on the ground were man's disruption of organic layers laid down in earlier millennia.

He never grew tired of seeing the earth from the air and often thought about why he hadn't followed his little boy's dream of becoming an astronaut. That was water under the 63-year-old bridge at this point, and he had even more important issues of discovery to deal with now. The jet leveled off, and Solomon turned his attention back to his computer.

A map of the world filled the screen. Sixteen red dots slowly blinked on the screen. They were primarily scattered around the United States with six clustered around Washington, D.C. A large number of orange dots and yellow dots also flashed at a slower frequency in multiple locations. The red dots were the highly important ones, and he was about to visit the one flickering in the Ozark Mountains north of Little Rock at a log cabin perched on the bank of a river.

The door from the flight deck opened and a short yet muscular man, code-named Twig by his peers, entered dressed in all black. Twig came down the center aisle and sat across from Solomon. The powerful man was one of many former Navy Seals in his employ, and his most trusted protector.

The man's code name of Twig belied his abilities, Solomon thought, a rather flippant nickname that had been earned years ago during a night training exercise. Solomon liked to picture Twig running down a path at full speed with night-vision goggles bouncing around, when a low-hanging tree branch had cold-cocked him across the forehead, knocking him unconscious and into the bushes alongside the path. Twig had staggered back into camp four hours late, and the ribbing from his fellow Seals never let up.

Twig slid the black stocking cap off his shaved head and held it in his lap. Solomon lowered his computer screen and focused on the bright blue eyes staring at him.

"You wanted to see me, sir?" Twig asked.

"How much time?"

"Touchdown in seven minutes. Hangar team is ready. Tower's been given our security rating. There'll be no record of our flight plan, as usual."

"I want you to come along on this one, on the inside with me, and posing as a civilian. I don't trust Hoffman, and if he pulls anything I might not be able to activate the failsafe. Keep your team outside, on the perimeter."

"Got it."

"Get changed. And you need to be armed."

"Yes sir."

Twig stood up and headed back to the front of the jet. Solomon packed up the laptop along with yellow file folders marked for Jacob and Jonathan Shelby.

He had never trusted Hoffman nor understood how the board of directors had become so enamored with this man. Sure, Hoffman was a very smart scientist and had taken more than one biotech company public, significantly enriching himself along the way, but that's exactly what made him dangerous. He was cocky and had resources. Solomon had pushed the board for a more focused candidate, given the responsibilities inherent in the job, but he'd lost that battle.

Hoffman was a wild card. And now, after the cryptic calls from the son-of-a-bitch, including an invite to dinner at his cabin no less, Solomon's thoughts stayed firmly on the defensive. Something was up, and he didn't like it.

He pocketed his reading glasses, checked his watch, and touched a small button on the side of it. The digital watch dial disappeared and was replaced with a login pad for his thumbprint. He pushed his right thumb onto the small screen.

Within moments it flashed the color green and refreshed, populating a list of names with blinking red lights next to each one. He scrolled down to the name

Neil Hoffman and pushed the button again. The red dot stopped blinking, and a capital letter A appeared after the selected name. The small screen returned to the watch mode with a small red dot next to the number 4 on the watch dial.

The failsafe device was armed—an unfortunate but strategic system to ensure compliance with secret protocols that simply could not be ignored. It was the first time in years that a need had arisen to arm the deadly system against an Otter One team member.

Solomon cinched his seatbelt tight and closed his eyes for the final approach. He let his mind drift back to his boyhood dreams of spaceflight.

23

DAY 29 – Las Cruces, NM

Matt looked up at the large clock hanging from the food-court ceiling. The four-sided clock reminded him that he'd been stuck there a full six hours already and still had an hour before another bus departed to Tucson. He almost felt trapped inside the Las Cruces truck stop that did double duty as a Greyhound bus terminal alongside the cross-country ribbon of concrete called Interstate 10.

He was still mad at himself for missing the first bus, but the sleeping pills hadn't worn off in time. He'd slept right through the PA announcement with his head on his backpack on top of the food-court table.

After coming out of the mental fog, he had at least used the unplanned extra time to update new pages of notes in a looseleaf binder bought in Austin. He hoped chronicling recent events would help him unravel what had happened, or at least explain the crazy dreams and visions for posterity. Maybe at some point Lisa and the kids would care about what had happened to him.

The open binder in front of him had only eight or nine pages filled out so far, including one page for the recurring dream that was leading him to Tucson. Additional pages noted other repetitive dreams or broken visions of varying clarity. Most were just bits and pieces of unfinished sketches created from a tattered mind.

Matt had used a few pages as the beginnings of a diary, a daily account of all the events he could recall since taking the Cecilimate drug. He flipped through the diary notes that included his escape from Kyle and Lisa in Austin and the nights spent in various places about the city. He actually had fond memories of the couple of days he'd spent sitting by the small fire inside the utility truck, until a sympathetic employee found him and kicked him out rather than calling the police.

One entry covered the sale of the baseball-card collection from the storage locker to a dealer. Matt nursed that $1,300, spending as little as possible except for one night's stay in a grim San Antonio hotel where he managed a relatively hot shower before the next leg of his bus trip to Tucson.

He closed the binder, pushed it into the backpack, and stood up slowly, taking time to stretch his sore lower back. He wanted to buy a few snacks for the ride. And he was fresh out of sleeping pills.

Securing the snacks and bottled water was the easy part. A large checkout counter had a few aisles of shelving nearby stocked with random toiletries, varieties of candy, the ubiquitous Corn Nuts, plenty of cough drops, but no sleep aids. He fell in line behind a trucker buying a box of cigarettes and a bag of Gummy Bears.

"Next?" said the wiry old clerk behind the counter.

The man had a couple of teeth missing and had age-spotted arms of skin turning to leather from way too much sun. Matt dropped a couple of candy bars and a bottle of water on the counter.

"Any sleeping pills here?"

"Nope, but Seven-Eleven has 'em across the street."

"Thanks."

He paid for his items and stuffed them into the backpack.

"Next?" said the leopard-armed man.

***

Matt guessed the line of customers inside the 7-11 had to be twelve deep. The sleeping pills were easily found in the first aisle inside the door to the right and across from the magazine racks whose overall content leaned more towards motorcycles than Martha Stewart. There were a couple of brands of sleeping pills that Matt studied before sliding the complete supply of six bottles of his choice off the shelf and cradling them on one forearm.

He slowly made his way to the back of the checkout line that now extended up against the rear wall of refrigerators holding cold drinks. He glanced at each person ahead of him as he progressed towards the end of the line. Some had lottery tickets ready to go, filled in with their own special set of numbers likely derived from some important date or meaning in their lives. Young and old, poor and poorer, all hoped for a big score. At least he knew he had a much better chance of winning than they did, but his payoff waited for him in Tucson, if he could ever get there. He sure hoped the next bus would be on time.

A man patiently standing fourth in line looked a lot like Matt. He was heavier and a touch taller but with the same baby-faced features and salt-and-pepper hair under the sweat-stained brim of a baseball cap. The man's bulging overalls covered in paint splatters gave away his thicker build, and he sported a scruffy goatee of mostly white. A long ponytail hung out the back of the cap down between the man's shoulder blades. They could practically have passed as brothers if the guy were cleaned up, or if Matt had let himself go.

Matt passed by a tiny Asian woman wearing very short shorts and an oversize t-shirt and dragging a case of beer on the gritty floor near the end of the line. She bent down to scrape the heavy box forward in front of the hypnotic revolving circles of the Icee slush machine, its bright blue-and-red cylinders of iced pleasure rotating in unison.

Then Matt felt it. A bolt of pain shot behind his right eye.

He had seen this before!

The scene matched snippets of a recurring dream from his binder and completed the full vision that flashed through Matt's brain. His body jerked, and the hair on the back of his neck stood up straight. He reached the end of the line and bent over, putting his hands on his knees and releasing the pill bottles onto the hard floor. Everyone in line turned around at the sound of bouncing plastic bottles. Matt kept his eyes closed and let the bits and pieces of the vision play out on the inside of his eyelids.

The Asian woman. She's driving too fast. Empty beer bottles on the floorboards. Screaming children in the back seat. A spinning crash. Ejections. Small bodies in the roadway. Matt stood up straight, sweating, and breathing hard. He winced and groaned as another spike of pain coursed through his head. The Asian woman slid the box of beer forward as the line moved. Matt looked up and outside through the big glass windows at a small car parked out front with three kids swatting at each other in the back seat.

He had to stop her, but should he? Could he?

Matt felt sick to his stomach and dropped down again on one knee amid the scattered sleeping-pill bottles. He let the backpack slide off his shoulder with a thud.

As the line of customers turned to watch Matt's ongoing distress, they didn't notice a rusty pickup truck brake hard into a parking spot near the entrance. A trio of masked gunmen jumped out and rushed through the front door.

The leader of the group, in a colorful ski mask, stuck his pistol in the face of the clerk before pointing the gun at the cash register.

"Give it up, man, and we'll be gone!"

The other two thieves waved their guns at the line of customers, a strong signal to stay out of it. One of the men was tiny in stature and clearly uneasy. The Batman Halloween mask was too big for his face, and it jiggled with his nervous tremors.

Most people in line quickly recoiled at the waving of firearms--most, but not all. The paint-splattered man with the ponytail saw the fear in the small shaking thief standing to his side. Matt sensed the man was going to make a move, and he cringed at the pending unraveling of the already bad situation. His mind raced through the available options. None was free of human cost.

Matt quickly dug through his backpack for the gun. This was his chance to stop the Asian woman and maybe, somehow, control the coming carnage. And if it all went very wrong, at least he would be put out of his own misery.

Matt raised the handgun, pointing it at the Asian woman. He didn't want to kill her, just stop her. He lowered the gun a bit, closed his eyes, and squeezed the trigger.

The preemptive shot startled everyone, especially the leader of the gang. The Asian woman screamed in pain, grabbing at her wounded thigh. The ponytailed man took advantage of the sudden surprise and lunged for Batman's gun, trying to wrestle it from his grasp. Customers dove to the floor yelling in fear. The flustered ski-masked leader turned his attention to the struggle with Batman. The clerk reached under the counter.

The remaining gunshots rang out within split seconds of each other. The ponytailed man hurled Batman into a display of DVD movies, and the gun discharged, hitting the slush machine. Blue liquid from the damaged machine spilled out onto the floor. The ski-masked leader shot the ponytailed man in the face, knocking him backwards towards Matt, and splattering blood all over little Batman. The store clerk raised a sawed-off shotgun and fired point-blank into the ski-masked leader's temple, killing him instantly. The third robber fired at Matt, hitting the backpack in front of him. Matt returned fire and hit the thief in the shoulder, spinning him around. The guy somehow stayed on his feet, pushed his way out the front door, and stumbled into the parking lot. The clerk emerged from behind the counter and chased the wounded thief out the door.

Matt quickly turned towards little Batman. The small thief had yanked off his bloody mask to reveal the terrified face of a kid no older than fifteen. Matt pointed his weapon at him for a moment before waving the gun towards the door. The kid slowly got up, slipping on the blood, and ran out the door.

A few seconds passed before the frantic customers watched Matt put down the gun.

"Go!" he yelled at them.

One by one they scrambled to their feet whimpering, then dashed out the door screaming and fanned out in every direction. The Asian woman, petrified and crying, tried to drag herself to safety behind the front counter.

The ponytailed man lay on his back directly in front of Matt. The damage to his face was extensive. Blood slowly pooled on the floor beneath his head. Matt put two fingers on the man's neck. Only gravity was at work now, no pulse remaining to push blood through the man's veins.

The clerk would be back at any moment. Matt had to get out of there and fast, but a thought kept him kneeling beside the dead man. He pulled hard on the body, dragging it around the end of the aisle and out of view of the front door and the security camera. Once most of the body was hidden, he dug through the man's pockets.

He found a set of keys on a Ford F-150 logo keychain, then a wallet that he flipped open. The Colorado driver's license was for an Alex Trotter.

"Wrong place, wrong time, Mister Trotter," Matt whispered.

There was yelling outside and then more gunshots. He quickly pocketed the wallet and the truck keys. He scooped up a couple of the bottles of sleeping pills and stuffed them in the backpack. A rear door at the end of the aisle led him into a crowded storeroom with no obvious exit.

Matt bounced around the room, looking between piles of boxes for a door. Anything. A small window would do. More yelling out front. The Asian woman wailed for help. He found a metal door behind the last stack of cases of beer and pushed his way outside.

Faint sirens sounded in the distance. Waiting at the bus station for another forty-five minutes was out of the question. He opted right and slid down the rear of the building, knelt low, and peeked around the corner at the side parking spaces. No pickup truck in sight. With his luck, it would be parked right by the front door.

Matt gingerly moved to the other side of the building. There was an old pickup on this side, and it looked to be a Ford. An old shell covered the truck bed. Luckily it wasn't parked up against the side of the building near the front entry. It sat across the side driveway, its front bumper pushed into scrubby half-dead bushes facing the KFC store next door.

A few parking spaces closer was a cinderblock enclosure hiding a rusting Dumpster. There was more than one siren close by now, no time to waste. Matt dashed across the lane, the backpack bouncing on his back, and ducked behind the Dumpster wall. Thirty feet separated him from the truck.

The key better fit!

He stumbled through the planter bed and up to the old F-150, a late 1990s model. Matt closed his eyes and turned the key. The lock popped, and he jumped inside.

The dirty cab was a mess, with papers on the dash and high piles of stuff on the passenger seat. Matt looked over his shoulder and through the window into the covered bed of the truck. It looked like the guy had been living back there. A crumpled sleeping bag lay in the middle of boxes and trash bags. No matter now. He tossed his backpack onto the pile next to him and inserted the key in the ignition. The rough-running engine sputtered to life.

He put the pickup into gear and rolled it forward over the curb and planter bed and onto the KFC parking lot. He drove around the other side of the fast-food joint and onto the street as a police car arrived at the 7-11 in front of an animated clerk waving his arms.

24

DAY 137 – Southern Iowa

The drive south from Swisher on I-380 past Iowa City was uneventful for everyone in the motorhome except Bob. He had already demonstrated his affection for girls on TV and now had a live specimen in Nikki at the steering wheel. As soon as Nikki had settled into the driver's seat, Bob climbed down onto the headrest behind her, pawed at her black-and-pink hair, and rubbed against the back of her head. Matt remained unimpressed yet mildly jealous at the same time.

After some initial stressful moments, Matt decided Nikki wasn't such a horrible driver. She had picked up the nuances of handling the motorhome quickly, and although she felt nervous at first, they had made it out of the metropolitan area and into the open countryside with a little daylight still left. As much as he wanted to stay awake and watch her drive into the evening, his energy level was fading fast, and he still had not yet prepared himself for the night to come. He reclined the seat on the passenger side as far back as it would go and settled in, trying to keep his shoulder from moving too much.

Matt found a bag of potato chips on the floor, jammed a handful into his mouth, and chased them with the leftovers of a cheap beer in the cupholder. Nikki snatched the bag out of his hands and helped herself.

"So this is it? All you have is chips and beer?"

"There's other stuff."

"Like what?"

"Like ice cream. And Red Bull. There might be a few Pop-Tarts left."

Nikki shook her head while munching on a handful of the golden chips. She gave him the bag back.

"And cat food. There's cat food in a pinch," Matt said, working what was left of his wry sense of humor.

He got the reaction he was after as Nikki nearly blew a few chip pieces onto the dashboard.

The motorhome's headlights lit up a passing road sign announcing 22 miles to Mount Pleasant, the next notable town on Route 218 South. Nikki pointed at the sign as it passed.

"Can I stop for some real food?"

Matt thought about it for a moment and decided that before pulling over for food or anything else, it was time for a serious discussion on ground rules while he could still think straight. As much as he really didn't want the burden of having her around, he was stuck with her for the time being. He handed the bag of chips back to Nikki and downed the rest of his beer.

"Yeah, we can stop, but we need to get a few things straight first."

"Lemme guess. More Pop-Tarts?"

"No, like house rules."

Nikki realized by his tone that he was serious. She stared straight ahead, focusing on the two-lane road as it disappeared into a small dot in the distance, the early-season cornfields flying by on both sides. She took her time responding.

"Okay," Nikki said.

"Number one. I don't want you touching my stuff. No reading through my notebooks. They're off limits. Period. Number two. I'm headed to Cincinnati, and that's the end of the line. After that you're on your own."

"My sister lives in Evansville. Can you drop me there?"

Matt thought about it for a moment. Evansville would be close enough along the route to accommodate that.

"Only if you don't break any rules."

"Got it, captain."

"You have a phone?"

"What?"

"Come on! A cellphone!"

"Nope! Been trying to save money."

Matt turned to look down at her purse on the floor between them and realized he couldn't reach for it to check for himself. The sling made any attempt difficult and likely plenty painful. Nikki could guess what he was thinking.

"Open it."

"Don't trust me?"

"Just do it."

Nikki reached down and unzipped the top of the purse. She lifted it up and dropped it in his lap, all without looking.

Matt dug around inside the large bag containing few actual items. He finally nodded, and Nikki grabbed it and put it back on the floor between them.

"Satisfied now, are we?"

Matt yawned before responding.

"Rule number three. No calls. You can't make any calls from anywhere without asking me first."

"What's next, can't use the bathroom?"

"They can track you. They're going to figure out you're here with me sooner or later."

"You mean police?"

"Let's just say I'm wanted in a few places and leave it at that."

Nikki stared at him and suddenly felt trapped.

Had she hitched a ride with a serial killer? The guy was running, but from what?

As long as they were clearing the air in a sense, she had some questions.

"I'm gonna need to call my sister. She's waiting for me." It was a half lie.

"Only when you get the okay from me and not before. We only use prepaid phones one time and then toss 'em. No exceptions."

"What did you do, Trotter, or whoever you are?"

"Not important."

"It is to me!" Nikki said.

"You wouldn't believe me anyway."

"How 'bout you try me?" she grumbled.

He wasn't going to give her any more information or attempt to explain himself, the crazy events, or the drawing he'd made of her until he could figure out how best to deal with this. He was stuck with her for at least tonight, and she continued to be a big risk to his current freedom.

"Number four. You get to bunk with Bob. I sleep on the floor."

Matt struggled to stay focused. The pain radiating in his shoulder from the occasional bump in the road was significant. He hoped the sleeping pills would kick in sooner rather than later.

Nikki squeezed the steering wheel tight and pressed the accelerator a bit. She waited for the next rule to be announced, but nothing came. She was awfully hungry and now pretty angry.

"What, no more rules of the road?"

"None for now."

"Great!"

"I'm not going to hurt you, but if you break a rule or talk to anyone, anyone at all, you're out on the street."

"Fine!"

What is the deal with this guy? Why all the secrecy? Was he a hardened criminal? Had he killed someone?

Nikki's mind raced through the possibilities, but something just didn't add up. After all, this man did stand up in Maybelle's to defend her, a perfect stranger, from a vicious attack. Not many would stand up to Travis. He saved her from a nasty beating at the very least.

But he had a gun! Why?

Then there's the broken glass. How, just how, did he know what Travis was going to do before he drove the truck into Maybelle's? It's not possible. He even had a drawing of her tattoo! Had she met him before in a casino somewhere?

Nikki wondered how Travis had found her in Swisher. He knew she was there. He came in with a purpose. Family or old friends? At least she felt good about putting some distance between herself and Travis. She needed to focus, think straight.

Nikki suddenly had another chilling thought. Someone did shoot Travis, and she knew it wasn't this guy in the seat next to her. There must have been someone else at Maybelle's, outside and watching.

What if that someone was after Travis, or this guy Trotter, and even worse, following them right now?

She checked her mirrors and could see headlights behind her in the distance. She wondered if Trotter would already know that she was thinking about ditching him at the next stop. Nikki needed more information to speed up her decision.

"What do I call you? Is it George, Trotter, or something else?"

No response came back, and Nikki looked over at the man. He was asleep with his mouth half open. His head softly jiggled with the motion of the motorhome. He didn't look evil, but there was trouble lurking somewhere inside him, a gray shadow following him wherever he went.

She checked the mirrors again, and the headlights were further behind this time. Bob rubbed up against the back of Nikki's head, helping to calm her nerves. She reached back and scratched behind the kitten's ears. Bob responded by stepping onto her shoulder with both front paws and rubbing against the side of her head.

"Hey, buddy. Who names a cat Bob?"

Nikki could hear the kitten purring loudly. She couldn't understand this guy, whatever his real name was. He had saved her but was running from something himself. He scared her a little.

She started thinking about a Plan B.

***

Sam kept the driver's side window cracked open to let the cigarette smoke escape. In between passing cars on the two-lane road, he could sometimes hear the crickets cranking up the volume as evening descended on this part of Iowa. The radio was off and stayed off most of the time. Nothing made him long for a trip back home to Europe more than listening to American country music.

The small tracking receiver wobbled slightly as it balanced on the steering column. He estimated the location of the pulsating blue dot on the small directional display at about eight miles straight ahead of him. He compared it to the separate GPS display in the dashboard of his rented SUV and determined he was following the motorhome directly south on Route 218 and getting closer all the time. A quick stop for gas had almost put him out of range.

Sam was happy with the choice of radio tracking instead of a cellular GPS device, even though the shorter radio range was a drawback. A tracker could easily become the tracked with a GPS-enabled system. Intercepted signals that could pinpoint both locations weren't covert enough for this task. Radio was old school, dependable, and kept the tracker in the shadows.

He would catch up soon and then make the call to the fisherman. Maybe Hoffman would finally let him grab the guy, take him to Amanda, and finally end his tortuous tour of the American Midwest.

25

DAY 106 – Rockville, MD

Kevin was already running late for work, and now electrical problems with the Metro Red Line train into Rockville were adding another twenty minutes to his commute from inner D.C. A loud thunderclap had awakened him at 3 a.m., and he had listened to the rain for a while, turning over current issues with the Cecilimate case in his head. He finally fell back into a deep sleep, a little too deep, one that kept him dreaming right through the radio alarm. A soft Fleetwood Mac ballad wasn't enough to do the trick at the appointed time.

The extended train ride did allow him to organize his thoughts on the case and what he could possibly do to get the investigation back on track. Wade was at a conference in Boston and wouldn't be back for two more days. Kevin's emails requesting an update had not been returned. Erin hadn't seen any data arrive on the FDA email chains or phone records regarding the two Shelby brothers that Wade was supposed to secure for them. What had been a hot topic had suddenly cooled off, and Kevin was frustrated that he could do practically nothing about it.

If Wade was right, and the citizen deaths related to Cecilimate were somehow connected to the FDA, then whom could he trust? He wanted to go over Wade's head and push to get the internal email logs and phone information, but these would likely be the same people Wade worried about, with an even greater incentive to cover up any agency culpability. He was new and lacked leverage with the I.T. Department to force them to scrounge for the data. The Director of O.C.I. probably knew his name but only as the "new guy from the FBI" or "Wade's personal restoration project."

Kevin stepped off the train and passed through the station and out to the curb. He hailed a cab for the few miles' ride to the O.C.I. offices just south of town. He recognized the car number painted on the door of the distasteful lime-green cab pulling up to the curb. The wide grin of Manny Mackowski exploded beneath a thick moustache. He had ridden with Manny maybe twenty times or so but hadn't seen him in a few weeks. He opened the door and sat in the front seat. Manny looked Kevin over as he pulled away from the curb.

"I thought youse was buyin a car and takin the food out of my kids' mouths," Manny said, "like a month ago or somethin."

"You're in luck. I can't make a decision on a car."

"Youse government types is all the same."

Kevin smiled but didn't look up from his cellphone screen. He did need a car. The commute to Rockville was a hassle on public transportation, but he had been pretty tapped out before landing the job with Wade.

"Guess I have your vote for Congress then, eh?"

"Only ifs you buy my brother's Honda Accord. Got about a hundert forty tousand on it, and it runs."

"Just runs?"

"Runs pretty good," Manny said.

Manny made a hard right off Rockville Pike. The office building was close.

"Pretty good ain't good enough, Manny."

"So, now youse makin a decision?"

"An easy one, my friend. I can do those."

Manny jerked to a stop next to the building entrance. Kevin got out and dropped a $10 bill onto the seat for the short ride.

"Tanks," Manny said, "Guess I see ya tomorrow?"

"Maybe. Unless I buy a car at lunchtime," Kevin said.

"Goes ahead, see what I care!" Manny retorted before reaching across the seat and pulling the door closed.

Kevin waved as Manny sped away from the curb. He thought he saw something resembling an extended middle finger through the rear window.

***

By the time Kevin reached his cubicle it was practically ten. Still no email responses from Wade had showed up. It must be an exceptionally interesting conference to hold Wade's complete attention for a couple of days straight. He stared at a new pile of Cecilimate files stacked on the floor. More cases had been trickling in, and there were now nearly forty deaths tied to the unknown drug. And now the investigation was stalled.

Wasn't this the kind of situation that Wade brought him over here to clean up?

If he couldn't get any actual data to come to him, he would have to go out and get some data. It would make logical sense to anyone at O.C.I. if his next step were out in the field, actually interviewing families about what happened to their loved ones, trying to learn more about the drug and the criminals who sold it. He could even stop by and see the Cincinnati location used as a front for the sales of Cecilimate. He decided he needed Erin's help.

Kevin picked up the phone and dialed her extension.

"You made it in," Erin said. "I stopped by earlier to—"

"That's what I wanted to talk to you about."

"Being late again?"

"How about I buy you lunch at Popeye's and you help me pick out a car over on Frederick Boulevard? This public commute is killing me."

Erin paused, being largely a vegetarian, but answered him calmly, masking some otherwise minor excitement that could creep out in her voice.

"Okay. What time?"

***

Erin poked and prodded at her Cajun Chicken Salad, carefully avoiding any chunks of chicken that might cling to her black plastic fork. Kevin was otherwise fully involved with half a fried chicken.

She tried not to watch him devour it. The sight of it turned her stomach, seeing him get grease all over his mouth and fingers. He finally stopped and wiped his face and hands with a napkin from a neat pile of half a dozen or so stacked next to his plate. He was clearly a veteran of Popeye's, right down to an extra napkin tucked into his collar, protecting his tie.

"You heard from Wade at all this morning?" Kevin asked.

"No. Still waiting for the records."

"Feels like we've been left out in the cold, doesn't it?"

"Kinda."

Kevin leaned back and stared at Erin. She looked down at her salad and kept poking at it.

"We're out here like this because I'm concerned. It's not like Wade. This is clearly a serious case."

"I've been surprised it's taking this long," Erin said. "I thought the legal department was slow—"

Kevin glanced around the fast-food restaurant for anyone who appeared overly interested in them or their discussion.

"I know Wade said to keep a low profile and do nothing without telling him, but I can't just sit around and see more deaths pile up."

Erin slid her glasses up the bridge of her nose.

"What can we do besides wait for Wade?"

"I'm going out in the field and do some follow-up with the families. Maybe we'll discover something new. I want you to come along."

"Me? This whole thing scares me enough as it is," Erin said.

Kevin saw the concern in her eyes.

"It could be more dangerous to stay in the office with Wade off the radar. We don't know what's going on with him. Other personnel might be involved."

"I don't know—"

"You've talked to some of these families on the phone. They'll open up to you," Kevin said.

Erin jabbed at the salad and shook her head.

"I need you, Erin. A big black government agent show-ing up at a grieving family's door is not going to be, let's say, as effective as having you there."

"I guess, but—"

"Listen, I'm trained for anything and everything that could get in our way out there. I'm your partner, and I've got your back. I won't let anything happen to you."

"But I can't cover *your* back."

"I can take care of both of us," Kevin said.

He pushed his chair back and checked the time on his watch.

"All you have to do is help me find a late-model used car in the next forty-five minutes that doesn't make me look like a sissy."

Erin smiled at the comment. He seemed to be letting her get closer, and she liked it.

26

DAY 137 – Ozark Mountains, AR

The concrete runway at the Holly Mountain airstrip in the Ozarks was just long enough to accommodate Solomon Carr's Gulfstream jet. Although the abrupt braking required to land lurched him forward in his seat, it didn't bother him. He wanted the evening over as soon as possible, even though it was an important event. He never relished killing someone, even people he didn't like, and was thankful he hadn't been forced to make that decision often while running Otter One.

The sun hadn't quite dipped below the horizon, gracing the flattened top of Holly Mountain with an orange glow. A pearl-white Range Rover SUV pulled up near the jet as the stairs unfolded to the tarmac. Solomon shielded his eyes as he descended the steps with Twig close behind.

***

Neil Hoffman stepped out of his Range Rover and waited for Solomon to come across the concrete to him. The wind flipped Neil's comb-over hair up as he watched another man follow Solomon off the plane. He smoothed his hair down as the pair approached.

"Solomon, good to finally see you."

"Hoffman. You look well."

Neil's extended a hand that Solomon accepted half-heartedly. He quickly turned his attention to Solomon's companion.

"And I see we have a guest?"

"Yes."

Solomon moved to the side and the stolid man stepped forward.

"Anson Howard, Mr. Hoffman."

Neil firmly gripped the extended hand and immediately realized that this man was much stronger than most scientists he had met. A man to be closely watched during the evening's activities.

"A pleasure, sir. Welcome to the Ozarks."

"Howard is new to Otter One. Just brought him over from D.C. as my senior assistant," Solomon interjected.

Neil directed them towards the SUV.

"I imagine Otter One is an upgrade over Washington, Mister Howard."

"I can tell you I don't miss D.C."

"He's well trained, Solomon."

"It's the first lesson they learn. Secrecy is paramount. No details about Otter One."

"I've obviously never been there myself, wherever it is. It would be nice to see it sometime."

The trio reached the SUV, and Neil walked with them to the passenger side of the Range Rover.

"I thought it would be good for Howard to see what our field operatives are involved in daily. I hope you don't mind," Solomon said.

Neil retreated to the driver's side and opened his door.

"Mind? Not at all. The river was good to me today, and there's plenty of trout to go around."

Neil did mind, but he tried not to show it. This was supposed to be a high-level private affair. He didn't like the tagalong guest, an unlikely scientist, who would now have to hear about his discovery. The man was just another obstacle that might have to be permanently moved out of the way.

He also didn't like this Howard character sitting directly behind him while he drove off into the heavily wooded hills to his cabin by the river.

***

A few minutes after the Range Rover drove away and out of sight, a pair of headlights lit up a swath of the tarmac. A windowless van rolled forward from between two metal hangar buildings and drove up alongside the Gulfstream jet. Six Navy Seals, dressed in black, quickly descended from the plane and into the open sliding side door of the van. The last man in slid the door partially closed and took one last look around the darkening airport, his blackened face scanning for possible abnormalities at Holly Mountain.

***

Solomon was impressed by the great room of Neil's cabin. It was a fantastic, two-story open space criss-crossed with rough-hewn log beams. A massive rock fireplace occupied one end of the room, while a staircase angled up the opposite wall to extra bedrooms above the kitchen. A sliding glass door opened onto a screened porch overlooking the river. A dinner table had been set up for the night's festivities.

The twenty-minute drive up the Red River canyon from the airstrip had been uneventful--mostly small talk about the area's quality fishing opportunities and the nature of Neil's regular commute south through Little Rock to the Pine Bluff Arsenal that housed the FDA's National Center for Toxicological Research.

Solomon watched from the great room as Neil Hoffman lit a cigar in the kitchen. The man appeared calm as he sucked a big drag and blew the smoke high in the air before turning his attention to the trout sizzling in a large pan on the grill.

Solomon looked over as Twig quietly came down the stairs from the bedrooms. He quickly returned to Solomon's side.

"No one else in the cabin, and the team is in place outside," Twig whispered.

"This might be easier than I thought."

27

DAY 31 – Tucson, AZ

Sam Asrani sat in his rental car waiting for a red light to change at the busy intersection. He was not happy. He didn't like Tucson, its dusty desert climate and cold winter nights, and he wanted to get back to Miami and his beach-front condo as soon as possible.

Neil Hoffman kept wasting his time. Randomly driving around Tucson hoping to find this Sizemore character was ridiculous. Hoffman said the guy would be on the bus, but he never got off. Sizemore could be anywhere by now, and Sam needed more information to go on before taking a next step.

At least Tucson happened to be a college town, and his one enjoyable activity last night had been visiting the college bars along East Speedway Boulevard. There was nothing quite like observing the American youth and the dance of raging hormones between the sexes when alcohol came into play.

Sam pulled into the parking lot of his hotel, a tired Best Western near downtown. He parked in front of the door to his room. He exited the car and stood outside, leaning up against the concrete-block wall, and lit a cigarette. He slid his cellphone out of his pocket and dialed.

"Anything?" answered the fisherman.

"Nothing. I need more to go on, Hoffman."

"Working on it. He got off the bus somewhere."

"No shit. He wasn't on the goddamn bus like you say. I don't wait around here any longer."

"Calm down, Sammy boy. My team is hacking into Amtrak to see if he changed plans in New Mexico."

"I'm going home to Miami tomorrow if I get flight."

"Wait a minute. Wait, Sam. Listen, One more task. It's important."

"*Govno!*" Sam sputtered. "What, what now?"

"The other Shelby brother, at Berkeley. It's time. He's acting erratic, strange. He's been searching online for flights to Costa Rica. I need him silenced, and I need proof for Amanda."

Sam rolled his eyes and didn't respond. His thoughts drifted to Amanda.

"You'll get double this time."

"Then I do South Beach?"

"Then your beloved Miami. I'll call you when we find Sizemore."

Sam closed his phone without responding. He could always use double. He finished his cigarette and put it out on the wall before letting it drop into the dried-up planter. He'd call the airlines first and see if there was a flight right away so he could avoid another crappy night in the hotel.

Then again, he thought, a late morning flight up to San Francisco would give him another night of trolling the college bars looking for a way to get the exotic Amanda out of his system.

28

DAY 137 – Mt. Pleasant, IA

Bob retreated to the overhead bunk as Nikki drove into the crumbling, mostly empty asphalt parking lot of the Pack N' Save grocery store. He watched with interest from the small rectangular front window above the cab as she directed the motorhome to a dimly lit parking spot. She carefully slowed to a stop, trying not to wake George, or whatever his real name was.

Nikki crawled out of the driver's seat and stood up straight and stretched. Bob looked down on her from the edge of the upper bunk. Nikki stepped closer and rubbed noses with Bob before turning her attention to the refrigerator.

It was as the man described, devoid of anything remotely edible. There was beer, of course, and two Red Bull energy-drink cans, but not much else. The freezer did in fact contain ice cream. There were even two kinds, a tub of Häagen-Dazs Pina Colada and a half-empty box of Drumstick ice-cream cones.

She checked a side cabinet looking for any canned goods or cereal boxes. Nothing for humans. Bob meowed.

"Shhh!"

She quietly searched through her small purse looking for money and went digging deeper for any coins left in the bottom. It all added up to seventeen dollars and thirty cents. The rush to get out of Swisher had its consequences.

There just wasn't enough cash to run for it. She wasn't far enough away from Travis to be stranded somewhere. For now, the seventeen bucks would at least get her something decent to eat, and she'd have to just keep driving the motorhome with this guy for one more day and hope nothing bad happened.

Nikki leaned over the dinette table and peeked out the mini-blinds towards the grocery store. Not all of the illuminated letters on the Pack N' Save sign were working, and many parking-lot lights were out. The darkness bothered her.

She still wondered if someone could be following them.

She decided a little protection while walking across the dim parking lot would be a very good idea. There was his gun, but she wasn't keen to have him catch her with it. She started to look for a sharp knife in the small set of drawers by the sink.

What she found in the third drawer down surprised her. There were no utensils, no knives, nothing Nikki could use as a weapon in case of an attack. Just cash, U.S. currency that seemed to gaze back at her as she stared at it.

Nikki slowly reached into the drawer and pulled out wads of crumpled bills of all denominations. She dropped handful after handful of bills on the dinette table, creating a small pile. Bob's little head moved back and forth as if he were watching a tennis match. The growing mound must have contained thousands of dollars. After clearing the loose bills out of the drawer, she uncovered freshly banded stacks of twenties and hundreds, neatly laid side by side in the bottom.

She flinched when Matt stirred and snorted a little, but he quickly settled back down. Nikki turned and started to refill the drawer with handfuls of the cash. Half the pile of cash on the dinette table was returned by the time she paused and closed the drawer. She stuffed the rest of it into her purse.

This makes the decision easier.

Nikki picked up her duffle bag, blew a kiss to a bewildered Bob, and carefully closed the door behind her as she stepped out of the motorhome.

29

DAY 53 – Tucson, AZ

Most mornings Matt dressed like a fireman, grabbing at random pieces of clothing draped around his studio apartment. A disheveled appearance was the natural result and a perfect disguise. He smiled to himself as he tied his shoes.

It had been riskier than he thought to hang out at the Pima County Library when he arrived in town a few weeks back. Questioning the library staff with sleepy eyes and always carrying a large backpack garnered him some unwanted attention from library staff, especially one frail and nosy old woman. She always seemed to be eyeing him--a praying mantis circling a bug.

He went to the library to use the internet. Apart from researching herbal medicines and attempting to find a Dr. Cecil Ross, it was the news from Las Cruces that worried him most.

When he finally decided to try the main library at the University of Arizona, he nearly slapped his own face in disgust. Disheveled, tired, and carrying a backpack? He fit right in with most of the student population. There were no sideways looks, no wondering what he was doing there, and no concerns about why he spent so much time on the internet.

He had made a number of visits to the campus library since those early misadventures at the public one, and today was no different--just his recurring check online for any news of what was, or wasn't, happening on the robbery and shooting back in Las Cruces.

He figured six more weeks was all he needed. He hoped that would be enough. Six weeks in Tucson and then he'd be set. Everything could work out as he imagined if the unidentified body currently on ice in the morgue simply stayed unidentified. That had been the case so far, based on the news articles. The very real and faceless Alex Trotter who had bled out on the floor of the 7-11 was still a mystery man to the Las Cruces Police Department.

Two of the three gunmen inside the convenience store on that day had been identified as local gang members. The one Matt wounded in the upper chest didn't make it very far before the store clerk caught up to him and finished him off. There was no mention of little Batman in the articles, and he hoped the scrawny teen had been scared straight by the encounter.

The Asian woman had attempted to describe the fourth assailant, the one who shot her, but to his relief she hadn't got a good look at him. She was the only person currently behind bars, arrested at the hospital soon after the robbery attempt. Wanted for abducting her three children from her ex-husband who had full custody, she was being held in the county jail and facing three to five years in prison. A front-page picture of a grateful father hugging his kids had

Matt consoling himself that he, in fact, had somehow done the right thing.

The police did give the newspapers what could only be called summary updates on the search for more gunmen. There were certainly "persons of interest" culled from roundups of known gang members after the shootout. Videotape from the store security cameras had been scrutinized, as well as tape from the border crossing with Mexico to see if the fugitives had escaped south or if there was a possible drug- or arms-dealing connection.

During Matt's most recent trips to the campus library, there had been nothing new to report from Las Cruces. But today a short article mentioned one new lead in the case, a lead that scared him.

The authorities were looking for a man who never made a ticketed bus connection at the Greyhound station across the street on the same day.

***

Matt nervously walked the long way back to his apartment from campus. Frequent glances in all directions made his neck sore. He had to be extra careful now, and his mind struggled to hold balanced thoughts.

After dropping the backpack on the floor next to his rumpled futon, he grabbed a beer out the small fridge and paced back and forth, thinking hard and trying to focus. He could only muster five steps in one direction at most, including having to dodge a beat-up round table covered in papers. His clouded mind tried to calculate whether staying in Tucson was a risk worth taking.

He could really use the money that was waiting for him. A new part-time job was paying for the basics—a roof over his head, some food, herbs and sleeping pills, but it wasn't going to line his pockets with enough dough to travel cross-country. He only needed six more weeks and now this!

The police knew his real name.

How could they not? He, Matt Sizemore, had purchased a bus ticket. They would find Lisa. They would learn about the unstable man who had refused help and tried to disappear.

Matt stopped, flipping a mental coin.

But he did disappear!

He wasn't Matthew Yastrzemski Sizemore any longer. He hadn't used that name since buying that bus ticket out of Austin. He tried hard to remember if he had used his old credit card since then. Nothing. Only cash. He went over it again and again while downing another beer.

Did he slip up anywhere? Even once since Las Cruces?

Nothing came to mind, nothing since leaving Austin. He was Alex Trotter as far as anyone knew, and so far the authorities weren't looking for him.

Trotter had been a surreal gift, neatly laid out on the floor of the 7-11. The man's whole unfortunate life turned out to be in the bed of that Ford truck. The guy actually lived under the shelter of the rusty camper shell. His documented life was mostly there, a smelly mess of various divorce papers, empty bottles of bourbon, coffee-stained tax returns, and ultimately a crumpled Social Security card.

Matt figured he'd be living on the streets if he hadn't used Trotter's identity to land the part-time job and sell the truck. He had even opened a bank account with no problem.

He was Alex Trotter now, a former gypsy handyman turned permanent resident of Arizona.

Six weeks!

As long as the dead man's real identity wasn't daylighted by the police back in New Mexico, he just might pull it off and land the money he needed to get him to the Midwest, to Cincinnati and the source of the drug called Cecilimate.

30

DAY 137 – Ozark Mountains, AR

Solomon liked the setting. The company for the meal was another matter. The screened porch was lit by small strings of white lights woven around its rafters on the exposed underside of the wood roof and cleverly draped along the top frame of the exterior screens. A nice touch that, despite attracting all manner of light-loving insects to cling to the screen, also allowed Twig's men in the woods to have a very clear view of the festivities going on inside.

The porch also allowed the soothing sounds of the river below to infuse the dinner with a fleeting sense of calm. The emotional undercurrent was exactly the opposite. The small talk had been increasingly forced, and Solomon was getting impatient.

The trout tasted as good as advertised, but he assumed the real reason for the invitation to the cabin was to smooth over the furor over the disappearance of one of Neil's researchers at Pine Bluff, a scientist named Jonathan Shelby, and his likely involvement with the Cecilimate cases. He would let Neil offer his explanation and then push him on what he knew about Jacob Shelby's death in Berkeley. If he didn't buy Neil's story, he would have to seriously consider activating the deadly failsafe device before dessert.

Neil Hoffman touched a napkin to the corner of his mouth. He leaned back in his chair, obviously content with the clean plates before him and his guests.

"Is it what you expected?" Neil offered.

Solomon thought for a moment while clearing his palate.

"The setting, the fish. So far, yes, it is and more. Yet I didn't expect the invitation."

"Something wrong with having a colleague over to discuss a scientific discovery?"

"Your invitation was more of a demand if I recall, Hoffman. I don't respond well to demands."

"And yet you came. How nice."

"It's the least I could do for Jonathan Shelby."

"Carr, you're priceless!"

"Just tell me what's on your mind, Hoffman," Solomon said.

He pushed his plate out of the way and noticed Neil closely watch Twig take a last bite of trout.

"I have news to share, rather private news."

"Anything you say to me, he'll be privy to."

"His clearance level is unquestioned?"

"Yes."

Neil pushed his chair back and walked over to a side table, opening a small carved wooden box. He fingered a large cigar from the box and waved it towards his guests. Solomon and Twig both declined to join him.

"You don't know what you're missing," Neil said, returning to his chair, "A good quality cigar can make for a very relaxing habit."

Solomon leaned forward putting crossed forearms on the table. The wristwatch with the little red light on the dial angled for his clear view.

"One of our--rather your main scientists is missing, suspiciously so, and you're relaxed?"

"Is that what you think this is all about?"

"Is it not?" a frustrated Solomon asked.

Neil stood up and slowly paced near his chair as Twig closely watched. Hoffman carefully dipped the end of the cigar in his drink.

"Indirectly speaking, yes. But there's more, much more."

Solomon tried to stay composed and positioned his fingers near the buttons on his wristwatch.

"Very thin ice you're skating on, Hoffman."

"I'm a responsible man, Carr. I value my relationships and my staff," Neil said. "But sometimes people get in the way of progress and have to be dealt with."

"What are you saying? Did you--"

A stunned Solomon was interrupted by a cigar-twirling Neil.

"I will admit, with some minor regret, that I am responsible for Jonathan Shelby's absence and also for the untimely death of his brother Jacob. They both failed to cooperate in a manner consistent with my plans, refusing generous offers, I might add, and had to be dealt with accordingly."

Solomon sat astounded at the cocky straightforward confession. It meant something worse was coming down the pike than what he had even imagined. Twig pushed his chair back and stood up and at the ready.

"You might want to have muscle boy here sit down until I'm finished."

Neil caught a glimpse of a translucent red pinpoint of light dancing on the screened side of the porch. He looked down at his chest to see three laser dots shimmer on his shirt. He brushed a hand down his chest as if trying to wipe them away.

"I give you credit for preparation, Carr. I expected nothing less."

"If you've jeopardized this agency and the country in any way, this night will not end well for you."

Neil remained totally calm and dipped the cigar in his drink for a second time. He touched the soaked end to his tongue.

"Your brother Harrison, in Cannonsburg--I take it he's well?" Neil said matter-of-factly.

"What?"

"Tending bar tonight, I would imagine. Busy night probably, lots of people. Oh, and my man is there too, talking to your brother right now over a pint of beer. He's there, waiting and watching, and most of all, expecting a call."

Solomon wished he were younger and could simply lunge across the table at Neil. His face flushed red, and he pushed his chair back hard. Twig reached behind his back and touched the semi-automatic handgun tucked in his belt.

"You don't want to make this personal, Hoffman."

Neil slowly reached in his pocket and tossed a book of matches on the table. Solomon spun the matches around, seeing the familiar logo of The Honey Creek Inn of Cannonsburg, Michigan, stare back at him.

"My man has instructions, if somehow I'm unable to reach him at the predetermined time."

A confused Solomon calmly motioned to Twig to sit. This news hit far too close to home in more ways than one, and it was ultimately his fault. He'd held a lingering fear that a moment such as this would ultimately come, ever since Otter One set up shop near his brother's little town.

He'd make Hoffman pay for this transgression, he'd make sure of that, but maybe it couldn't be tonight. Solomon still had the active failsafe ready to go, but there were many unanswered questions, important ones, and he needed more details out of Hoffman before using it. And most of all he had to make sure of his younger brother's safety first.

"I assume I now have your attention?" Hoffman said.

"Yes," Solomon responded.

Twig tapped his ear and barked a sharp command in two short bursts. The red lights disappeared from Neil's chest. Twig did not sit. He backed away from the table and moved to a corner of the porch behind Solomon.

Neil Hoffman calmly lit his cigar as he sat back down and stared across the table at Solomon.

"Some regrettable recent events were all handled in the name of science. Nothing more. Important findings are now within our grasp."

"Jesus, Neil! What have you done? Killing a highly prized scientist is not part of this research platform, nor is threatening someone in my position!"

"That will depend on your point of view once you hear all the facts."

Solomon slowly removed his eyeglasses and laid them on the table. The buzz of the insects circling the porch matched the growing buzz of a headache inside his head. He propped an elbow on the edge of the table and ran his hand around his face, rubbing his eyes and massaging the day's scruffy beard growth covering his chin.

"Then let's have it," Solomon said without looking up at Neil. He stared at the red dot on his watch and wondered how soon he could make it go away.

He didn't know what Neil planned next or how the night would end for his brother, but the floodgates had been opened, and he tried to prepare himself for the worst.

31

DAY 137 – Grand Rapids, MI

The West Michigan Whitecaps were not a very good base-ball team. Randy sat through the evening game at the mi-nor-league park just north of Grand Rapids and witnessed four errors and no shortage of poor pitching in the 10-2 loss. The stadium was nice, pretty new as far as minor-league parks go, and the local Polish sausage had been a pleasant surprise. The place even served the Goldfinch hard apple cider he had enjoyed at The Honey Creek Inn a few nights before.

The crowd had been energetic for at least the first few innings but really started thinning out after the 7th inning stretch with the Whitecaps behind 8-2. But it was more about the darkening sky and the rumbling of thunder that brought a collective groan from the crowd and more foot-steps headed to the exits. He stayed to the end and fol-lowed the remaining faithful fans out of the stadium, some of them scampering, hoping to beat the coming deluge.

A flash of lightning against the black clouds got Randy's attention as he sat in his SUV. It was nearing nine o'clock in the evening. There would be time for a pleasant cider or two with Harry before the call came in from Sam with his instructions.

He went over a mental checklist of the supplies in the back of the Suburban. He had chloroform, if he needed it, and a black fabric hood among the many other useful items of his trade. He had straps for restraints and various medical tools and devices designed to get someone to talk. Folded tarps were ready for any clean up or disposal duties. He wasn't looking forward to using any of the items this time.

Randy started the engine and backed the SUV out of the parking space as more thunder rolled in overhead. Fortunately, the 20 minute drive east to The Honey Creek Inn and Cannonsburg would get him there ahead of the storm.

There had been no additional calls from Sam since he'd arrived in town. He had followed Harry around as the man worked long hours at his various businesses. He had only taken a few notes on Harry's schedule, as the guy basically worked twelve to fourteen hours a day in the small village and then drove back to his cabin on the shore of a nearby lake each night.

Who could this bartender possibly be related to that would be in Sam's path of destruction?

The whole situation was unfortunate. Randy already liked Harry after meeting him and now wondered if he could bring himself to follow through with Sam's unsavory instructions.

He thought about bailing on this job, but the prospect of Sam Asrani ultimately hunting him down wasn't a good feeling either. Randy realized he had a tough, likely life-defining decision to make in a few hours. He liked Harry. The man was unique.

A little internet research back at his hotel room had turned up local newspaper articles about Harry. The guy had stumbled down the path of owning the town starting about thirty years before, in the early 1980s. He'd practically bought the old Honey Creek Inn on a dare from his old college buddies looking to help him with another new career idea.

The rundown tavern in Cannonsburg had been a dive for years and a haven for bikers, a status that the local residents weren't too happy about. The building itself needed significant repairs along with most of the old center of the village. Harry struggled at first with his decision but, not wanting to give up and eat crow with his friends, he ultimately settled on trying to clean up the town and put Cannonsburg back on the map--which it hadn't been for 150 years.

Fixing the old building with the help of his college buddies had been the easy part. Getting rid of the bikers and their noisy Harleys became the making of the local legend named Harrison Carr.

Step one was not carrying Budweiser any more. That only helped a little and tended to make the biker gangs a little feistier than usual with more frequent calls to the police. Harry ratcheted up the creativity to get them to move on. The answer was simple yet brilliant.

Step two involved Harry arriving at his bar a few hours early each morning and pumping handfuls of quarters into the jukebox, selecting the same Debbie Boone song with each coin dropped. The bikers would arrive later and pop in quarters of their own hoping to hear "Wild Thing," "Stairway to Heaven," or some Southern rock come out of the jukebox first. Instead, the bikers had to suffer through hours and hours of "You Light up My Life" to get there.

The plan ultimately worked, and the bikers moved down the road to a substitute bar in the neighboring town of Lowell. It took a few months for Harry to get the irritating ballad out of his head after that. Parades of bikers still liked to purposefully rev their engines when passing through Cannonsburg on their way to Lowell. Harry took it as a loud salute to the victor.

Harry the bartender became the talk of the small town and greater Grand Rapids. The Honey Creek Inn became a destination with Harry's knack for funky marketing, including the now famous VW bug with the nasty shag-rug hairstyle. Randy hadn't yet figured out how the big bronze giraffe fit into the picture.

Raindrops began to splatter the windshield just as Randy pulled into The Honey Creek Inn's parking lot. He raced up the front steps, past the disturbing Volkswagen parked in front, and into the tavern just as the heavens let loose.

He found an empty barstool and waited. He watched as Harry finished a conversation with a big laugh and wide smile before making eye contact and moving in his direction. Randy stared into his hands, unable to fathom the prospect of possibly killing this man in a few hours' time.

32

DAY 113 – Washington, D.C.

Kevin jogged on a treadmill and stared up at the flat-screen TV on the wall in front of him. The big gym was five blocks from the FBI headquarters in Washington proper and rather conveniently located a half block from the International Spy Museum. He wasn't coming to the gym as often since the move to the FDA, and he felt the gradual reduction of his endurance level.

The monthly handball match with his few remaining FBI buddies kept him from becoming a total slug. This was the core group of guys who'd stuck with him through it all, friends and colleagues who knew he was innocent and thought he got a raw deal from the agency.

The only downside of coming back to this gym was putting up with the other less sympathetic agents who routinely flashed disgusted looks in his direction. They thought they knew the truth, but it wasn't that simple.

Kevin was eight minutes into his twelve-minute treadmill warm-up routine before the match when a woman with a dirty blond ponytail, big sunglasses, and a lavender "Life Is Good" cap stepped onto the treadmill next to him. He didn't even notice Erin at first, his mind still busily turning over open issues with the stagnating Cecilimate case, including what steps to take next.

"Ignoring me won't get me to leave," Erin said softly. "I still want to help you."

He recognized her voice and nearly stumbled on his own treadmill.

"I'm not sure that's a good idea. You've got a career to think about."

"Back with the Administrative Law Department? Not the career for me. I'm going to resign and apply to the FDA O.C.I., or maybe the FBI."

"Wade sent you back there, remember? He'll really support that maneuver after the dressing-down he gave us."

They both stared straight ahead at the big TV. The sound was off, but the CNN broadcast had subtitles that were easy to follow.

The unapproved road trip to Albany in Kevin's newly acquired used car had not gone over well. Wade was still very concerned that an internal FDA conspiracy might be at work. The trip also left Kevin without any of the Cecilimate drug itself, because the victims or their loved ones typically flushed remaining pills down the toilet after a negative reaction. An angry Wade had broken up the team, sending Erin back to her law-clerk job and reassigning Kevin.

But it wasn't just that bothering him. Wade seemed genuinely less interested in this case than before, no matter who worked on it. Maybe competing priorities vied for Wade's attention and got in the way, but this was serious. There had been no press on it yet, a requirement Wade insisted on until the investigation could be fleshed out more thoroughly. More than forty civilian deaths certainly demanded more attention from the FDA in Kevin's opinion, and future outbreaks of this drug hitting the larger market had to be stopped. His frustration with the process had been growing as the investigation slowed, and Wade hadn't helped by sending Erin back to her old department.

"Do we leak information to the press and let them run with it?" Erin asked.

Her voice was barely audible above the deep hum of the treadmills.

"I'm not a fan of going to jail," Kevin said.

"I can't just drop it, can you?"

He knew she was right. He couldn't turn his back on the Cecilimate case either. But he also couldn't risk his already damaged career by doing something stupid again. If he screwed up, he'd lose all access to the information already collected on the case to date.

They would pursue it. Play it smart. Work on it outside the office, on their own time and off Wade's radar.

"We won't drop it. We just have to be very careful. Evenings and weekends only. How much vacation time do you have left?"

"Uh, I don't know, maybe eight or nine days."

"Any trips planned?"

"Just heading home for July Fourth."

"Have a boyfriend?"

"What?"

"He'll wonder about us getting chummy after hours."

"No. Nothing—current," Erin answered shyly, turning her attention to the TV. She nearly froze.

Side-by-side photos of Kevin and a pretty black-haired woman with honey-colored skin were being shown on CNN. The subtitles described the woman as the daughter-in-law of the Israeli ambassador and a former Mossad agent.

"Okay, so if you get questions at work or someone sees us together, tell them we're dating. I'll do the same," Kevin said.

He waited for a response then realized why it hadn't come.

The TV now showed the pretty woman being escorted through an airport.

Kevin sensed Erin staring directly at him.

"I used to know her," he said in a monotone.

"Pretty obvious on that score."

"They're deporting her today."

"You arrested her for something?"

"Not exactly,"

A moment later he decided to elaborate.

"They arrested me for knowing her."

33

DAY 137 – Mt. Pleasant, IA

Nikki didn't make it very far before she thought twice about what she was doing. She stood still, leaning heavily against a parking-lot light pole, looking back at the motorhome barely a hundred feet away. She kicked at clumps of dead grass growing from large cracks in the asphalt.

One of the lights above her head flickered and hummed, as if also undecided on a course of action. The duffle bag still hung on her shoulder, and she pondered the cash stuffed in her purse.

There was just enough light from another pole near the motorhome for her to see through the windshield at the man trying to sleep in the front seat. She watched as he lightly jerked sideways and tried to settle again into a comfortable position.

He had wanted to give her some cash to go away back at Maybelle's, so maybe he wouldn't miss the money. He probably wouldn't miss her either. After all, she had been the instigator of their partnership, forcing herself on him in order to get out of Swisher and away from Travis. He'd be happy to have her gone, she thought. He was in some kind of trouble anyway, something that she didn't understand and didn't want to be wrapped up in.

Nikki looked around the dark parking lot. Even with the newfound cash this wasn't the best place to make a break for it. It was getting a little cold, and she felt exposed standing there in the open. Looking for help in a rundown town at night wasn't that appealing and pretty risky at best, even with money in your pocket. And she needed to call her sister and let her know she was making her way home.

As she looked back at the motorhome, Bob's little face popped into view in the window above the cab. Nikki paced near the light pole still toying with the dead grass.

The man had saved her from Travis, in fact twice in one day, and she owed him for that. He was pretty strange, with his herbs and notebooks, his ability to know in advance that Travis was going to smash into Maybelle's with his truck. And the guy had a cat. Not a dog, but a cat.

What normal single guy takes a cat on a road trip?

Maybe the man had saved Bob too.

Nikki adjusted the duffle-bag strap on her shoulder and kicked hard at a grass clod one last time before turning towards the motorhome.

***

Sam tossed the Grateful Dead lighter onto the passenger seat before pulling a long drag. He brought the pair of binoculars up to his eyes. From his vantage point across the Pack N' Save parking lot, it did appear to be the same young waitress with the black-and-pink hair he'd met that very morning at the diner, then saw running from the Hospital later in the day.

What was she doing with Sizemore?

She carried a large bag and paced in circles around a light pole before walking directly back to the motorhome. He watched her as she slowly opened the door and placed the large bag inside. After carefully closing the door, she turned and walked swiftly towards the grocery store with a purse tucked tightly under her arm.

Sam took one last drag and tapped the butt out in the SUV's ashtray. He opened his door and stepped outside, keeping an eye on her progress. It was a risk following her into the grocery store, but he needed to confirm that she was really the talkative waitress with the big brown eyes.

***

Nikki had about twenty minutes left before the entire store closed, and the large flower stand near the entry had already been abandoned. The photo-processing counter next to the flowers was also unmanned. A telephone caught her eye, sitting on the end of the counter behind a display of batteries.

She stopped in place and thought about it for a second. This might be her best, her only chance, to make the call to her sister Jill. There was no telling what tomorrow would bring.

The store wasn't busy, and the remaining staff seemed to be made up exclusively by tired, disengaged teenagers. She decided to go for it.

She tried to conceal herself behind the battery display rack while reaching over the counter. She spun the phone to face her and quickly dialed Jill's cellphone number from memory.

"Come on," she whispered as she listened to the rings until the voicemail message kicked in. She fidgeted while waiting for the end of the message.

"Damnit, Jill! Crap is going down here with me, but I'm okay. Travis found me, but I ditched him again. I'm on my way to you. Call you later."

Nikki replaced the receiver and casually walked towards the deli section of the store.

***

Sam peered through the automatic doors before stepping through. He didn't see the waitress immediately and quickly surveyed the front of the store, looking for a good vantage point to watch her exit though the checkout lanes. A vacant florist stand stood just inside the entry, and he moved to hide behind it. He walked around the side of the stand and stiffened.

There she was! Very close by and at the photo counter. He quickly turned his back to her. She was definitely the waitress from the diner and luckily not looking in his direction. She stood not fifteen feet away, talking on the phone. She abruptly hung up and walked away.

After she disappeared around the end of a grocery aisle, he walked up to the photo counter and looked at the phone. He pulled a pack of batteries from the display and tore a piece of the cardboard package off. He reached for the cup full of ballpoint pens on the counter and selected one. He scanned the store for any signs of the waitress emerging from the end of an aisle.

Sam lifted the receiver and pushed the redial button, quickly writing down the displayed number on the scrap of cardboard before hanging up. He pocketed the number and quickly eased back out the front door unnoticed.

34

DAY 98 – Tucson, AZ

Matt pushed though the double swinging doors, pulling a bright-orange apron off over his head as he entered. The employee break room was a fairly large room, close to square in appearance, with full kitchen amenities along one wall. Tables and chairs were placed against another wall with a few more groupings of furniture dotting the middle of the room. Sets of stacked lockers, half-height and gray, lined the other two walls.

Clear ownership of each employee's locker was literally stuck on each metal door using a length of masking tape marked with a red or black felt tip pen. The longer an employee's tenure, the more curled up their taped moniker became around the edges. Four employees sat at a table eating brown-bag lunches, while two others stood by their lockers getting ready to start a shift or go home.

Matt walked over to the locker tagged with Alex Trotter's name and fiddled with the combination lock. He pulled out his backpack and set it on the floor between his feet. He hung the apron up inside, turned and sat on an old wooden stool, bending down to tie his shoe. He unzipped the top of the backpack and saw the rolled-up sweatshirt and its lethal contents still intact.

Another employee came in, a very big man, red-headed and with freckles everywhere. Larry to his friends and Lawrence to his boss, he had a big red beard and a matching big heart. Matt returned a friendly wave from his crouched position. He was actually going to miss working at Home Depot.

"Hey, Larry," Matt said.

"Trot-man. You takin off?"

"Yeah, just about. Big night."

Tonight was the night he had been waiting for, even though he wasn't completely sure how it would turn out. Pieces of a recurring dream were all he had, plus the few details written down in his binder. Dreamt clues that had finally added up and brought him here, to this specific time and place.

It was the recurring dream about a mildly attractive young woman, a wannabe TV news anchor standing on a studio set. The dirty blonde pointed at numbered ping-pong balls spinning in a round wire basket adorned with a **Pick 5** logo, a snapshot scene of a lottery selection show that could have been happening anywhere at any time. She weakly pointed as each of the balls tumbled into a clear plastic tube.

There were four numbered balls out of the five that Matt really remembered from his dreams. The fifth numbered ball would have to be an educated guess. With thirty-nine choices and four already known, all he had to do was play all thirty-five of the remaining combinations on the one specific night.

But which night?

He had at least remembered the all-too-common moving news banner at the bottom of the TV screen in his dream. That's all it took. The TV station call letters in the corner of the screen had stood out too, K-O-L-D, ironic call letters for an Arizona broadcasting station. Other remembered fragments from his recurring dream were the spring-training baseball scores on the moving banner along with the **Pick 5** jackpot amount in big colorful numbers on the screen.

After some internet research back at the Austin public library, he knew where to be and generally when to be there. And tonight the announced jackpot had reached $97,000—the same amount he remembered from the dreams had recorded in his binder.

Matt stood up and put a couple of bottles of powders from the locker into the backpack. He cleared the shelf of a few empty Red Bull cans drained during his ten-minute breaks. He pulled on his baseball cap, loaded the backpack onto his shoulder, and walked towards a trash can. He clanked the empty Red Bull cans in.

Today was finally the day, and the suspense had kept him upbeat and energized while he worked his shift. He walked towards the swinging door into the warehouse and stopped, turning to Larry who went about buttoning up his triple extra large shirt.

"You doin anything tonight?" Matt asked.

"Nah, othing special. What's the big night for you?"

"Hot date with a blonde," Matt winked at him.

"Nice. Good luck, my man."

"Thanks."

Matt nodded at his friend as he pushed through the door.

As he made his way to the front of the store, he thought about the blonde he'd be seeing on TV soon and smiled to himself.

Luck had little to do with it.

35

DAY 137 – Ozark Mountains, AR

Solomon watched Neil Hoffman stand defiantly on the screened porch with a cigar in one hand and a scotch on the rocks in the other. He hoped the blustery speech was almost over.

"You bureaucrats would have taken forever to do what I've accomplished in a matter months! And now, you have an opening, the opening you've been looking for. I've done the country a great service."

Solomon closed his eyes, still absorbing the unfolding tale of Hoffman's rogue experiment. He had listened intently, wringing his hands. His mind drifted from Neil's disturbing facts to worrying about his innocent brother. He checked the failsafe display on his watch and wished he could begin the final countdown to ridding himself of Neil Hoffman.

The reports of mysterious civilian deaths reported by Wade Kearns at the FDA were definitely Neil's handiwork. So was the heartless killing of Jacob Shelby, one of the two acclaimed scientists who had uncovered the chemical compound. Then there was the fake company Hoffman had set up in Cincinnati to sell the drug to unsuspecting residents of a few selected cities. A horrific, direct test on human beings, conceived without Solomon's specific approval and without a formal blessing from the Otter One board.

Solomon stared at Neil. His fingers toyed with the small buttons on his watch. A severe breach of protocol such as this was the ultimate reason for the failsafe device. Security was paramount, and any risk of exposure would need to be dealt with swiftly.

The high-tech failsafe units were covertly implanted into each field operative under the guise of required medical evaluations, oral surgeries—any procedure that required anesthesia.

Solomon hesitated to immediately use the failsafe on Hoffman because of his brother. He couldn't yet ensure that Harry was safe. As much as he wanted to see Hoffman die in front of his own eyes, he'd have to wait.

"I see you're speechless, Carr. I take that as a complement."

Solomon figured Neil would be prepared to negotiate. He had to want something, in exchange for the release of his brother.

But what?

"Hoffman, your only success to date was convincing enough board members to bring you on eighteen months ago, and I wasn't one of them. The rest of this, this so-called experiment, is an unmitigated disaster."

"Disaster? You're closer than ever to actually seeing inside the human continuum and you call this a disaster? I view sacrificing a few people with small, pitiful lives for the greater good as simple collateral damage."

Solomon understood Neil's point, but Otter One's work in researching the potential through-line of human consciousness over time and space was way beyond "super secret" status within the federal government. Every recent president's hair had quickly turned gray from knowledge of the possible implications of the Otter One program. Hoffman's stunt had risked public exposure that could change the course of human history.

"From what I've heard tonight, the only thing you're close to is a string of dead bodies and incapacitated people who provided you with no knowledge. You've collected no concrete data, made no controlled experiments with this new compound. You've simply put the whole program at risk. And to top it off, you've threatened my family, for some unknown reason."

"What if there was one?"

"One what?"

"One reason. One living, breathing reason out there, someone who's experiencing things we can only guess about. A single patient, one who took the Cecilimate drug months ago and has survived on his own to this day."

Solomon tried to stay calm but could feel his face flush with anger. A living subject meant a talking one.

If Hoffman's lone patient actually existed, he or she could be a serious threat to the social structures underpinning global civilization.

Solomon realized the absolute size of Hoffman's ego as the man paced the porch under the watchful eye of Twig. He had to probe further and determine what Hoffman ultimately wanted and why he was using his brother Harry as a pawn.

"This test subject—fully functional, I assume?" Solomon asked quietly.

"And using his newfound power on occasion to affect future events, from what I can gather."

"I see. While very interesting, this person is not currently in your hands, correct?"

"That will be remedied shortly, within hours. I have resources tracking him. He's being kept out of harm's way."

Solomon had heard enough and pushed his chair back. He struggled to stand after sitting for so long.

"So, tell me what you want, Hoffman, to get my brother's life off the table."

Hoffman started around the end of the table towards Solomon. Twig stepped forward and Neil stopped. He set the glass of scotch down and slowly put both palms on the table.

"I demand credit, formal worldwide credit for the discovery, and I want to be there every step of the way on the research. I may even be a test subject. I want to see what Sizemore sees, what he knows about the universe. You get the compound to test and synthesize to perfection. You get the patient to study, and your brother survives his shift tonight at the bar. That's the deal."

Hoffman stood up and gulped down the reminder of his drink. He turned away and walked to the side table to pour himself another.

Solomon Carr did his best to hold back a smirk.

He wants the credit?

Solomon fondled his watch, secure in knowing that none of this would ever become public in any way if he could help it. And to think Hoffman demanded to be one of the first to see what the brain is fully capable of, see the untapped potential of human consciousness! Essentially see, maybe, God? He was more than willing to help Hoffman see God, but only after his brother was confirmed safe. He would play along for now.

Solomon stepped towards Neil and offered his hand.

"You're a full-blown asshole, Hoffman, but you leave me little choice but to accept," Solomon said. "It's imperative that we study this live patient of yours."

Neil's face flashed brief surprise before he grasped Solomon's hand firmly.

"This deserves another drink! Can't I tempt you, Carr? To seal the deal, as it were?"

"Consider me tempted."

"Good!"

Neil set out a second glass, dropped a few ice cubes into it, and drizzled in some of the expensive scotch. Solomon accepted the glass and raised it in the air.

"To Project Otter."

"And to the unknown world that awaits us," added Neil.

They clinked their glasses, and Solomon took a measured sip while Neil fully drained his. Hoffman slammed the glass on the table and laughed out loud.

"How soon can you get this surviving patient off the streets and, say, to the airstrip here?" Solomon asked.

"Eight, maybe ten hours at the most," Neil lied.

"Then do it. And get enough of your drug ready for controlled tests. I'll have a jet pick you up in twelve hours and deliver you and the patient to Otter One."

***

Twig and Solomon stood impatiently outside Neil's cabin as the black van powered up the driveway at high speed. Solomon pulled out his phone and dialed his brother's cell number before leaning into Twig.

"Get a team to Honey Creek Inn right now and secure my brother," Solomon said.

The black van stopped abruptly and Twig jumped in, his phone already to his ear, followed by Solomon up front. There were four Navy Seals inside, leaving two in the woods for insurance. The van sped off back to Holly Mountain airfield and the waiting jet.

Solomon slapped the dashboard in frustration as Harry's cellphone rang once, then twice.

"Damnit!"

After the fourth ring, he finally heard the familiar voice.

"Hey, bro!"

Solomon could hardly hear Harry with all the noise in the busy tavern.

"Harry! Harry, listen to me very carefully."

"What? Sully?"

"LISTEN! Do NOT leave the bar. Stay right there!"

"Don't leave?" Harry laughed, "I can't leave. Why, the place is jammed!"

"Just keep serving drinks and stay inside! I've got some good friends coming over to see you. Got it?"

"Okey-doke. I'll be here!"

***

Neil Hoffman poured another scotch for himself and started to raise the glass to his lips. He stopped midway and set the glass back down on the table. There was some unfinished business to take care of before enjoying the rest of the evening. The matter of Solomon's brother needed attention.

He opened his cell and dialed Sam Asrani.

"Yes?"

"Where are you?"

"Southern Iowa, following him. Got girl with him now."

"Bring him to the safe house in Memphis. Amanda's waiting."

"And the girl?"

"Dispose of her."

"What about bartender?"

"Have your man grab him and bring him to the safe house. I'll meet you there."

Neil closed the phone and picked up the glass of scotch. He and he alone would control when and how his man Sizemore would be turned over to Solomon Carr, and Harry the bartender remained the insurance policy that a deal was a deal.

36

DAY 137 – Mt. Pleasant, IA

Matt awoke with a jolt as another violent dream flashed across the inside of his eyelids. His jaw felt sore from clenching his teeth, and he rubbed his face and eyes. He took a few deep breaths to slow his racing pulse. He needed to get his mind to focus.

A plastic dome light over the motorhome's sink lit the interior. The driver's seat was empty, and they were parked somewhere. The keys still hung from the ignition.

Maybe she took off and was gone.

He struggled to twist out of the passenger seat with only the one good arm. The stiff shoulder didn't want to cooperate, and he moved carefully to keep the pain at a minimum. He held onto the edge of the dinette table to get his balance. Bob greeted him with a soft meow. Matt noticed Nikki's duffle bag on the floor by the door.

So, she's still here after all.

He slid into the dinette booth and parted the miniblinds. He could barely see Nikki walking towards the motorhome across the dark parking lot. She carried a plastic bag of groceries in each hand.

He opened up his backpack on the seat next to him and made sure the gun was still there and all his notebooks undisturbed.

He needed to finish his entries about Day 137, which had turned out to be one of the more eventful days so far. But he was tired, awfully tired to try and write anything down. Maybe tomorrow.

The door opened, and Nikki stepped into the motorhome with the bags. She kicked her duffle bag to the side and put the groceries on the table.

"Cool. You're awake."

"I wouldn't go that far."

Nikki pulled prepackaged and frozen meals out of the plastic bags and opened the refrigerator to load in the items.

"You kinda passed out a while back."

"Where are we?"

"Mount Pleasant. Do you want a deli sandwich? I've got turkey or ham and Swiss."

Matt pointed to an upper cabinet.

"Open that one there, please. The medicine bottle with the red cap."

Nikki found it and read the label.

"You really need sleeping pills?"

He snapped his fingers and held out his hand. She put the bottle in his palm.

"I'll need one of those beers, too."

She retrieved two beer bottles from the grocery bag and tossed the turkey sandwich on the table. He twisted open the bottle of sleeping pills and poured five into his hand. He chased the pills down his throat with most of the beer.

"That can't be good," she said.

"No choice. Have to."

Nikki sat down in the dinette seat across from him and picked up half of the sandwich. She slid the wrapper with the remaining half towards Matt.

"You should eat something if you're going to throw those down like that."

She took a big bite of her half followed by a sip of beer. Matt stared at the sandwich in front of him but didn't pick it up. Instead, he finished his beer and reached across the narrow aisle and dropped the empty bottle in the small kitchen sink. He turned to the backpack and pulled out the notebook with **Day 131** on the cover. A ballpoint pen protruded from the wire ringlets running down the spine.

"Is that a diary?" she asked.

He ignored her while he flipped through the notebook to land on the blank page for Day 137.

"I've got about thirty minutes before these pills kick in to write things down about today, what happened."

"That'll take more than thirty minutes."

He watched her smile at him as she finished her beer. She was right, but he was exhausted and not up for the banter. He needed to get as many of the day's events down on paper before the sleeping pills pulled him under.

"Just drive and let me write. Can you do that, please?"

"I'll drive if you eat that," she said, pushing the sandwich even closer.

"Head south, towards Keokuk. Follow the signs. We'll cross the Mississippi River there. And find a safe place to park away from people."

Nikki saluted Matt.

"Yes, your highness!"

She picked up her half of the sandwich and pulled some turkey meat from inside and held it up to the overhead bunk for Bob. The hungry cat leaned forward to snag it and nearly fell out of the bunk and into her arms. He happily munched it down. She stroked Bob's back before settling into the driver seat.

Matt picked up the sandwich took a small bite. It wasn't half bad. He wanted out of Iowa after the crazy day they'd experienced. He followed Nikki's lead and pulled out some turkey meat from his sandwich. He winced as he held a pinch of it up over his head with his good arm. Bob gobbled it up and finished by licking Matt's fingers clean.

***

Sam let the cigarette dangle from his lips as he checked the clip of his Glock. He picked up the silencer from the passenger seat and screwed it in place. Satisfied, he laid the gun across his lap, inhaled a long drag, and surveyed the parking lot.

Not the perfect situation, but he had kidnapped people in open surroundings before. They were at least in a dark part of the parking lot, and the grocery store was closing. The only potential witnesses might be employees leaving the store— a risk worth taking in the small town. The sooner he got Sizemore to Memphis, the sooner he could enjoy a few days with Amanda before going home.

Sam opened the door and stepped out of his SUV and ground the cigarette butt into the cracked asphalt with his shoe.

Lights were on inside the motorhome. He'd have to kill the girl first to avoid having her scream alert anyone.

He flicked the gun's safety off and started to walk across the six rows of parking spaces separating him from his goal.

The rear brakelights on the motorhome suddenly flashed red, and the engine turned over. Sam stopped in his tracks. The motorhome backed out and turned to the right, down the parking aisle.

"Goddamnit," he cursed.

Sam retreated to his SUV, put the gun on the seat, picked up another cigarette, and lit it. He watched as the motorhome left the store parking lot. He touched the button on the tracking device display, and the blue dot began flashing. He twisted the key and jammed the gearshift into drive, angry about having to chase this guy for a little while longer. He circled the lot, heading towards the exit.

At least the displayed blue dot turned south on Route 218, moving Sizemore closer to Memphis and to Amanda rather than further away. He hoped they would find a remote place to park for the night, somewhere off the beaten path, which had been Sizemore's style so far.

He could then easily carry out the instructions from Neil Hoffman.

37

DAY 114 — Rockville, MD

Kevin decided to straighten up his desk to pass the last few minutes before his meeting with Wade. As he went through the mundane tasks of rummaging through his inbox, sorting paperclips, and wiping the desktop down, his mind wandered between deep frustration over the Cecilimate case and a growing uneasiness that he was about to be fired.

He scooped up a legal pad and a pen and made his way out into the busy thoroughfare outside his cubicle. As he slowly walked down the narrow aisle, the hectic human traffic backed up behind him, and the built-up pressure only released when Kevin turned a corner towards the conference room. He was in no rush to reach his destination.

Even though he was a few minutes late, he arrived first at the conference room that had been his quasi-second home. He dropped his pad on the table and looked around the room in disbelief.

They were gone. All the Cecilimate files were gone.

He took a lap around the large conference-room table, stopping periodically to look underneath in the faint hope the files were somehow hidden there.

Wade hobbled though the door and shut it behind him.

"Where are the files?" Kevin immediately asked.

Wade walked over to a chair without looking at him.

"Downstairs. In storage. Too risky to have them out in the open."

"You've shelved it, haven't you? Shelved the case," Kevin said as he paced back and forth across the room from Wade.

"They're simply locked up for safekeeping until the root of this internal mess is cleared up."

"I see. So everything stops. Give the big bureaucrats some time to figure out how to cover their asses for when news of it hits The Washington Post. Meanwhile, people are dying out there."

"You need to trust me on this, Kevin. Can you do that?"

Kevin kept pacing and didn't respond. Wade's patience faltered.

"Goddamnit, Sharpe! Sit the hell down for a minute!"

"Why? So you can look me in the eye when you tell me I've been terminated? Someone must be cleaning out my cube right now."

"You're not fired! You just need to listen to me and trust me. This is a complicated matter for the FDA."

Kevin stopped pacing, pulled a chair away from the table, and abruptly sat down across from Wade.

"You forgot to mention the devastated families out there. I'm sure they'd understand how complicated this is for the FDA."

"You don't realize the magnitude of what will happen if I can't sort this out internally. I need your help, and Erin's, to keep what you know under wraps. If the press gets hold of it, a nice little congressional over-sight committee will threaten jail time, cut our funding, and even worse, restrict the FDA's ability to do research, provide food-safety inspections, and approve life-saving drugs for market. How many people do you think that will affect?"

Kevin glared at the ceiling. Veins throbbed in his neck.

"And if this problem is internal and starts at the top, you think you're personally safe? They've killed already, or hadn't you noticed?" Wade added.

Kevin closed his eyes and tried to breathe normally. Getting fired was one thing, being hunted down another altogether.

"So then, where are you with this big internal investigation?" Kevin said.

"The Dallas FBI office is covertly investigating a Doctor Neil Hoffman and any of his associates there at Pine Bluff. It will take some more time before they have a profile of what occurred down there. I need that time for them."

"No Shelby email records forthcoming?"

"No, the FBI is scanning them first."

"Who at Langley? I might know them."

"I'm not at—I don't think it wise to say."

"I see. So, I'm not fired but—"

"Reassigned. Temporarily. I've got plenty of other tasks that need attention. That tainted ground-beef scare in Chicago is getting big."

"Do you trust me, Wade?"

"Yes. I trust that you want to do the right thing. And doing the right thing means you need to follow my lead."

Kevin kept looking straight at Wade while pondering the question. He did understand Wade's concerns about the risk of something unacceptable going on at high levels and behind the scenes at the FDA. But keeping a serious public-health threat covered up, one already shown to have caused dozens of fatalities, was seriously pushing it. More lives were at stake, including Erin's, and Kevin decided he had to go along with Wade, at least for the time being.

"People are dying out there. Tell me you give a damn," Kevin said.

"You think I don't know that? If this isn't stopped, there'll be plenty more. I just need a little more time."

"Okay, okay. But I have one request."

"Shoot."

"A trip to Cincinnati. I can at least check out the office they occupied for this scam."

"Already done."

"Indulge me, Wade."

"There's nothing to see. The FBI report said the place was wiped clean."

"That's the point. I want to go over it myself. It can't be that perfect a clean-up job. These scam artists aren't that sophisticated."

"I don't think it's necessary. I need you elsewhere."

"Cecilimate is my case. Would you prefer I just resign? I can get rather talkative when I'm sitting around unemployed."

Wade confidently leaned forward, his arms crossed on the table.

"Kevin, your name recognition in this town isn't, let's say, the best it could be after your rather public dismissal from the FBI. Frankly, you're lucky to be a free man. The dating a foreign-spy part, that's still a little fresh in a lot of important people's minds, so, you have to ask yourself this. Am I okay flipping burgers the rest of my life after a lengthy stint in prison? Do you really think you have the depth of support to challenge the government? You know what they're capable of. But while you think over the idea of going to the press, I'll humor you and allow a pointless trip to Cincinnati. Maybe you can catch a Reds game and relax a little. Becky can make the travel arrangements."

Kevin held his tongue after Wade's harsh yet valid analysis. Wade was right, it was too big a hill to climb to bust out and go public. He decided that for now his only choice remained to suck it up and stay in control if he wanted any shot at continuing to work on the Cecilimate case. He stood up and reached his hand across the table.

"Thank you for the invaluable history lesson. And I'll take that trip to Cincy."

38

DAY 122 – Pine Bluff, AR

Doctor Neil Hoffman's greasy fingers tapped out a nervous beat on the steering wheel of his Range Rover as he pulled out of parking lot of the fast-food joint. A lunchtime jaunt for a burger and a Frosty milkshake from Wendy's was supposed to help him calm down, but the stress of waiting for answers didn't disappear.

His mind reeled from the internal deliberation of possible outcomes in tracking down Sizemore as he drove on the wooded access road back to the campus of the National Center for Toxicological Research at Pine Bluff.

Yesterday's phone call from that Las Cruces sheriff's deputy with the significant gambling problem had brought good news. A Maxine Trotter had called Las Cruces to file a missing-persons report. Her brother hadn't picked up any mail at his post office box in months. With her help in describing a class ring and an ankle tattoo, the police now felt sure Alex Trotter was the faceless man on ice in the Las Cruces morgue. Hoffman had reassured the deputy that his gambling debts would be taken care of. All he needed now was confirmation that Sizemore was posing as Alex Trotter.

The update call from hackers employed by his investor in Taiwan hadn't come yet this morning, so his fidgeting had continued since breakfast and had devolved into aggressive tapping on the steering wheel after lunch. He was within a mile of the federal lab when his phone finally rang.

Neil braked hard and steered off the road and up against the dense tree line. He fumbled for the cellphone and answered.

"Give it to me."

"The identity. It's being used," a boyish voice said.

"Where?"

"Flagstaff, Arizona. Hotel room listed for Trotter. There's also a bus ticket reserved for tomorrow morning to Denver in the same name."

"Jesus!"

"Looks like he set himself up in Tucson. Driver's license, bank account, the works. Even landed a job at Home Depot. And get this, he won nearly a hundred grand in a lottery a few weeks ago. Been in Flagstaff since he collected the cash in Phoenix."

"Send me the encrypted packet."

"Already emailed."

"Good work," Neil said.

He quickly dialed Sam Asrani. Someone picked up. Music and women's giggling voices permeated the background.

"Well, well, Hoffman," Sam answered.

"We're back in the game. Get yourself ready to move."

"Not today. Too nice here at South Beach."

"There's no time to waste! I found him. You've already been paid to complete the deal."

"Where?"

"He'll be in Denver in about twenty-four hours."

"You don't know where he is right now?"

"Goddamnit! He's in Arizona, catching a bus to Denver soon."

"How sure? I don't want to be left at bus station again with no package to collect."

"It's him. He's using the name Trotter. The man shot in the face in Las Cruces was named Trotter. The guy's sister filed a missing-persons report with the police there, and the jerkwads finally figured it out. Sizemore lifted his I.D. at the scene."

"Could be anybody. How you know?"

"Well, this dead man Trotter somehow sold his truck in Tucson and won a hundred grand in an Arizona lottery game! The lottery win wasn't a coincidence, given his abilities. You get your ass to Denver and you can keep whatever cash you find on him. If he doesn't show, I'll pay you another fifty grand. Does that get your attention?"

"Keep talking while I order more beer."

39

DAY 137 – Cannonsburg, MI

Randy sat at the end of the bar and hoped the heavy rain would stop soon. The sound of it pounding the roof was loud enough to add a muffled hum above the boisterous conversations and the rock music pouring out of the juke-box. He wanted to take the predetermined call from Sam Asrani outside, where he could have some privacy. Ten minutes to eleven and the heavens were still letting loose overhead. Fortunately the lights in the tavern had only flickered once all evening.

Two pints of hard cider were having the desire numbing affect, but he was still very aware of the decision he would have to make after talking to Sam. Unusually nervous, he had eaten way too many peanuts after already consuming a big burger, and right now, more than anything, he needed a smoke. He raised his glass for Harry the bartender to see and pointed a finger into the voided pint, a gesture more than sufficient for Harry to understand from the other end of the bar.

Randy tapped a cigarette pack on the back of his hand as he made his way to the front door. At the tavern entrance he put the cigarette in his mouth and dug for the Honey Creek Inn matchbook in his pocket before turning the vintage doorknob to go outside.

A smoky haze filled the small, covered front porch, already a standing-room-only haven for nicotine addicts getting in their fix while trying to stay dry. Randy lit up in the middle of the cramped group and stared out at the raindrops persistently hitting the road.

This wasn't going to work.

He decided on making the dash to his SUV for the phone call but only after taking in a couple more drags.

"Send a search party if I'm not back in fifteen minutes," Randy joked to the huddled group.

He sprinted down the front steps into the rain and quickly circled right, passing the crazy Volkswagen, and inhaling the faint, musty smell of wet shag carpeting. He slowed to a stop at the muddy parking lot. He was forced to tiptoe on the high ground between the puddles to reach the driver's side door. The serpentine process exposed him to the rain longer than desired.

He swung the SUV door open and jumped inside. He found an old paper napkin in a cup holder and blotted his face and forehead dry. A few large drops from overhead tree limbs randomly whacked the metal roof of the Suburban. He checked his phone. Almost eleven. He watched the rainwater run down the windshield, and the flowing movement somehow soothed him. His mind was made up.

The cellphone rang and he picked it up before the first ring was finished.

"Yeah."

"The snatch is a go. Grab the target and head south towards Memphis. Don't kill him. Call me when you're fifty miles out."

"Confirmed."

The line clicked off, and he was instantly blinded by a set of headlights turning into the parking lot. A van passed his SUV and drove around to the rear of the tavern. Four men jumped out and dashed to the back door. A second set of headlights turning off Cannonsburg Road lit up Randy's windows again. This time the headlights stopped, remaining fixed on his location. Three men exited the idling sedan and raced up to the front door of the tavern. Then the car parked right next to his SUV.

As the sedan driver opened his door and stood up, he swung his long raincoat around to protect himself from the rain and briefly exposed a shoulder holster. Randy remained perfectly still, hoping he wouldn't be noticed watching the action of what he guessed were undercover police or security forces arriving at The Honey Creek Inn. The sedan driver ran up the front steps, dodged the congregated smokers on the porch, and disappeared inside.

Whatever Sam wanted done with Harry, there were stronger forces at work that wanted to prevent it. Whoever they were, they knew what Sam was up to. Not a good thing.

Randy sat in the Suburban and debated what to do next. The safe bet was bugging out at that moment, driving home, clearing out his apartment, and going into hiding. But there was an unpaid bar tab, and he didn't want to stiff Harry Carr, the Mayor of Cannonsburg.

***

The four Navy Seals entered the dining room from the rear and fanned out after methodically checking the kitchen, storage areas, and bathrooms in the back of the tavern. They surveyed the customers sitting at tables and booths for potential risks as they worked their way towards the bar.

The three Seals who came through the front door duplicated the others' effort. A minute later they were followed inside by the driver of the sedan, a tall, lanky man who stood at the doorway shaking the wetness off his coat.

Harry recognized him from across the room.

"Hey, Stewie!" Harry yelled.

Stewart Crites nodded from behind his John Lennon glasses and made his way through the crowd to the bar.

"Howdy, Mister Mayor," Stewart said while reaching a hand across the bar. Harry gave him a hearty handshake.

"Been a while, my man."

"Had to bring some buddies down to see the place and have a drink."

Stewart draped his arms over the shoulders of two Navy Seals arriving next to him.

"Great! What'll you boys have?" Harry asked.

"Bring 'em one of those bird ciders. I've been selling it in the car all the way over here."

"Goldfinch, eh? Good choice!"

***

Randy stepped through the front door and saw the sedan driver talking to Harry while the other men went about casing the joint. These were no policemen, and he was taking a big risk by coming back inside. He calmly returned to his barstool and the now semi-warm pint of cider waiting for him. He quickly drank half of it and picked up a couple of peanuts. He cracked a few shells open, all the while attempting to eavesdrop on the conversation a few seats down the bar.

Harry brought the fresh pints of hard cider for the three men. The men all took a sip and nodded in unison. Stewart jumped into the conversation first.

"Hey, your big brother's flying in tonight. Wants to see you. Brought something back from Mexico for your collection. In fact, he's landing in about thirty minutes."

Harry jumped with excitement.

"The bronze peacock I wanted?"

"You know, you might be right, Harry. How about we run out to the factory and meet the plane?"

"I dunno. A little busy—"

"Isn't Scotty here?"

"Yeah, was slower earlier, so I let him off. But he's around here somewhere, though."

Stewart looked around and spotted Scotty, the son of one of Harry's old college buddies, sitting at a table with two girls.

"Scotty!"

A young man stood up and looked for the source, then waved. Stewart pointed to behind the bar.

"Can you cover?" Stewart blared.

"Sure!" Scotty responded.

He said something to the young women, who clearly liked that he was the man in charge now. Scotty came around the end of the bar, and Harry tossed him his bar towel.

"Cool, man! Thanks! Bro's landing soon."

"Gotch your back, Harry. Go."

Randy watched as the sedan driver and the two other Navy Seals drained half of their pints while their eyes continued searching the tavern. They escorted Harry Carr to the back of the main room, through the swinging doors and into the kitchen. The remaining Seals in the tavern split up with a few leaving through the front door and the rest following out the back, all the while constantly surveying the room.

Randy dropped a handful of peanuts back in the bowl. His stomach had had enough. He wished he had antacid tablets for the drive back to Chicago. He nursed the rest of the cider for another ten minutes, waiting for the coast to fully clear, before he dropped a wad of cash on the bar that included a sizable tip for Harry.

He stood up and walked to the front door, turned and absorbed one last look at The Honey Creek Inn of Cannonsburg, Michigan, a comfortable place he could never return to. He paused at the bottom of the front steps to laugh at the sight of the ugly VW one last time.

After a hasty drive back to Chicago to permanently close up shop, he figured he'd cruise around the country on back roads for a while and see what he could find.

There must be a few small towns in need of a new mayor.

40

DAY 124 – Denver, CO

Matt's attempt to splash water on his face wasn't overly successful. The small bathroom tucked into the rear corner of the Greyhound bus constantly jostled around so that more water landed on his shirt than on his face.

Another passenger pounded on the bathroom door.

"Any time now!" a raspy male voice growled.

"A minute, okay?" Matt responded.

He gave up the fight with the water and toweled himself off as best he could. More significant pounding rattled the flimsy door.

"Jesus Christ!"

"Doubtful he can help you in there," the voice cackled from outside.

Matt snatched his backpack off the covered toilet seat and opened the door.

"Sorry," Matt said sarcastically to the old-timer as he slid out of the way.

The old cowboy pushed his way past him and his bulging backpack. Matt let the encounter with the old man go. The last twenty-four hours on the bus had been tougher than he expected. His old hotel room in

Flagstaff was better than this cramped busload of people of all nationalities. There were whining children and no shortage of personal aromas to deal with. Thankful the bus was arriving half hour early into Denver, he anxiously awaited getting out of the sardine can and stretching his legs.

Flagstaff had been helpful. He had focused on trying to get some quality rest while also filling out pages detailing recurring dreams and images trapped in his head. He updated the daily events and descriptions in his notebooks. The confusing dreams and nightmares had continued, and the overnight hours were still rough to get through, but he'd made progress in dialing in the best cocktail of herbal substances to help him deal with the lack of REM sleep and recover the next day.

There were new herbs to try on his visits to the local health-food store after the frequent stops at the Flagstaff public-library computers to look up any news on Las Cruces. It had been more than forty-eight hours since he'd last checked the news on the internet, and the Denver library would be his next stop after finding a place to stay for the night.

The bus coasted down the freeway into metropolitan Denver. Matt looked out the window at the suburban sprawl engulfing the flat plains around the city center. The bus driver's voice crackled over the PA system.

"Folks, we'll be arriving in Denver shortly and ahead of schedule by twenty-five minutes or so. Check the overhead monitors in the terminal for your connecting bus. Our through passengers will have a little over an hour before we depart for Chicago. Thank you for riding Greyhound."

Matt smiled at the thought of actually riding a Greyhound dog.

Probably just as uncomfortable as riding this bus.

He hoped to find a decent hotel within walking distance before his next leg of confinement to Kansas City.

***

Sam Asrani walked out of the bus terminal after checking on the arrival time for Sizemore's bus and headed back to his rented SUV. He had thirty minutes to wait, more than enough time for a smoke. He reached his vehicle and sat inside.

His vantage point a few blocks away from the back side of the bus station was perfect. Approaching buses were easily seen coming down the street behind the terminal and turning into the designated parking slots. He picked up his binoculars and double-checked his bearings. All he had to do was watch space #27, the sixth spot from the end. The slot was occupied now but slated to be vacated any minute. He set the binoculars down, powered his window halfway open, and lit a cigarette.

Something caught his eye in the rearview mirror. Sam watched intently as a Denver metro police cruiser approached and slowly rolled past. The patrol car paused at the next intersection, and the white reverse lights came on. He slid his fingers around the gun in his lap just in case, but the cop car turned and backed into a warehouse driveway between parked semi-trailers.

He quickly picked up his binoculars after noticing another police car moving towards him from the front, a few blocks directly ahead. He watched the black-and-white cruiser slow down and park against the curb, a full block short of the bus terminal. Sam tossed the binoculars on the seat. He knew what was happening.

He checked the silencer to make sure it was locked in place, then opened the glove compartment and took out two more clips of bullets and shoved them in his coat pocket. With the local police clearly setting up surveillance of the terminal, he felt certain the package he was sent to collect would actually arrive this time, just as Hoffman said.

Whether he could get to Sizemore before the police did was another matter. He pocketed the Glock in his coat and stepped out of the SUV. There was just enough time left to take another stroll through the terminal to see what he was up against.

***

The bus driver rolled past occupied arrival lane #27 and looked for an alternate. He saw an opening ahead and made the final turn into slot #16. The PA snapped to life again.

"Welcome to Denver. Please be careful as you collect your belongings. Items stowed overhead may have shifted."

The bus came to a halt under the protective metal canopy, and most of the passengers immediately stood up. The bus driver opened the door and exited first. The line of passengers began to move, and Matt stood up and stretched his tight back muscles. He swung the backpack over his shoulder before falling in line.

The late afternoon sun was bright as he stepped off the bus, and Matt pulled the brim of his baseball cap further down over his eyes. The concrete concourse was a grinding mixture of exhaust fumes, bodies, and baggage. Departing passengers were forced to merge with arrivals emerging from their own buses, and all were randomly weaving together near the entrance into the terminal itself.

He passed one policeman standing to the side and up against the terminal wall. The cop seemed distracted, looking away and not interested in Matt's group of passengers. But as he reached the automated double doors into the terminal, he caught a glimpse of a grouping of six police officers standing further ahead near an angled parking slot where a bus was slowly backing out. He looked up at the overhead signs. They were all standing beneath the sign for #27. Something didn't feel right.

Matt followed the masses into the big terminal and exited out of the oversized conga line and over to a wooden bench in the middle of the large room. He set his backpack down on the seat and unzipped the side pocket and pulled out his bus ticket.

It was right there, clear as a bell.

The preprinted and planned arrival slot for his bus was #27.

Matt spun his head around, gazing into the large room full of people. His heightened focus tried to pick out any odd movements or persons possibly converging on him. He saw one policeman by an exit door, but the cop wasn't looking in his direction. He stopped scanning the room and focused on the large display screen hanging from the ceiling.

He found the illuminated data line with his bus information. The arrival time shown was still twenty minutes out and the parking slot number was #27. The monitor data suddenly changed and displayed his bus number as having arrived in #16.

A loud disruption outside shocked Matt. He heard yelling outside near the buses, the sound echoing off the metal canopy. The Denver policemen ran past the open double doors, aggressively motioning to the congested passengers to move out of the way.

A dazed Matt didn't feel the bus ticket slip through his fingers and float to the floor. He snapped out of the momentary panic and quickly surveyed the room again. They would be on him within seconds. The jig was up. He had to clear out of there. The police had to be after a ticketed Greyhound passenger named Alex Trotter.

***

Sam wouldn't have to wait the extra twenty minutes for the bus to arrive after all. Based upon the overhead monitor, the man he was looking for was here already.

His well-trained eye stayed focused on the crowd inside the terminal when the commotion started outside. Most passengers inside the terminal reacted to the policemen running and yelling by stopping whatever they were doing and taking a step closer to the action, the seemingly universal human trait of ambulance chasing. But there was one passenger who picked up his belongings off a bench, pulled his baseball cap lower, and began to move in the opposite direction.

Sam watched the disheveled passenger shuffle between people.

That had to be Sizemore.

He watched as a policeman guarding the east exit let his eyes land on a weaving Sizemore making his way through the sea of people. The cop took a step forward to try to keep a view of the retreating man. Sam needed a distraction.

The original 1970s decor of the terminal was intact, including the four rows of large round light fixtures hanging from the ceiling. The opaque white globes were an easy target. Sam slid the Glock out of his pocket and held it close to his hip. He picked out a globe away from Sizemore's path.

He tilted the gun upward and squeezed off a silent shot. The globe burst like a balloon, raining thin feathers of glass that drifted to the floor. The terminal passengers gasped in unison. The sound got the attention of the policeman watching Sizemore. Sam made sure he could be seen by the cop and then sprinted towards the south doorway. The officer moved off of Sizemore and gave chase towards Sam, pushing to get through the shocked crowd.

"You! Stop! Police!"

Passengers stumbled out of the way as the policeman followed Sam. Sam neared full speed upon reaching the south entrance, leaving no time for an officer stationed there to react. The cop had just turned away from looking at the ceiling when Sam lowered his shoulder and rammed him squarely in the sternum, spinning him hard into the wall. The force of the impact left the cop gasping for breath on the floor.

Outside on the busy sidewalk, Sam ran to the left. He had to get around the building and secure Sizemore at the opposite doorway, now vacated, before more policemen joined in the search. He rounded the corner of the building on a full run and nearly decapitated a college girl pulling a small suitcase on wheels. She shrieked as he somehow danced around the obstruction and stumbled forward, catching himself just before arriving at the north entrance.

He quickly looked around for the man Hoffman wanted. There was no sign of Sizemore. A field of parked cars spread out before him with many people coming and going. He ran towards the parking lot, weaving back and forth trying to find the man in the baseball cap.

Where was he?

Sam frantically scanned spaces between parked cars hoping to find his package hiding and quivering in fear. Nothing. No sign of him, and time was running out. A policeman came around the building and began to survey the parking lot. Sam crouched low and dashed between parked cars towards the edge of the parking lot bordering the four-lane city street.

At the edge by the sidewalk, Sam quickly stood up. The policeman was looking between cars on the other side of the lot with his gun drawn. Two new cops swarmed out of terminal in support. Sam checked the lot one more time but still no baseball cap was visible. He knelt down again and leaned from behind the hood of the last car, looking up and down the sidewalk. He tightly gripped the handle of the Glock in his coat.

Govno! I can't lose him!

It wasn't exactly a prayer, but it somehow was answered by a UPS delivery truck passing by on the street. A man carrying a backpack was hanging on the rear step of the brown van, his arm looped through a side handle and holding tight to the rim of his baseball cap.

Sam sprinted through an opening in traffic as he watched the van turn at a cross street. Once on the opposite sidewalk he realized chasing him on foot would be a lost cause. He had to get back to his SUV.

He retreated down the first side street to avoid police detection and circled around the terminal. From there it was an open run for half a block, followed by a sharp turn down an alley. A final sprint brought him to his SUV. He leaned against a brick wall, briefly catching his breath before carefully looking both ways on the street. With the coast clear, he casually walked out and over to his vehicle. A quick U-turn pointed him towards the last known path of the delivery truck.

***

The boulevard was big, and the traffic lights seemed to be favoring the UPS driver. Matt held on tight with his eyes closed. The wind was cold, and his arm felt numb. At least he was putting some distance between himself and the bus station, but the consistent flow of traffic gave him no opportunity to jump off.

A car following the truck started honking, the concerned woman driver waving her hand out the window, trying to get the UPS driver's attention. Her car was about to pull up next to the driver's side when the UPS truck turned right, leaving the honking woman behind.

***

Sam was barely able to keep the top of the UPS truck in view above the traffic as he raced to catch up from a few blocks away. An inconvenient red light stopped him abruptly, and he slammed his fists on the dashboard.

"Ahhh! Come on!"

He watched the roof of the UPS truck continue for another block and then, miraculously, make a turn to the right. At the green light Sam jerked the rented SUV right, cutting off another car waiting on the inside lane, and accelerated into the residential neighborhood on a parallel street three blocks away from the brown truck.

***

The UPS truck slowed to a stop in front of one of the small, densely packed brick houses in the leafy working-class neighborhood just north of downtown Denver. Matt jumped off the back of the truck and hid behind a row of dense bushes framing the corner of a front yard. He rubbed his arm as he witnessed the UPS driver step out of the truck and walk up to a front porch with a small package. The driver quickly retreated to the idling truck and drove off down the block.

It would be dark soon, and Matt didn't know where he was. The prospect of spending a cold night behind a garage or under a porch wasn't appealing. He exited the bushes and walked down the sidewalk. He stopped at the next corner. Just more rows of houses in both directions.

He walked another block straight ahead, passing more small brick homes. Some were well kept with nice land-scaping, while others were overgrown, a few even boarded up. He exchanged a friendly wave with a curious old man sitting on his front steps drinking a beer.

After a turn to the left at a corner, he stopped to relieve himself behind a tall hedge. He was tired. Nightfall would arrive soon, and he had to prepare. He pondered his limited options. As he blankly stared across the street thinking, Matt's eyes finally landed on a beautiful sight.

FOR SALE!

A large FOR SALE sign showed through the windshield of an older mini-motorhome parked in a driveway. Matt quickly zipped up and walked over to the house.

***

The neighborhood streets all looked the same to Sam, and it seemed like he was driving in circles. He pulled up slowly to the next stop sign, undecided on his next move. He put his head against the steering wheel for a moment but a loud honk snapped him upright.

What the hell?

Sam looked up, but there was no car in his rearview mirror. To his right, a UPS truck driver waved him to go first through the intersection. The hairs on the back of his neck stood up in anticipation. He picked up his Glock.

He motioned for the UPS driver to go first, which he did, while he anxiously waited for the rear of the brown truck to pass. The rear step was empty. He looked both ways down the street. Sizemore could be anywhere.

Did he talk his way into a house? Was he simply hiding somewhere close by until sunset?

Sam turned down an alley behind the rows of houses, and it was dark enough that the SUV's headlights came on automatically. He decided to do a few more circuits through the neighborhood streets in the hopes of finding Sizemore. There wasn't much time left before he would have to make the call to Hoffman sharing the news that his prized possession had gone missing.

***

"That there switch is for the generator," the older black man with the short white hair instructed Matt from the open driver's side door of the small motorhome.

"What's this toggle switch?" Matt asked from the driver's seat.

"You got two gas tanks, that's how you change over from one to the other."

"Okay. Anything else?"

"Can't run the A/C unless the generator's running or you're plugged in. Fridge works on propane, tank is outside over here. Compartment behind the driver's door. Should last 'bout a month between fill-ups."

"Thanks. Everything else here looks normal to me," Matt said as he scanned the dashboard.

"Just a regular van cab, 'cept there's a bed over your head."

Matt turned the key and the motorhome came to life. He closed the door and rolled down the window. The old man had tears on his cheeks.

"Mary and I had a good time in this rig before she got sick, but I gots to let her go."

"Tell your daughter I'm sorry if I upset her," Matt said.

"She'll be fine. I'll talk to her. We're all thankful you came along when you did," the old man said.

He reached and put a hand on Matt's arm. Matt shifted the idling motorhome into Drive.

"Be good to that ailing wife of yours, Richard, and best of luck to you and your family."

"Godspeed to you, George."

Matt took the FOR SALE sign off the dashboard and dropped it on the passenger seat. He waved at the man as he slowly pulled out of the driveway.

He hoped Richard's daughter would follow through on his unwanted comments and go get the mammogram he sensed she needed. Her life and her ability to care for her elderly parents might depend on it.

***

Sam looked for a Wendy's fast-food restaurant as he cruised down the four-lane boulevard after the unsuccessful search of the neighborhood. His one addiction to American fast food, courtesy of Neil Hoffman, was the malt-flavored chocolate Frosty. He was hungry, too, and before making the call to Hoffman with the disappointing news, a big burger followed by the obligatory Frosty chaser sounded good.

Sitting first in line at a stop light, he saw McDonald's golden arches up ahead on the right and a Red Lobster restaurant on the opposite side. Not his first choices, but there wasn't a Wendy's in sight.

Headlights slowly pulled up behind him at the red light. The headlights on the vehicle were higher off the ground and were blinding Sam as he looked in the rearview mirror. He flicked the mirror up as the light changed green.

Sam decided to pass on the current food options and see what might lie ahead on the next few blocks of the boulevard. Before the next stoplight, he moved into the slow lane as he thought he recognized a tall Wendy's sign further ahead on the right. The truck with the headlights pulled up next to him at the red light, and he realized it was a van, actually a camper of some sort.

The domelight in the motorhome cab suddenly went on, illuminating the interior. A barely recognizable figure in a baseball cap fumbled with a folding map.

His craving a Frosty would have to wait.

***

The passing headlights and overhead streetlights were already lulling Matt to sleep. He had to find a place to park for the night and get himself prepared to deal with the dreams that would surely come. He turned into an entrance of a large city park dotted with manmade lakes that he had seen on the map. He followed the curvy access road until he found a quiet corner near the water and backed into a parking space.

He turned on a light inside and set his backpack on the counter. He downed the required sleeping pills with a palm-ful of water from the small kitchen sink. Matt attempted to convert the dinette table into the bed but couldn't figure out how to do it. He kicked off his shoes and started to climb up onto the bunk above the cab but thought better of it. A fall from up there during a violent dream would hurt.

He pulled the seat cushions from the dinette and arranged them on the coffin-sized floor, followed by a blanket and pillow off the bed above the cab. He set the backpack on the floor nearby in case the police started whacking on the door in the middle of the night.

***

Sam Asrani sat in his car and watched a group of teenagers goofing off along the lakeshore in the park. They were laughing and jumping around near the motorhome. One of the boys tossed something into the lake. Sam lifted his binoculars and saw the boys each holding a kitten. They tossed them one-by-one into the lake and then laughed some more as the kittens tried to swim.

His cellphone rang for the third time within fifteen minutes. He'd ignored the previous two calls from Hoffman while following Sizemore. The fisherman obviously was wondering if the package had been picked up.

"Goddamnit, Asrani! Where have you been?" Hoffman barked.

"There were complications."

"What complications? Do you have him?"

"Law-enforcement complications. At the bus station. They waiting for him. I helped him escape."

"DO YOU HAVE HIM?"

Sam watched a light come on inside the motorhome. Sizemore stormed out, waving his arms and yelling at the teenagers. The boys ran off. Sizemore bent down and pulled the kittens out of the water one by one, tossing them onto the grass near a terrified mother cat.

"Yes. I observe him across parking lot now. Area appears secure."

Sizemore stood watching the soaked kittens take off across the grass, following their petrified mother to safety in some thick bushes--all except one. Sizemore picked up the shivering kitten and took it back into the motorhome.

"Where are you?"

"City park. He stole a vehicle, a motorcoach."

"He's going to drive there," Hoffman said.

"What you say?"

"Drive! Drive to Cincinnati. He can't use his bus ticket if the police are onto him."

"I grab him now?"

Sam saw the lights go out inside the motorhome.

"No, not yet. Follow him out of town, away from the city. The less potential attention the better."

Sam wanted to slam the phone on the dashboard. He was tired of chasing the man. He took a deep breath.

"At least get me the friggin surveillance unit so I don't have to be awake day and night."

"Fine. I'll send it ahead. Don't screw this up until—"

Sam hung up on the fisherman and powered off the phone. He had almost had enough of the fat man.

Only one thing would make him feel better right now, a quick drive back to Wendy's before a long night watching the motorhome.

41

DAY 137 – Keokuk, IA

The pleasant hills and valleys of the Iowa plateau gave way to much steeper ravines the closer Nikki drove to the monstrous Mississippi River. She didn't like the prospect of parking for the night on any nearby side road as the man had requested. A dark road in one of these steep wooded gullies felt more scary than private, a bad slasher movie set ripe for a victim's demise. She opted to keep driving and see what the town of Keokuk had to offer. It was just after 11 p.m., and although she'd been up since before five, Nikki remained anxious to at least make it to the riverside town.

The motorhome's headlights soon flashed on a passing road sign, confirming that the destination city of Keokuk lay 17 miles ahead. She relaxed deeper into the driver's seat and kept her tired eyes on the road.

Nikki stretched an arm up over her head and yawned, bumping into Bob as he sat on her headrest.

"Sorry, Bobby boy."

She took a look over her shoulder at the sleeping man in the dinette booth. He was bent forward onto the tabletop, his head draped over his one good forearm, covering up the scribbles he had been writing in his notebook.

Trotter, George, or whoever he was had been through a lot that day too, including an injured shoulder courtesy of Travis.

She reached behind her head and lifted Bob off of his perch, against his will, and dropped the cat into her lap. Momentarily frozen stiff with panic, Bob finally curled up content and enjoyed the extra attention for the duration of the ride into Keokuk.

***

The tracking device tucked into the ladder of Sizemore's motorhome was working well. The blinking blue dot on Sam's monitor showed the vehicle just a couple miles ahead of him. With luck, they would pull over soon and find a private place to park for the night. Sizemore usually avoided heavily populated areas, parking off the beaten path when possible. Sam hoped tonight would be the same.

Sam tossed his cellphone on the passenger seat. He had finished the quick call to Randy in Michigan with instructions for kidnapping the bartender. He could now concentrate on his own part of the next phase, securing Sizemore and bringing him to Hoffman's safe house outside Memphis. The big-eyed waitress with the pink in her hair was an unfortunate obstacle that had to be dealt with. Of the many ways to get rid of her body that had crossed his mind, the wide expanse of the nearby Mississippi River seemed to provide the best opportunity.

Sam cracked his window in preparation for another smoke, something to take the edge off before his final assault on the man and his companion.

Proclivity

***

The large "Welcome to Keokuk" sign on the side of the road announced a population of over 12,000 in the historic river town separating Iowa from Illinois. Nikki looked for a suitable place to park. She passed suburban homes on large lots before she found herself in more densely packed neighborhoods near downtown.

A billboard five miles back for a Best Western hotel had caught Nikki's eye as a good potential place to stop and use the parking lot for the night. But a sizable glow from a brand new Wal-Mart ended up being even more attractive.

"Here we go," she said, braking for the turn.

A dozen other motorhomes of all sizes were already parked in a row on one side of the big parking lot. She circled in front of the grouping and then carefully backed in between a converted school bus camper and a larger, much more expensive motorcoach. It might not be what she had been specifically told to do, but parking here felt safer than somewhere out in the countryside. And the Wal-Mart was open twenty-four hours in case she needed anything, anything at all.

She shifted into park and turned off the engine.

"Okay, Bobby, up you go."

She stood and put the cat back up on his bunk. Both of them stopped for a second and stared at the sleeping man at the table.

Nikki turned the light on over the kitchen sink before closing the curtains in the front along the windshield, and then followed suit with the mini-blinds covering the side windows. She flicked the light off again for a second, happy to see that it would stay dark enough inside to sleep in the well-lit parking lot.

With the light flipped back on, it was time to deal with him. Sleeping that way at the table, his one arm in a sling, couldn't be comfortable or a good idea.

She grabbed the seat-back cushions from the dinette, laid them on the floor, and added the other seat cushion to complete a makeshift mattress. She pulled a sheet out from under Bob, draped it on the cushions, and added a pillow and blanket from the bunk.

Now came the hard part. She stood over the man wondering how to move him without hurting him. Nikki turned to Bob for inspiration.

"This will be interesting. Any ideas?"

Any jarring movement might wake him up, even after his big dose of sleeping pills. She also had to be careful of the injured shoulder. She decided to try and slide him to the edge of the seat, cushion and all, and then lower him onto the floor from there.

Nikki knelt low and grabbed the end of the occupied seat cushion. The first weak tug on the cushion yielded no movement. Her second attempt moved him an inch. She pulled again hard and he slid even further, notebook and all under his arm, towards the end of the booth seat. He stirred just a bit, the sleeping pills doing a good job of keeping him under.

For the next step, she reached around his waist from behind and locked her arms around him tight. She twisted his torso slowly and pulled him towards the edge of the seat. He teetered on the edge and, as much as Nikki tried, she couldn't hold back gravity. She fell backwards with him onto the cushions with a small thud, the man landing on her lap.

The jolt got him squirming, and he started waking up. She managed to wiggle out from under him as he mumbled something.

"Just lay down, okay?"

The man relaxed in her arms, and she carefully laid him out on his back. Crawling over to his feet, Nikki lifted one leg onto the bedding, followed by the other, and took off his dirty tennis shoes. She unfurled the blanket and spread it over him last.

She stood up at the opposite end of the motorhome from Bob and stared wide-eyed at the cat, and in her best wrestlemania pose, flexed her arms in a circle with fists facing each other.

"Grrrr!" she grunted.

Bob turned his little head to the side, the quizzical equivalent of 'What the hell was that?'

"Mission accomplished!"

She turned and stepped into the bathroom as Bob watched. A minute later she came out in her panties and carrying her jeans, which she promptly tossed on top of her duffle bag on the floor. She pulled one of the two layers of t-shirt over her head and tossed it on the dinette seat.

The man's open notebook balancing on the edge of the table invited her to look, even though he had warned her not to. Nikki paused over the pages with "Day 137" scrawled at the top. She needed to know more.

Was she in danger? What had he done? Why was it Day 137?

She glanced at the man on the floor and then turned to Bob.

"I'm not too good at following rules."

Nikki put her elbows on the table and started to read.

The man had recapped the day's events in a jumbled way, some pieces out of sequence as far as she remembered, and she struggled to read his messy handwriting.

The interior décor of Maybelle's Diner wasn't favorably described. He recounted being "drawn" to Swisher as he crossed into Iowa from Nebraska. He mentioned her, as "tattooed and talkative" and "irritating," and wrote about the vision of broken glass after seeing the snakehead tattoo on her neck—a scene he had dreamt before. Nikki pursed her lips at the thought of being irritating, as he was the one that had the bad attitude upon their meeting.

He wrote about the tense encounter with Travis and the subsequent crash of the truck into the diner. He described his escape from the hospital before being questioned by the police. He took a cab back to Maybelle's. Then he mentioned her again.

He said she "had a strong will" and that she had forced him to take her with him. But he did also note that she had "big brown eyes" and "a nice smile," and he would let her drive a while as it helped him until he could get stronger.

Nikki closed the notebook and pushed it to the side. She was too tired to read more. She looked down at the man on the floor and wondered how he ended up this way. There had to be a regular person in there somewhere, behind all the internal terrorizing his mind seemed to be absorbed with. She didn't know how long this funky partnership would last either, but maybe tomorrow she could coax some more history out of him.

After a quick drink of water at the sink while straddling the comatose man on the floor, she turned off the light and started to climb up onto the bunk above the cab.

"Move over, Bob, you've got a roommate now."

***

It took Sam a few minutes to find the motorhome in the Wal-Mart parking lot, and he wasn't happy about it. Not happy at all.

A new store, one of those mega-monster places you don't find in Europe, was right here in this small town. "Open 24 Hours" meant activity, too much of it. "New" also meant a bright parking lot and no shortage of security cameras to contend with. And once he saw the roving security guard in the golfcart, Sam knew he'd have to change plans.

He was tired of waiting. Tired of driving. Tired of endless cornfields and open prairie. But the professional in him knew better than to let his own frustrations get in the way. As much as he wanted to secure Sizemore once and for all, he would have to be patient and pick the right moment.

Sam drove out of the Wal-Mart parking lot and across the street to a Denny's for an overdue meal. He parked and walked up towards the front door. He spied a vacant auto-repair shop next door to the restaurant with a side parking area that was dark and industrial. He judged that a good view could be had from an inconspicuous spot under a corrugated-metal cover jutting out from the side of the building. He decided he would park there for the night and exact his growing frustration on Sizemore in the morning.

Before walking into Denny's, Sam stopped at the newspaper rack and thought about buying a USA Today to see what the weather was like back in South Florida. He decided against it, knowing it would only piss him off.

42

DAY 137 – Washington, D.C.

Erin accepted her roommate Pam's hand in helping her get up off the deep couch as movie credits rolled on the TV. Erin rubbed her suddenly taut stomach as she slowly stood erect, all the while silently cursing the evening's trifecta of Taco Bell, Orville Redenbacher's, and brothers Ernest and Julio Gallo.

"I told you not to do it," Pam said. "If I didn't know better, I'd say you're looking kinda pregnant."

Erin twisted her face.

"I'm not sure how to take that."

"You know what I mean. The second bag of popcorn did us in."

"No kidding."

Pam stepped into the kitchen but quickly reappeared in the doorway holding up the empty popcorn bag.

"If I'm wrong, you and Kevin can always name it Orville."

"Never shoulda said anything about Kevin, huh?"

"Nope!"

A cellphone began to vibrate on the coffee table as Pam came back into the room. Erin reached for it, but Pam

245

lunged and got there first. She snatched up Erin's phone and looked at the screen before showing it to Erin.

"Speak of the devil. A Mister Sharpe for you."

Erin stared down at the screen for a moment. Pam handed it to her.

"Aren't you going to answer?"

Erin nodded and touched the screen. She tried to hold back her excitement that the trip to Cincinnati with Kevin was the day after tomorrow.

"Hello?"

Erin immediately wished she could have brought more energy to the salutation.

"How's unemployment treating you?" Kevin said. The background noise on Kevin's end crackled in Erin's ear.

"Okay, I guess."

"I heard the law judge asked you to come back."

"Word gets around."

"I have my sources, gotta keep tabs on the team."

The scratchy noise was getting worse.

"Where are you?" Erin asked.

"Charleston, South Carolina. Another one of Wade's temporary assignments. Trying to find a flight back to D.C. That's what I'm calling about."

Erin's mind quickly calculated the possibilities.

"Need me to pick you up?" she asked as Pam jumped up and down in front of her.

"No, no. I'm good. About Cincinnati, I can't drive you to the airport tomorrow. Wade's got some meeting he's forcing me to attend. Just meet me at Dulles at four."

"Okay, see you there."

"Great. Thanks, Erin."

Kevin hung up, and Erin closed the cellphone and set it down.

"So?" Pam asked.

Erin felt her stomach.

"I think I'm gonna puke."

43

DAY 137 – Above Indiana

Solomon Carr stared out the window of his jet at the twinkling city lights of South Bend, Indiana, from 10,000 feet up. The golden dome at the University of Notre Dame glowed beautifully just north of the city, a nightly beacon shinning for all to see. He always looked forward to this view while descending into Grand Rapids and back to Otter One.

He turned his attention to his wristwatch and the still-illuminated red light next to the number 4 on the dial. The armed failsafe was ready to go. And he was ready, more than ready, to end the exasperating life of Neil Hoffman.

Twig entered the cabin and quickly sat across from him as Solomon fondled the watch.

"Harry's safe, sir. Stewart and the team have him at the hangar."

Solomon looked out the window, seeming indifferent to the news. He tried not to show any emotion. He covered his eyes with his hand for a moment before taking a deep breath and stared up at the cabin ceiling, hoping to keep a tear from running down his cheek.

"We're about twenty minutes out, sir," Twig said, "Do you plan to activate?"

He turned to Twig and composed himself quietly without responding.

"I should alert the men on the ground if that is your plan," Twig offered.

Solomon looked down at the watch. He could freely activate the implanted failsafe now with no repercussions. Harry was safe and waiting on the tarmac for his return. Men were in place to do any clean up necessary at Hoffman's cabin in Arkansas. Any covering details of Hoffman's demise could be easily fabricated and distributed to news outlets. He was tempted, but it wasn't quite time yet. A chance existed to learn more.

"No. No, this time we wait. We'll see what his next move is tomorrow. Who he calls. Who he talks to and what he does at the office. He has to have help."

"Understood, and wise, sir."

"Do we have active surveillance on all his phones and official devices?"

"Yes, we have him covered."

"Then get a new team ready at Pine Bluff for clean-up duty when I do activate. Have your men at the cabin stay close to him and follow him to his office in the morning."

"Yes, sir," Twig said before retreating to the front of the plane.

Solomon looked down at his watch again. Almost midnight. He closed his eyes and leaned back on the plush headrest. The stressful day was nearly over, and he could soon get some sleep, knowing his brother was safe.

Tomorrow the fun would begin.

44

DAY 137 – Cedar Rapids, IA

The sutures holding his neck wound tightly closed allowed Travis Whitacre to rotate his head only so far. He could feel them pull and didn't want to test their strength. He managed just enough of a turn to see the glowing time display on the digital clock in his dimly lit hospital room--11:30 p.m. The hanging IV bag of heavy sedatives and painkillers had been full an hour ago but was now completely empty.

Travis cringed with pain as he reached across his body with his right hand and arched his back. His fingers probed the wet area under his left hip. He felt around for the open end of the plastic IV tube. He could replace it now that the solution from the IV bag had drained directly into the sheets. He could deal with the pain. It was a clear head that he needed most.

It took some manual dexterity to hold the small tube between his large fingers. The uncomfortable tugging of sutures kept his movements slow and deliberate.

He finally slid the open IV tube back onto the host needle taped down tight to his left forearm. He had made sure the nurse would think he'd pissed the bed, having gingerly pulled the urinary catheter out from his member minutes after she left his room.

A half-eaten dinner sat on its tray on the rolling table next to the bed. The food was generally abysmal, and rather than eating most of it, he instead dreamed about finding a nice big steakhouse after busting out of the hospital. He had to escape soon. His options would be severely limited once the police moved him to a county jail.

Travis touched a finger on the bullet wound in his shoulder to gauge sensitivity to movement. The pain at the entry point wasn't as bad as he'd thought it would be. His neck actually felt worse.

The door to his room opened slowly, and Travis quickly closed his eyes and lay still. Light from the hallway cast a thin bright ray into the room. The portly Cedar Rapids police officer guarding him peeked in first before stepping inside. He listened closely as the officer tip-toed up to his bedside. Travis barely opened an eye and watched the officer scan the tray, pick up a leftover dinner roll, and tear a bite out of it. He then grasped the juice box of apple cider and sipped on the small straw sticking out the top.

The officer then quietly walked around the end of the bed, holding the juice box in one hand, the dinner roll lodged in his mouth, and picked up the TV remote off the side table. He silently looked it over for a few seconds before pointing it at the TV hanging from the ceiling. The officer quickly pushed the mute button as the TV sprang to life. He reached up and swiveled the TV a bit to face an oversize leather armchair across from Travis's bed.

Travis peeked out of the corner of his eye as the officer slowly settled into the armchair by the window. The cop glanced over at him for a moment to make sure the light from the TV hadn't awakened him. Satisfied, the cop flipped through a few channels before landing on a baseball game. The policeman smiled as he looked up at the TV, munching on the roll and washing dry bites down with swigs of the apple juice.

A St. Louis batter stroked a double off the center-field wall, and the guard pumped his fist. The officer was clearly a Cardinals fan. Travis hoped tonight's game was the start of a three-game series.

An escape plan, newly rattling around in his drug-free head, depended upon it.

45

DAY 138 – Keokuk, IA

Matt straddled a makeshift litter box made from cereal boxes on the floor and leaned in closer to the bathroom mirror while holding a small pair of scissors. His left arm still in a sling, he carefully snipped away at his goatee with his right, trimming ever closer to his skin, the white hairs floating down into the tiny sink. It was time to say goodbye to Alex Trotter for good.

The Cedar Rapids police would certainly learn about Trotter's narrow escape from the authorities in Denver a couple of weeks before after yesterday's wild events in Swisher. The expanding identity trail across the West left by Trotter had to end.

He had plenty of cash left to get him to Cincinnati, to track down the elusive Dr. Cecil Ross, and to find any conspirators involved in selling him the mind-altering drug called Cecilimate. He thought less about outright revenge and considered letting them live long enough to fix this with an antidote of some kind.

Most of the goatee whiskers were already in the bottom of the sink when Matt heard the disturbing sound. He cringed and nearly stabbed himself with the scissors.

He turned slowly sideways and looked out the bathroom door into the motorhome. Curled up in blankets on the bunk above the cab, Nikki the waitress snored like a water buffalo.

That such a guttural sound could emanate from someone so slight in stature surprised even Bob the cat, who moved away and off the bunk altogether, leaping down onto the back of the dinette seat. If a cat could look disgruntled, this one was the poster child for it.

He turned back to the mirror to finish his shaving job. Having Nikki around brought a mixed bag of feelings. She helped with the driving, but she hadn't parked the motorhome out in the country like he told her to. He felt tired, and his shoulder was stiff as a board.

He wondered why having more people around somehow led to more dreams and disturbing visions playing out like movies projected on the inside of his eyelids all night. Difficult dreams that included the recurring one about broken glass and the waitress. A bad sign that what was in store for her hadn't happened yet.

And how exactly had he ended up on the floor?

The plugged-in razor whirled to life, and Matt pressed it against his remaining gray stubble. He leaned out the bathroom door while still running the razor around his face. Bob cocked his head as Nikki rolled over on the bunk. She lifted a hand to rub her eyes and thumped her knuckles into the low ceiling above the bunk.

"Crap," she exclaimed.

She turned onto her side and rubbed her hand. Bob patted at her bare ankle. She yawned and gave Bob a quick backrub before swinging her legs around and dangling them over the edge. After another constrained stretch due to the ceiling height, she slid off the edge of the bunk and dropped onto the floor with a thud.

Matt started to say something to Nikki but the words didn't come. She stood there in her panties, pink no less, and a short white t-shirt that rode up on one hip and left her belly-button exposed. The small bandages remaining on her arm and thighs didn't distract from her form. Unaware of his presence, she locked her long legs and planted her feet on the floor. She pressed her palms against the low ceiling, stretching with her head tilted back. Matt stepped back into the bathroom.

He tried not to think about it. He hadn't been curious about things female in a while, and there was no time for that now. Didn't he remember she was kind of a pain in the ass? But at that moment, he was more intrigued by her than embarrassed for her.

"Mind turning the TV on? Bob seems to like it," Matt barked over the sound of the razor.

Nikki finished her stretch then knelt down to pick the cushions up off the floor and put them back in place on the dinette seats. She bent over the kitchen sink and cupped a few slurps of water using the palm of her hand.

"Gotta remote?" she asked as she wiped her mouth on the shoulder of her t-shirt.

"Magazine rack under the TV."

Nikki found it and plopped down in the booth to poke at the buttons. The cat put his front paws on her shoulder and stood erect with his tail in the air. She rolled through a few channels of snow before finding a fuzzy morning news program. Bob rubbed his head against her ear.

Matt finished shaving and stepped out of the bathroom. Nikki looked up at what appeared to be a totally different man. This one looked much younger without the deceptively gray goatee. The hair was still a matted mess, and he still looked strung out, but she couldn't believe it was the same guy.

"You look a bunch better than when you walked into Maybelle's yesterday."

"I thought I said find a quiet place to park."

"Sorry. I saw the other motorhomes and--it felt safer."

"I can't sleep at these places. Too many people."

Matt decided not to waste his limited energy complaining further and pointed at the floor.

"How did I--?"

"Bob and I managed to get you laid down without much problem."

"Thank you. And Bob too."

Matt slipped into the booth across from Nikki. He struggled to reach into a plastic Wal-Mart bag.

"Shoulder?" Nikki inquired.

"Stiff as hell. Was up early and made it to the store. Got something for you."

He slid a prepaid phone across the table.

"You can call your sister after breakfast. Lady in Wal-Mart said to try the River City Grill on Main Street on the way out of town. I could use some eggs and coffee."

Nikki was a little surprised by the gesture. He was, after all, following through with what he said he would do earlier. A little unexpected but appreciated. He didn't know she had already tried to call her sister from Mount Pleasant.

"Thanks, George," Nikki said.

She pushed the phone to the side and pointed at the bathroom.

"Maybe I'll call after a quickie shower in there."

"Uh, I'm not sure that works. Haven't tried it yet."

"I know."

Matt stared blankly back at her. Nikki smiled and slowly got up from the table, realizing she was hardly dressed. It didn't bother her and never had.

"After lifting you onto the floor last night, it was clear you hadn't used the shower in a while."

Matt tried not to follow her movements as she collected her clothes and turned to the bathroom.

"Might be why Bob stays up on the bunk all the time," Nikki said with a wink before closing the bathroom door.

46

DAY 138 – Little Rock, AR

Navy Seal David Dobson drove one of Twig's tag-team of two nondescript sedans trailing Dr. Neil Hoffman as he drove from his cabin in the Ozarks to his office in Pine Bluff. A fellow Seal was in the backseat watching his laptop screen for any incoming data on phone calls Hoffman was making from his SUV.

The trip had been uneventful so far. The cars had shadowed Hoffman's white Range Rover for the last hour as he headed south out of the mountains on the cloudy morning. The caravan had already left Route 65 and joined up with Interstate 40 at Conway, and they were now approaching the northern outskirts of metropolitan Little Rock.

Dobson had the two vehicles trailing the Range Rover make various tactical moves. Each car alternated approaching the SUV, completing a slow pass, before falling back and allowing Hoffman to overtake them again. During these repetitive maneuvers, the Navy Seals did not see Neil Hoffman talking on his phone at any time, yet the fat man's head was observed slightly bobbing, likely in unison to some tune playing on the radio.

The morning traffic flow wasn't as bad as Dobson expected through downtown Little Rock, allowing an easier than usual merge into the righthand lanes to catch the upcoming Interstate 30 South towards Pine Bluff.

But the Range Rover didn't merge. The SUV didn't slide into the right lanes to make the I-30 exit and work its way south to the FDA research facility.

Neil Hoffman stayed in the fast lane on Interstate 40 and proceeded at speed underneath the large green sign with white arrows pointing down at multiple traffic lanes flowing east to Memphis.

47

DAY 138 – Rockford, MI

The sizable wraparound front porch on Solomon Carr's re-stored farmhouse was more than sufficient to hold the oval glass-topped dining table surrounded by eight chairs. The two brothers ate a quiet breakfast, sitting together at one end of the table. The mustached Harry immersed himself in reading the local newspaper, while Solomon sipped cof-fee and stared out across the expansive lawn at ducks float-ing on the small private lake adjacent to the house.

Solomon wasn't interested in the newspaper this morn-ing or necessarily what was happening around the world. It seemed all so immaterial. He looked over at Harry, who frowned into the paper, clearly straining to read something. Having Harry safe was all he cared about at the moment.

The recent threats on his brother's life had taken a toll, leaving Solomon to question bringing the headquarters of his secret government agency so close to Harry and his beloved little village. What was once perceived as a safe and secure location for Otter One had somehow been exposed by an internal problem named Neil Hoffman. Solomon took a deep breath as he watched a small deer step out of the dense woods on the opposite shore of the lake and dip its nose into the water for drink.

Twelve years ago it had all seemed like such a good idea. The overall security risks were perceived as small, and the set-up was universally viewed as ideal. Other available options for locating Otter One had been explored, vetted internally over many months by senior members of the board, before the group finally arrived at the reasonable and unanimous decision to locate the Otter One headquarters just north of Cannonsburg, Michigan.

"They have no pitching," Harry said firmly.

The random comment brought Solomon out his contemplative stupor.

"What was that?"

"Pitching. The Whitecaps have no pitching. Got clobbered again last night."

A large man appeared from the front door of the farmhouse carrying a silver pot of coffee. The exposed shoulder holster over a white shirt and tie delineated him as another security team member on servant duty rotation. He approached the table with the coffee and silently exchanged the new pot for an old one.

"We should go to another game some time soon," Solomon said.

"Not while they suck. Not worth the time."

"You used to like it."

"Too busy, man. More fun to be at Honey Creek with my peeps and maybe just watch the bums on local TV. I can yell at the screen all I want, and I can't get thrown out of my own place!"

Solomon smiled at his brother's enthusiasm.

There had simply been more time in the early years, Solomon remembered, back when he took vacation time to visit Harry while his brother struggled to fix up the little town he had adopted. There were more baseball games taken in back then, plus occasional fishing trips together up north. It was during one of those visits that the genesis of locating Otter One in the local area took root in Solomon's mind.

The man's name was Peter Rockford, and he had joined a few of Harry's friends, along with Solomon, on one of those fishing trips years ago. Peter was the great-grandson of Hiram Rockford, a local pioneer and founder of monstrous Chippewa International Corporation, located in a town named after him on the Rogue River seven miles north of Cannonsburg. Originally a small tannery and mill operation founded in the 1870s by Hiram, the company known as C.I.C. had grown into one of the largest manufacturers of work boots in the world. The company had started selling boots to the army during World War I and became a major supplier of footwear items to all branches of the U.S. military.

Chippewa grew and expanded beyond its riverfront location within the Rockford, Michigan, city limits, eventually owning more than four thousand acres just east of downtown. The new corporate site swallowed a number of area farms and woodlands as it expanded. An enormous corporate complex had been constructed over the decades, including a private airstrip for corporate use. All of it was surrounded by an abundance of excess land, or buffer space, comprising leased cropland or thick hardwood forest dotted with lakes, including the area around Solomon's farmhouse.

What Peter shared with Solomon on that one fateful fishing trip was something unique--a general comment made in passing, a piece of local trivia noted as part of a wide-ranging discussion over beers. But that one piece of information turned out to be the catalyst that had captured Solomon's interest and ultimately led to the relocation of Otter One to Michigan from suburban Washington, D.C.

The random comment from Peter Rockford was that Chippewa International Corporation's land holdings had once been home to a Cold War missile-defense base designed to protect Chicago and Detroit from Russian bombers.

Locating the missile silos and bunkers on Chippewa owned land in the 1950s was a convenient and mutually beneficial arrangement that deepened the somewhat incestuous ties between a major Defense Department supplier and the federal government.

Ultimately the adaptive reuse concept that knocked around in Solomon's head made enough sense to lead him to formally pursue the idea with the board. The Chippewa land provided a nice private location away from Washington, and the sizable underground bunker complex was deemed perfect for Otter One's secret research. Getting Chippewa International Corporation to cooperate was the simplest part. Few things are quite as easy as holding huge military supply contracts over a CEO's head in order to get a favorable decision.

Harry knew nothing of Otter One or what Solomon really did for work. He was just happy that Solomon had wanted to be closer to him after their parents passed away, and that he apparently had an important job with

Chippewa International Corporation. All Harry knew was that Solomon's work included traveling often to military facilities as part of his supposed quality-control duties for C.I.C.

"All the good pitchers get called up to the big leagues, don't they?" Solomon asked.

"Yeah, but that's no excuse. So do the hitters!" Harry said as he crumpled the sports section into a tight ball.

The front door of the farmhouse opened again, and security chief Stewart Crites walked briskly onto the porch, followed by another armed servant holding an empty tray. The lanky man's sport coat covered up a fit frame with minimal body fat--an efficient fighting tool given his tall stature.

"Urgent call for you, Solomon. About the project in Little Rock," Stewart said.

"Thank you."

Solomon stood up and dropped his napkin on the tray as the servant cleared the table. He hoped the call was relaying some good news about Hoffman's likely accomplices and his future plans. If enough intel had been secured this morning, he would enjoy activating the failsafe device imbedded in Hoffman's chest.

Harry remained immersed in the local section of the newspaper. Stewart sat down next to him. He had kept an eye on Harry for years at Solomon's request, and they had become friends. Harry folded the page over and found the daily horoscopes.

"What kind of day am I going to have, Harry?" Solomon said.

Harry read quietly before slapping the page with the back of his hand.

"Crap! It says I get a lousy two-star day, while you guys get five!" Harry said.

"A five-star day sounds good to me," Solomon said from by the door. "Maybe you should go back to bed, Harry."

Solomon held the door open for the man with the tray full of dishes and then followed him inside the house.

"What does mine say?" Stewart asked.

"Says you should keep an eye out for a friend in need." Stewart patted Harry on the back and laughed.

"Sounds like that would be you, Mr. Two Star!"

***

Solomon followed the man carrying the tray down the center hallway of the farmhouse. Solomon stopped short of the kitchen and opened a door on the right and entered his office and library. He circled the dark hardwood desk and approached a wall of bookcases. Solomon reached for a faded yellow textbook on geology and opened the book to page 57. Imbedded in the book was a thumbprint scanner. He pressed his right thumb on it, and a green LED light came on. An adjacent section of the bookcase slid open to reveal elevator doors. Solomon replaced the geology book and walked up to a retinal scanner. The successful optical scan opened the elevator doors, and he stepped inside.

The elevator descended directly into a concrete tunnel below the farmhouse that connected to the underground research complex in the former missile silo and bunker via a rail line. Solomon stepped out of the elevator and around the small tram car sitting on the narrow tracks that led to the bunker complex a half-mile away. He opened a heavy metal door on the opposite side of the tracks, walked into the secure vestibule, and pulled the door closed behind him. A green light came on above the door a second after the electric latch clicked shut. Another door in front of him automatically swung open into the communications room under the house.

Twig was there, sitting in front of a laptop computer at a small conference table, a speakerphone nearby.

"Carr is here now. Go over it again," Twig said.

A voice came over the speakerphone.

"He didn't make the turn, sir."

"Who do I have?" Solomon asked.

"Dobson here, sir. Following the Range Rover. Hoffman didn't make the turn south to Pine Bluff."

Solomon leaned over Twig's shoulder to look at the map on the computer screen.

"Where are they now?" Solomon asked Twig.

Twig zoomed in closer on the one red dot, followed by two pairs of yellow ones, on a moving map of the state of Arkansas.

"Just east of Little Rock on the I-40. He passed up the interchange to Pine Bluff about ten minutes ago."

"Any other surveillance update?"

"No calls into his voicemail at the office or calls out from there."

"Cellphone?"

"One call right after we left the cabin. An international number located to a cellphone currently in Iowa. No other calls since. He left his cellphone at the cabin."

"Who the hell did he call?"

"Working on that, sir."

Solomon paced behind Twig. He didn't really expect Hoffman to adhere to their handshake agreement but had hoped for the best. A radio-silent Hoffman worried him. The man was up to something.

"Sir, any orders?" Dobson inquired.

"I don't like it," Twig said.

"I don't either," Solomon responded.

Nothing was left to gain from waiting if Hoffman wasn't communicating and providing leads. From what he'd seen of Hoffman already, the man was crafty and driven, driven to go beyond reasonable--a classic Type A personality who would only be comfortable in total control. Solomon understood the need for control. The failsafe existed to ensure control over individuals with detailed knowledge of the Otter One program.

Clearly Hoffman couldn't be comfortable yet. He didn't have Harry as a bargaining chip any more, and Solomon would bet serious money that he was executing a back-up plan of some kind. The man had to be stopped, even if they lacked more information from him on the Cecilimate drug. They would have to get it through other means.

Solomon said as he looked down at his watch. He leaned over the speakerphone.

"Dobson, I'm going to execute to failsafe protocol now."

"NEGATIVE! WE HAVE COLLATERALS!" Dobson said. "Heavy traffic here, school bus next to him! HOLD, I say HOLD!"

"CONFIRMED!" Solomon said. "Where are they exactly, Twig?"

"Eastern suburbs, fairly dense."

"How soon till they're out of the city and into rural areas?"

"Half-hour," Twig said pointing at the screen. "About there."

"What is that green patch a bit east of that spot?"

"State forest, De Valls area."

"Okay, we wait for that. Dobson?"

"Yes, sir?"

"I'm delaying failsafe activation until you get to De Valls State Forest. Less than an hour. Let us know immediately if he changes course off the I-40."

"Roger that."

Twig pushed a button on the speakerphone, ending the call. Solomon moved to a small desk in the corner and opened his laptop.

"Get your men in Pine Bluff mobilized. I want that lab facility locked down before the hour is up. No one in or out. And have a team turn that cabin inside out. We need that drug."

"Sir, a thousand people work at Pine Bluff."

"Then fabricate a story, a radiation release of some sort. Everyone has to be decontaminated. That will buy us some time."

Twig nodded and started to punch numbers into the speakerphone.

Solomon leaned back in his chair and stared at the blinking red light on his wristwatch.

This would be one long hour to wait.

48

DAY 138 – Rockville, MD

Kevin looked up from his desk as Becky walked into the cubicle waving a FedEx package. He would have instantly commented on her bright-red dress if he weren't on the phone. She appeared to be two pigtails short of being Dorothy from the Wizard of Oz.

"Yes, 11 a.m. works fine. Hotel? Yes, all set. No, I have directions, we'll meet you there."

"We?" Becky said.

He held up a thumb and forefinger, a half-inch apart, signaling he had almost wrapped up the call.

"Thank you, Mister Knowles. Yes, I do have your cell. Okay. Eleven it is. See you then."

Kevin hung up and turned his full attention to Becky.

"That for me?"

Becky held the package just out of range of his grasp.

"Someone going with you? I only booked flights for one."

"I didn't think you cared."

"I don't. Just curious."

Kevin quickly came up with a weak explanation for his slip-up while on the phone. He didn't want her to spread the news to Wade that Erin was going with him.

"Well, there's three actually. Me, myself, and I."

"You always refer to yourself in the plural?"

"I'm a multilayered man of action."

Becky rolled her eyes, happy to give up the fight. She stepped closer to his desk and handed him the FedEx.

"Came this morning, priority."

"Thank you," Kevin said.

Becky backed out into the aisle.

"And Doctor Kearns says there's a change of plans. He can't meet later today. He's been called out of town for a meeting. Wants you to call him on his cell with an update on your Charleston trip before three."

"Got it. Where did he go?"

"I booked him a round trip to Chicago."

Becky and her red glow twirled away and disappeared.

Kevin stared down at the FedEx package in his hand. It was very light and felt almost empty, except for a small bump he felt in one corner.

The sender was a Rachel Smallwood. The name sounded familiar, and Kevin remembered her name as one linked to the Cecilimate cases. The handwritten note inside the envelope confirmed it. The woman's daughter had been a victim of the drug scam, dying of exposure in a wooded area near Albany. He and Erin had visited the mother briefly a month before or so, during their unapproved road trip in his newly purchased used car.

The note was folded around a small Ziplock bag containing three yellow triangular pills. She had found them strewn under the front seat of her daughter's car. The woman's note asked Kevin to have the pills tested, to see if they were the same drug that had driven her daughter insane so that she ran practically naked into the winter wilderness.

Kevin fingered the Ziplock bag. The pale yellow pills had the letter C stamped on one side only--not much help in identifying its potential origin. They were rough around the edges, as if handmade in a crude mold.

In a normal situation he would turn the pills over immediately to his superiors for testing. But there was nothing normal going on here, not with Wade and not with the FDA if an internal problem was at the root of the deaths from this drug. Kevin quickly pocketed the bag of pills and jammed the note into a side pocket of his briefcase.

The next logical step would be to find a third-party lab that could be extremely discreet.

49

DAY 138 – Keokuk, IA

Matt quietly cursed Nikki, with her bobbing head and pink fingernails, as she poked at the buttons on the small tabletop jukebox jutting from the wall. He thought it was way too early in the morning for the rock and roll classic "Johnny B. Goode" by Chuck Berry to be blaring inside the River City Grill.

The irritating music was giving him a headache. He was trying to come out from the aftereffects of the sleeping pills, and the rock and roll wasn't helping. He closed the notebook on the table in front of him. There simply wasn't enough energy yet to write down more dreams and any final thoughts related to Day 137. Unfortunately, Nikki was ready to punch a few more buttons.

"Do you have any more nickels?"

"Not for you."

"Party pooper. Some Elvis would help wake you up."

"It'll take more than that."

"A shower might have helped, in more than a few ways."

"Stop with the hygiene police."

"Don't look at me. Bob mentioned it."

Matt ignored her attempt at a joke and looked out from their bay-window table at the street scene. Old brick buildings lined Main Street in Keokuk, half of them vacant storefronts with torn awnings. The heavily crowned street had high curbs on each side. The shape looked odd, but he guessed it was practical in this land of torrential rain from summer thunderstorms.

Just down the street, he could see Bob sitting in the window above the cab, a testament that someone forgot to leave the TV on for his amusement. The frustrated cat appeared a little askew in the window, given the sideways slope of the motorhome towards the curb.

Matt turned his attention back inside the diner and to the waitress loading a tray with their breakfast order at the kitchen window. Nikki kept scanning the jukebox.

"They have Steely Dan on here. Does that make sense to you?"

He didn't respond to Nikki and instead dug through his backpack for the bottles of herbs that would help him clear his foggy head.

"If it's a Fifties diner, it should have Fifties music. Not the Seventies," Nikki announced.

Matt watched a couple of middle-aged men eating at the counter together. They passed sections of a newspaper back and forth while they ate. One booth held a worn-out father attempting to control a pancake-and-sugar-infused frenzy of three boys, all of them under five years old. The occasional high-pitched chorus from that direction tore at Matt's ears.

The waitress arrived with their plates, and Nikki dove right into her breakfast. Matt worked to unlock his silverware assortment with one hand, his utensils trapped inside a rolled-up napkin taped tight with a paper ring. He finally freed the knife and tried to slice a sausage link one-handed but only managed to flick the greasy torpedo off his plate and skid it across the table towards an oblivious Nikki. The waitress returned with more coffee and then dug into her apron pocket.

"Looks like your friend could use some help," the wrinkled woman said with a grin, "and here's more nickels."

Nikki looked up from her plate at the sound of the coins hitting the tabletop. She snorted a short laugh at Matt's attempts to stab the slippery sausage.

"Let me help--"

"I got it!"

"Here--"

He let her skewer the greasy link with her fork and return it to his plate. Matt sat back reluctantly as she proceeded to cut the sausage into bite-sized pieces for him. He waited as she completed the two-handed job.

"There you go."

He wondered if the waitress thought they were a couple. Her choice of words, "your friend," was noncommittal yet tactful, and only mildly accurate. Nikki had been the one to force herself onto him and join his journey. He initially resented the unwanted passenger but was getting used to her and the assistance she provided. Watching Nikki cut the sausage link reminded him of better days.

"I used to do that for my kids," Matt said calmly.

Nikki paused for a sip of coffee, clasping the mug with both hands, taking her time.

"Kids, eh?"

"Two."

He spooned a piece of sausage and ate it while a suddenly quiet Nikki sipped more coffee and returned to her breakfast. He wondered if she would push him about who he really was, what the notebooks were all about, and how he acquired the unnatural talent to see certain events before they happened.

Matt flipped over a slice of the buttered toast and grimaced while reaching for a tiny tub of grape jelly. He tried to open the foil tab with only one hand. He paused, contemplating the problem. Nikki swallowed some eggs and reached across the table to help.

"Here, let me," she said.

"I'll need four of those."

"Four? On one slice of toast?"

"It's not a crime in Iowa, is it?"

Nikki shrugged and then peeled open all four little tubs and started spreading the purple mounds across the slice of toast. Matt pointed a finger at the wads of jelly.

"Corners. Make sure you get all the corners. I don't like dry spots."

Nikki shook her head and completed the masterpiece. She held it up for him to see.

"This is practically pie!"

He enjoyed her warm smile, even if some personal embarrassment was required.

"I like pie."

"I guess so!"

She handed over the creation. Matt opened the top of one of the bottles and shook cinnamon all over the smeared slice of toast. He worked it into the jam with a knife. He lifted the slice to his mouth and took a bite. Some of the jelly plopped back down on his plate. Nikki smiled at the scene before picking up a few nickels for the jukebox.

Matt kept a wary eye on the street scene. Bob still occupied the window above the cab. Traffic was light, and the town was quiet so far. He returned to observing the movements inside the restaurant, watching customers and staff. His eyes drifted back to Nikki.

She flipped though song choices in between forkfuls of eggs and hashbrowns. He had only known her for one whole day, but of all the potential threats circling him, she had already proven herself lowest on the risk meter.

She could easily run off. He knew she had taken some of his lottery money. He had been in the drawer before going to Wal-Mart earlier and noticed some of the cash was missing. He wasn't sure when or how much she took, but whatever the amount, she hadn't left him when she had the chance.

"Boy and a girl back in Austin."

"What?" Nikki asked.

"My kids."

Her cool eyes stayed focused on the miniature jukebox.

"They have names?"

"Megan, she's nine, and Timmy is six. They live with their mother."

"Missus Kaplan."

"Who?"

"Your wife. Sorry, maybe Missus Trotter?"

He decided to go all in.

"An ex-wife. The former Missus Matt Sizemore."

"Real names now?"

"Yes."

"So, Matthew Sizemore, eh?"

"Yes."

"You do look more like a Matt than a George."

Nikki waited a moment as he took a bite of his "pie-toast." It was her turn. She thrust her forearms across the table, showing him her wrists.

"I actually don't like tattoos, but these were kinda necessary."

Matt slowly focused on the tattoos, finally seeing the raised scarring underneath the flowery pattern.

"Got them in high school to cover up--a bad experience."

"You don't need to tell--"

"My uncle, well, he hurt me. My dad couldn't take it and went after him. He's in jail for stabbing my uncle, like a hundred times. Mother bolted, remarried, and lives in Maine. My sister Jill is all I really have left."

"My God, Nikki--"

"It's okay, ancient history now, and I'm mostly good."

Matt watched her return to her eggs and pick up a couple of nickels. He didn't know what to say next. She flipped through more song choices until he came up with something.

"The snake. The one on your neck."

Nikki snorted a laugh.

"That one? The jerk Travis pushed me to get it after partying one night. Wish I hadn't. Too drunk to care at the time. At least I can't see it."

Matt sat a bit stunned and poked at his eggs. Nikki dropped a nickel in the jukebox and then abruptly reached across the table for the **DREAMS** binder, snagging it before he could react.

"So, Matt, why am I in here?"

Matt flinched at first but let her flip though the pages in the binder without a fight. He was in no shape to stop her, and it was a valid question without a reasonable answer.

"I don't know why you are in there."

Nikki stopped on the page with the drawing he made of her and stared down at it, taking it all in. She'd hardly had any time to look it over back at Maybelle's. The detailed pencil sketch of her from behind was surrounded by scribbled notes including one about breaking glass.

"I have dreams, mostly vivid nightmares, and I try to write down the ones I can remember. Sometimes I can draw pictures of what I've seen."

"This, this is from a dream you've had?"

"Yes. Months ago. I don't know exactly when. I've had that same dream a few times."

"And you came to Swisher to save me from Travis?"

"No. Not exactly."

"Then how--"

"I don't know how! It's like--I'm just attracted to certain places. Sometimes I'm driving and come to a rural crossroads. I can turn either way, but I'll feel an odd, weird sensation, a pull, to turn one way or the other. That's what happened when I saw the sign for Swisher and when I turned into Maybelle's parking lot. I was somehow drawn there."

"Sounds crazy, but I know you're not."

"Ever had déjà vu moments?" Matt asked.

"What is that?"

The waitress was on her way over again. Nikki leaned back in her chair.

"You folks done here?" the waitress asked.

Nikki waited, motionless, as the woman stood over them.

"That'll do it, thanks," Matt said.

"Any more coffee for you two?"

"One more refill will set me straight," Matt said.

He held up his mug for more while Nikki covered her mug with her hand. The waitress filled Matt's mug and loaded the dishes up on one arm. He waited for her to move away.

"Déjà vu. It's when you have a dream one night, a strong one that comes back again and again on future nights. A nice clear one that you can remember in the morning. Say it's about a place, a room like this one. A place with unique details that stick with you. Then, maybe years later, you actually walk into that exact setting, a situation just like in your dream, and you feel chills come over you. The hair on your arms stands up. You're absolutely sure it's the same place you saw in your dream many times before. That's déjà vu."

"I've never--I don't think that's ever happened to me," Nikki said.

"I've had that déjà vu feeling sometimes, maybe half a dozen times in my adult life. Every time I would feel funny, almost woozy, and I'd get hairs standing up on the back of my neck. I never knew what it meant and still don't. It's just happening much more often now."

Matt stared at the ceiling, pondering a next step. Random conversations with Bob aside, he hadn't been able to confide in anyone, trust anyone, or just share thoughts with anyone for months. No one to really talk to, no one to hear his side of the story. He looked over at an uncomfortable Nikki. She seemed to care. She hadn't run off. She'd stayed. This strange girl, this young woman helping him, would be gone tomorrow anyway.

Matt stirred two sugar packets into his coffee and took a large gulp. It was a risky step, opening up to her with the truth, as best he knew it, but he almost didn't care any more.

Nikki leaned over the table, her brown eyes searching his before he looked away.

"What--happened? I mean, one minute you save my life from out of nowhere, then act like a total criminal with these different names--and you've got a gun!"

"Shhh!"

"What is all this?" she said, holding the binder high and pointing at the bottles on the table.

"You wouldn't believe it."

"You know that already? That I won't believe you? I mean, for some crazy reason you see things before they happen, so really Matt, will I believe you or not?"

"I don't know--"

"Try me. I'm not going to rat you out. I owe you. Maybe I can help."

Matt opened a bottle while Nikki waited. He sprinkled some ginseng powder on his omelet and carved off a bite. He pulled some aspirin out of the backpack while he chewed on the eggs, popping four pills into his mouth and swallowing them with a gulp of coffee.

"The police are after me. I shot someone," he said quickly. "I walked into a situation, another dream that unfolded before me. Something bad was going to happen."

"Like you saw the broken glass with me?"

"Yes. All thanks to a goddamn drug I ordered off TV. A so-called antidepressant called Cecilimate. I had a bad reaction. It gave me these confusing nightmares, and I can't make them stop."

"And those pills made you see, see these things?"

Matt nodded.

"Writing stuff down, in these notebooks, helps me try to sort it all out."

"These herbs then, they help you?"

"Mostly the sleeping pills help. Keep me from falling into deep sleep, REM sleep, where the nightmares are the worst. The herbs help me snap out of it in the morning and keep me somewhat alert. Problem is, you need REM sleep to survive, and I feel like I'm slowly unwinding."

"We have to get you help. Someone will understand. A doctor. Maybe you can explain it to the police."

"My ex-wife and the cops didn't believe me. Thought I was crazy and tried to have me committed, so I took off. Been on the run for months. I'm going to deal with this in my own way."

"You're planning on killing the doctor, aren't you?"

"Not any more. I need to find these people, find a cure. I want my life back."

Nikki looked at the bags under his eyes. She'd only known him a day, and she could tell his energy was fading. She wondered if he could make it.

"You need sleep, real sleep."

"I wish I could get some."

The waitress was closing in on them again with her refreshed coffeepot. She passed by the front door just as a sheriff's squad car pulled up to the curb outside. She stopped in her tracks and retreated to the cash register at the counter.

Nikki started to speak, but Matt held a finger up to his lips, stopping her. Two deputies entered the diner, one made a beeline for the bathroom. The other walked up the cash register.

"All set to go, Ron," the waitress said.

She handed him a to-go order of two coffees and a brown paper bag.

"Thanks, Annie. This will do the trick."

The deputy handed her a twenty and she made change.

"Seems like you got here just in time."

"I know. Buster's been dyin out there in the car."

The deputy turned, left the diner, and got into the patrol car. A few seconds later the other deputy walked past Nikki and Matt and out the door. The squad car did a U-turn and was gone.

Matt started to pack up his bottles.

"Time to hit the road. We can talk while you drive."

***

It would have been a simple task for Nikki to pull the RV out of a normal parking space. The crowned street was another matter. Nikki didn't think about the slope of the street to the curb. The back end of the motorhome behind the rear wheels was long enough to stick out and scrape against a rectangular parking sign affixed to a sturdy metal pole when making a turn.

As Nikki pulled away from the curb, the immovable sign edge dug into the thin sheet-metal exterior of the motorhome. The loud scraping was followed by a final pop as the sign caught the rear metal ladder of the motorhome, tearing the ladder's roof supports from their anchors.

Nikki stopped the RV and exited the driver's side to see what had happened. She walked around to the curb side to find the motorhome free of the obstruction, the parking sign still wobbling with the aftereffects. The gash in the side was about two feet long and a foot from the rooftop. The top section of the ladder had pulled away from the back of the coach by six inches or so, but was still solidly attached at the bottom and at the midpoint of the rungs.

Nikki closed the driver's side door as she climbed back in.

"Are we hung up?" asked Matt.

"Uh, not any more."

"I better take--"

"No, no. It's just a scratch. On a dumb street sign."

Matt stopped fiddling with his seatbelt.

"Your driving leaves--"

"Don't start with me."

"All right. Just get us moving."

Nikki slowly merged into the traffic flow headed towards the bridge over the Mississippi River and into Illinois.

50

DAY 138 – De Valls Bluff, AR

Dobson liked the setup at De Valls Bluff. The dense woodlands of oak and hickory within the Wattensaw State Game Area crowded up against the lanes of Interstate 40 just after the Hazen exit. He watched as the opposing traffic lanes gently spread apart, leaving a hundred-yard-wide stand of trees between them. It would make a suitable safety buffer from any oncoming traffic, in light of what was about to occur.

There were only minutes to spare before the woods retreated and the lanes reconvened to a side-by-side configuration. It was time for him to call in his location. Dobson speed-dialed Solomon Carr.

"Are we good?" Solomon said.

"Yes, sir. Light traffic. Few civilian vehicles now. He's just ahead of us. Ready when you are."

"Executing now."

"Copy that."

Dobson looked in his rearview mirror at a Navy Seal in the back seat with an open laptop, his focus on the screen.

"Status?" Dobson asked.

"Just started blinking, sir. Target has thirty seconds."

Dobson scanned the traffic in the immediate area. Two vehicles and one truck were in front of Hoffman's SUV by a good distance. Three additional vehicles could be seen behind his own car, one of them another sedan carrying Navy Seals that began swerving across the lanes, blocking cars further behind from gaining on the unfolding scene.

Dobson focused again on the white SUV ahead of him and waited.

***

Frank Sinatra had just finished "New York, New York" on Dr. Neil Hoffman's iPod—a rousing song, a favorite of his, that had left him uncomfortably warm for some reason. He fiddled with the air-conditioning controls before checking to see if his heated leather seats were switched on by accident.

The next random song that jumped into his earbuds was "Five Guys Named Moe" by Joe Jackson—another upbeat and entertaining tune to help occupy the next hour until he reached the outskirts of Memphis and called Sam Asrani about the "package" being delivered to the safe house.

A deeper warm feeling spread through his torso, and he cranked up the air conditioning another notch before opening a second button on his shirt. He hoped he wasn't coming down with the flu. There was so much he needed to do.

Beads of sweat appeared on his brow, and his fingers began to tingle. The music morphed into a monotone buzzing in Neil Hoffman's ears. The afternoon sunlight suddenly seemed too bright, even with his expensive sunglasses. He blinked and blinked again, but the glare remained bothersome. He wiped his forehead again. Little white stars flickered in his field of vision. He felt faint and thought of pulling over.

Neil Hoffman's chin dropped to his chest.

***

Dobson watched intently as the Range Rover lightly swerved for a moment before slanting abruptly to the right, off the freeway and towards the thick woods at speed. Dobson slowed in preparation and glanced down at his own chest. He had never seen a failsafe device activated and hoped the one inside him never would be.

Neil Hoffman had no way of knowing that his 55 year tenure on the planet was rapidly coming to a close. The failsafe device, a pea-sized ceramic-coated ball implanted near his aorta, had sprung to life as designed, unwinding a thin layer of sharp ceramic like an orange being peeled. The high-tech weapon unwound into a two-inch-long hypersharp knife that no aorta could withstand. The aortic dissection allowed large quantities of blood formerly headed through Hoffman's arteries to pour out into his chest cavity.

Dobson watched Hoffman's front right bumper connect first with a large oak tree, sending bark flying and tipping the Range Rover onto two wheels as the rear end ricocheted around. The SUV rolled three times through brush and undergrowth until impact with a dense stand of trees collapsed its roof. If the sheer force of the collision didn't kill the driver, the resulting explosion and fire completed the termination.

Dobson pulled over a safe distance away from the fire and got out of his vehicle. He stood still to watch the billowing smoke and flames rise from the SUV and spread into the brush. The second carload of Navy Seals pulled up behind him, followed by a private car that quickly braked and stopped just ahead.

The civilian driver, a bearded man chewing tobacco, jumped out and took one step towards the burning SUV only twenty yards away. The man looked over at Dobson, who waved him off. It was obvious that nothing could be done for the Range Rover's occupant.

51

DAY 138 – Keokuk, IA

It took the sound of a heavy metal lid clanging hard against its host dumpster to jolt Sam Asrani out of a deep sleep. He abruptly sat up in the reclined driver's seat of his SUV and rubbed his sore neck as a dark-green garbage truck jerked its way out of the Denny's parking lot next door. A quick look at his imitation Rolex brought fear.

Almost nine!

The corrugated-metal shade attached to the old auto shop had blocked the sunrise! He scrambled into action.

Sizemore might be out of range! He couldn't lose him again!

Sam furiously fumbled with the power seat control as he tried to focus on the tracking display screen balancing on the steering column. Seeing the blinking blue dot within range, he noted it had only moved one mile. Relieved, he quickly started the engine while closely watching the dot's location.

Sam took a deep breath to calm down and performed the final trim job on the power seat. There were no messages on his cellphone. The battery was low, so he plugged it into the dash. After a stale gulp from his water bottle he picked up the binoculars off the adjacent seat and verified that the motorhome had left the Wal-Mart parking lot across the street.

Thank God Sizemore and the waitress were still nearby. He could end this odyssey soon and, after some fun with Amanda, head home to Miami for some real rest. Sam grabbed his cell and dialed Randy Knox. Randy should have the bartender secured by now and headed towards Memphis. Voicemail picked up his call.

"You know the drill, go."

"Need location status now," Sam said then hung up.

He next dialed Hoffman. Four, five, six rings and still no answer.

Sam retried Randy's number with the same result. He nearly threw the phone at the dashboard.

"Jesus!"

He was mad, mad at himself for oversleeping, mad that he couldn't reach Hoffman or Randy. He slammed the SUV into reverse and backed out of the protected parking spot. At least he knew where Sizemore was.

After turning east out of the parking lot onto Route 218 into downtown Keokuk, he could see the blue dot was only a half-mile ahead. A soft curve brought him into the central core of commercial buildings lining Main Street. The blue dot was very close now, and he scanned the street for the old motorhome. Nothing. A few randomly parked cars sat on either side of the street but no motorhome.

The display showed his SUV practically sitting on top of the blinking blue dot. Sam hit the brakes and pulled over against the high curb.

"Tell me no!"

He stepped out of the SUV and slammed the door. Sam walked forward past one parked car, looking down at the street, knowing what he would ultimately find.

A vacant parking space in front of a restaurant yielded the prize. He bent down and snatched the little tracking device from the gutter by its wire antenna and tried in vain to crush the unit in his fist. He seethed with disgust and stomped the pavement as he turned back to the SUV.

Sam jumped inside and checked his cellphone. No messages. He wasn't ready to try Hoffman again with this bad news. He stared straight ahead and tried to think.

Sizemore must have hours on him, a radius of hundreds of miles to consider. He was likely across the river somewhere in Illinois, but where was he headed? He threw the tracking device onto the passenger seat.

Sam wondered if the waitress was still with him. Or maybe he'd left her behind. She could be around Keokuk somewhere, and maybe he could find her and make her talk about Sizemore's plans.

The waitress! The phone call from the store!

Sam dug deep into his pants pocket for the little piece of cardboard with a phone number scrawled on it. He needed to know the location of that phone.

Only once before had he talked to Hoffman's hacker team. He searched his cellphone for the international number to call. A young voice answered.

"Yes?"

"I work for fisherman, need help."

"Wait."

That was the last thing Sam wanted to hear.

There wasn't time for passwords!

Sizemore was further away each second. He ran his fingers through his matted hair.

"Favorite food?" the voice said.

"Peppermint meatloaf!"

"Confirmed."

Sam read from the scrap of cardboard.

"Need location of this number. 812-555-1072."

"That's it?"

"Yes."

"Too easy."

Sam could hear typing in the background. There was no response for fifteen seconds, and he was about to say something when the voice returned.

"Cellular phone, Evansville, Indiana. Registered to a Jillian Cook, 1412 Taylor Street. Phone location is at the premises."

Sam hung up and quickly jotted down the information on his palm. He reached into the back seat and rummaged through a few folded maps piled there before finding one covering Illinois and Indiana.

52

DAY 138 – Cedar Rapids, IA

Travis's wait was over by the 7th-inning stretch of the game on the TV. The portly Cedar Rapids policeman, mouth agape, was slipping inch by inch out of the leather chair, his legs splayed wide. The cocktail of sedatives Travis drained from his IV bag and into tonight's juice box was having the desired effect. The now-empty juice box tucked between the cop's legs was being pushed ever so slowly to the edge of the chair cliff and would soon topple onto the floor.

The big man snorted in his sleep, and Travis softly chuckled with satisfaction, even though it hurt his neck a little. Freedom lay close at hand. It was time to get out of bed and complete his escape plan.

He rolled the bed sheets off his legs and slowly sat up. He turned his back to the policeman, swiveling himself onto the edge of the hospital bed. The sutures tugged at his neck, but fortunately he felt little pain. He stood up quietly and steadied himself for the next phase of the operation.

The combined vital-signs monitor and IV stand by the bed was a mobile one, similar to the one he'd been hooked up to a military hospital in Germany after being wounded in Iraq. A battery pack allowed the patient to walk with the wheeled unit to the bathroom, down a hallway, or during rehab, all the time remaining connected to an IV drip as well as to the heart-monitor leads.

Travis grabbed the IV needle and jerked it out of his arm. He let the plastic drip line dangle to the floor with the needle still attached. He dabbed a Kleenex at the blood droplets on his forearm.

He reached behind the bed and unplugged the monitor from the wall. Travis turned and dragged the unit alongside as he shuffled towards the bathroom. One wheel squeaked and he stopped, turning to check briefly on the comatose cop. He touched the offending wheel with his toe, pushing it around a half-revolution, and restarted his slow walk to the bathroom. The wheel cooperated and kept quiet.

Travis quietly lifted the toilet seat and prepared himself. He wasn't looking forward to taking a leak. He knew the act of urinating would burn after he'd removed the catheter for the second time in two days. He gritted his teeth and let it flow. The initial spike of pain slowly subsided after he finished. He turned to the small corner sink and splashed some water on his face.

He lifted a fresh washcloth from the towel bar and dried off. He turned back towards the room, to the slumped cop in the chair. The man's legs were fully extended now with his feet jammed up against the tray table. The juice box teetered.

He quietly shuffled over to the sleeping cop with his beeping heart monitor unit in tow. He stood over the policeman and carefully rolled up the washcloth into a tight tube.

In one fluid motion, Travis lifted his thick leg and dropped his knee heavily across the man's lap, pinning him down. He thrust the washcloth tube deep into the cop's open mouth. The victim sputtered to life just as Travis landed a heavy punch to his jaw, knocking him back into unconsciousness. A rivulet of blood oozed from a corner of the cop's mouth. He released the washcloth, listened for the cop's shallow breathing, and checked his pulse. A glance at the wall clock told Travis he had twenty-one minutes before the nursing shift change.

He returned to the bathroom and untied his blue gown and unsnapped the sleeves. He was careful not to pull off the heart-monitor leads taped to his chest. A small closet next to the sink held what was left of his clothes, the few items that survived the crash and that the paramedics hadn't cut off. The pair of jeans hung there, still dotted with blood splatters, as well as his work boots. The shirt he wore was gone, and he didn't need it anyway, as the Cedar Rapids cop was going to lend him his. He sat on the toilet and pulled his jeans on, followed by the steel-toed boots.

He pushed the monitor unit out of the bathroom ahead of him and rolled it up next to the officer. Travis pushed on the back of the cop's head, doubling him over onto his own lap. He removed the Cedar Rapids Police Department jacket one arm at a time and then pulled the cop's body back upright by the shirt collar. Travis unbuttoned the standard-issue blue shirt and then bent the man forward again to remove it. He dug into the front pocket of the officer's pants and pulled out a set of car keys. He followed by opening the cop's wallet and snatching what looked to be close to sixty dollars. The last item he claimed from the limp body was the police-issue handgun.

Travis checked the wall clock. Sixteen minutes before the new night nurse would check in on him. The last part of his plan would draw attention, and there was no way around it.

He looked down at his bare chest, the two heart-monitor leads still taped in place while the monitor continued beeping. Taking the leads off would trigger an alarm at the nurses' station. He hoped to walk out of the hospital quietly but was prepared to take an unsuspecting hostage if required.

Travis leaned in close to the policeman and listened to the cadence of the heart monitor. He listened some more and waited for the right moment. Fourteen minutes on the clock now.

In one quick motion, he ripped the leads off his chest and stuck them firmly on the policeman's chest in the same general locations. A red light appeared on the heart monitor followed by the momentary squeal of a high-pitched alarm. Travis struggled to get the blue shirt on before someone came. Three, four, five seconds passed. And then the alarm stopped.

A regular pulsing rhythm returned to the monitor. Had it worked? Or was the nurse on her way? Travis laid his hospital gown over the officer like a blanket. He moved next to the door and finished tucking in his shirt as best he could. He tossed the Cedar Rapids jacket over his shoulder to hide the blood-stained neck bandage and held the gun at the ready, then waited for the nurse to come.

He focused on the door handle for any movement, but nothing happened. A good three minutes passed, and now he had less than ten minutes before the new night nurse would certainly check in on him. Had his plan really worked? Could he just walk out of the hospital? It was time to find out.

He put the handgun in his belt and adjusted the jacket on his shoulder, pushing it up against his neck. Travis turned the door handle and stepped into the brighter light of the hallway. The corridor was empty except for the small metal chair next to the door.

***

Travis reached the parking lot opposite the hospital's emergency entrance and looked for a Cedar Rapids Police cruiser. A fading twilight greeted him, the parking-lot lights were not yet on. He found the police car easily on the second row in.

He started to open the door when he heard someone crying. Parked two cars down from the cruiser, a woman sat in a minivan with the windows down, smoking a cigarette between sobs. He watched her for a second. She folded down the visor mirror and dabbed at her makeup. She looked to be in her forties or fifties, and her minivan appeared newer, a late-model Dodge, a nice inconspicuous choice of a vehicle. Travis pocketed the keys to the police car and turned. He walked over to her window.

"Are you all right, ma'am?"

She fumbled with her makeup case before looking up. Travis fingered the gun behind his back.

"Oh, yes, fine, officer. Just upsetting, these test results and all."

"I'm sorry to hear that, ma'am."

"It's okay. What can you do, right?"

"You can get out of the car--now."

The dumbfounded woman looked down the barrel of the gun inches from her face. Travis opened the car door and grabbed her by the arm.

"Come on, lady! Out!"

Before she could let out a scream, he flung her hard against the neighboring car's door. The woman slipped to the ground stunned from the impact. He jumped in the minivan and started the engine. He quickly backed out of the space and drove out of the parking lot.

Travis smiled as he merged into traffic. The gas tank was three-quarters full, a good start for the eight hour, overnight drive to Evansville to get reacquainted with Nikki's sister.

But first he needed a big fat steak at a sports bar. The least he could do for the unconscious cop was cheer for St. Louis to win the baseball game.

53

DAY 138 – Evansville, IN

Nikki maneuvered the motorhome through the sluggish evening traffic while a light rain fell on downtown Evansville. Lights were still on in some of the office buildings, but the brightness was no match for the vibrant lights on the riverboat casino docked on the Ohio River. Visible from the freeway, the thousands of small white lights framed the outline of Casino Astar.

"Check it out!"

A dozing Matt shifted in the passenger seat. Nikki backhanded a swat at the side of his leg, jostling him awake.

"What?"

"The riverboat down there, Jill got me my first casino job at that place."

His weary eyes found the riverboat. It looked more like a big rectangular barge than a true side-wheeler.

"We must be close, then," he said.

"Yup. Ten minutes away."

"She picked up yet?"

"Nada, no answer. Tried a half-hour ago."

Matt didn't think Nikki looked tired after the long drive on back roads across Illinois. With a few pit stops thrown in, they'd been on the road about nine hours. He guessed the excitement of finally seeing her sister had kept her going.

He didn't remember much of their drive after breakfast. He dozed most of the time until an occasional rough patch of road inflamed the collarbone break. Not having to drive and getting some rest was helpful, but now that was ending. Ten more minutes and she'd be back at home with her sister, and he'd be left to make it to Cincinnati on his own.

Nikki exited the Veterans Memorial Parkway and turned north towards the working-class Goosetown neighborhood on the bluff above the Ohio River. Matt surveyed the streets lined with plain wood-frame houses with dirt alleys in the rear. A few updated Victorian homes remained, mixed in with random vacant lots tall with grass. Nikki turned onto Taylor Street.

"Why do they call it Goosetown?" Matt asked.

"Birdshit. Lots of it. Every year the stupid things fly across the river from the Kentucky marshes and they strain to get up over the bluff--"

"I get the picture."

"They should have called it Splatter City."

Nikki slowed and pulled the motorhome to the curb midblock. Yellow police tape was drawn across the front door of her sister's house.

"Oh no!"

She bolted from the motorhome and sprinted up to the house. Bob sprang to life with a loud meow when she slammed the door. Matt squirmed out of his seat and opened his door to join her outside in the rain. Nikki bounded up the front steps and onto the wraparound porch.

"Jill!"

She turned the doorknob, to no avail. She hopped from window to window, trying to get a glimpse inside the house. Something she saw made her gasp, and she started pounding hard on the front door.

"Jill!"

Matt arrived on the porch as Nikki paced back and forth.

"The place is torn up!"

He handed her his prepaid cellphone.

"Try her again."

She dialed as Matt looked through one of the windows. A phone began to ring inside the house. They looked at each other knowing it was not a good sign. Nikki tore the yellow tape off the door and started banging on it again.

"Jill!"

Matt looked out at the evening street scene. A few homes had lights on inside. He touched her shoulder, and she stopped hitting the door and started to sob. She hugged him briefly before she slumped down onto the porch floor. He took the phone from her hand.

"What about neighbors?" he asked.

Nikki sat stunned for a moment before she jumped up and pushed past Matt.

"Miz Andy! Around the corner! She'll know!"

Matt watched her run down the porch steps and jog across the grass. She disappeared around the corner a few houses down.

He stood there, pondering his options. Clearly her sister was in trouble, and the police were involved. He debated how long to wait for Nikki's return or whether it was best to avoid the goodbyes and simply drive away, leaving her belongings on the front porch.

***

Nikki caught her breath as she rang the doorbell of her former grade-school teacher, Ms. VanAndersen. She could only hope Ms. Andy was home and would know what had happened.

A porch light came on, and a short, white-haired woman pulled a curtain aside from an adjacent window and looked outside. The door soon opened.

"My dear, Nicole!" she said as she hugged Nikki.

"Where's Jill?"

She fought to keep tears at bay. The woman released her and held Nikki's shoulders.

"She's okay, honey. Glenn took her up to French Lick. Come, sit down."

The older woman directed her inside and closed the door. Nikki plopped down on the familiar couch, which had been a place of refuge for both her and Jill during some difficult teenage years in the Cook household.

"All I know is that a man came looking for you, a big man with tattoos, and he beat up Jill pretty bad."

Nikki jumped to her feet and paced with her fists in knots.

"Travis! Oh my God!"

"You know the man?"

"I ran away from him months ago! I never thought--I'll kill him!"

"The police will want to know about him. I'm so glad he didn't find you, dear. Jill worried about you after she woke up. She rested in the hospital for a few days. We tried calling you in Iowa, at the restaurant, but only left voicemail messages."

"That asshole found me, all right, and tried to kill me! A man--another man--saved me."

Nikki realized Matt wasn't nearby. She opened the front door and checked the street. She saw him standing down at the corner in the rain.

"Matt!" Nikki yelled out.

***

If he couldn't find her in the next ten minutes, Matt figured he would park somewhere close by for the night but away from the police crime scene, maybe try for Cincinnati in the morning. He heard a noise and didn't recognize it at first. He turned and saw Nikki waving at him.

Matt walked up the block and met Nikki on Ms. Andy's porch. He winced in anticipation as Nikki embraced him again, pushing her wet face into his neck. Nikki's friend held the door open.

"Travis got to Jill. That's how he found me," Nikki sobbed.

"Come inside, you two," Ms. Andy said.

"Is Jill--?" Matt asked slowly.

"Miz Andy says she's okay. God, I hope she's okay. If I ever see Travis again I'll--"

Matt guided Nikki through the door and back into the small living room. She sat back down on the couch, and Matt lowered himself into a chair nearby.

"Welcome, Matthew, is it?"

"Yes, ma'am."

"Let me get Glenn on the phone for you, Nicole," Ms. Andy said before walking out of the room.

"Who's Glenn?" Matt asked.

Nikki blew her nose before responding.

"On-off boyfriend of Jill's. He worked with us on the riverboat and then moved up to the casino at the French Lick Resort a year ago. We can head up there in the morning."

Matt had no plans for a detour to a place called French Lick. He wanted her to come with him but knew she wouldn't now. He figured a clean break would be best. He looked away from her big brown eyes.

Their hostess had returned carrying her closed cellphone.

"He's at work now but says Jill's fine. He'll tell her you're okay when he gets home."

"I'm pushing on to Cincinnati in the morning, Nikki," Matt said. "I was hoping you'd want to--"

Nikki quickly turned to him.

"Please take me up there tomorrow! It's not far."

"Come with me instead, help me figure this out."

"French Lick is a couple of hours north at most, in the hill country," Ms. Andy said. "You can both stay here tonight."

"I have to see Jill! I need to see her for real. Make sure she's okay."

Matt realized he wasn't going to win her over.

"I can't take you there, Nikki. I just hope you understand."

"Understand? Well, I don't! You're so stubborn! I've been helping you this far, now you can help me!"

He took a deep breath before responding. She was the one who had pushed him to take her in the first place.

"The deal was, I'd drop you in Evansville, and we're here," Matt said as he gingerly stood up. He started to shuffle towards the front door. The older woman put her hand on Nikki's arm.

"You can take my car, Nicole, after breakfast. Matthew? Please stay."

"Thank you, but no, I have accommodations."

Nikki followed Matt to the door. She bit her lip and tried to hold her emotions in check.

"You just want to be rid of me," she said while jutting out her hand, "Well, thank you, Matt, George, or whatever you call yourself today. It's been real--"

Instead of grasping her outstretched hand, Matt looked down to reach into his sling. He retrieved his prepaid cell-phone and placed it in her palm. Nikki looked up at him. Matt smiled and pointed at his chest.

"Me, Matt Sizemore. I know that number."

54

DAY 138 – Rockford, MI

Stewart Crites entered Solomon's paneled office at the farmhouse with two small glasses of twenty-year-old port. He reached across the large desk and placed a glass near an open file folder as Solomon flipped through the pages.

"Thought you could use this tonight."

Solomon picked up the glass and studied the amber liquid.

"The thorn that was Hoffman is gone, but I can't celebrate it. Additional problems lie ahead."

"Then be happy Harry is safe."

"That I can do."

Stewart raised his glass, and Solomon followed suit. They savored the port in silence. The sound of crickets chirping outside echoed in the room and nearly masked the ticking of the grandfather clock standing in the corner.

Solomon set his glass down and returned to the file.

"Has Wade Kearns been through this?" Solomon asked.

"He has a copy. I imagine he's going over it now."

"Nothing at the cabin? We need more to go on than this!"

"No, sir. Clean. We're tracking down a missed call from a cellphone in Iowa. No message was left."

"And nothing at Pine Bluff?"

"Not yet. The employees are still being processed through the lock down and we're still working on contractors including former ones. We know Hoffman closed down Shelby's lab a month before the scientist disappeared, but we don't know where any of the source material is."

"I cannot believe he didn't have help. He had to manufacture the pills somewhere. He could do that at Pine Bluff."

"No indication that happened, sir. Shelby's lab was professionally cleaned. No residue of any type."

"What else have you got?"

"I've got the FBI checking the travel history of the Shelby brothers. Trying to find a supply chain for the drug. Same with Hoffman and his close business partners. Waiting on the results."

Solomon slammed the file closed.

"Damnit! With all the resources at our disposal, we've got nothing! Unbelievable! Tell me you've had some luck with Sizemore?"

"We'll find him, sir. He's quite the character. We have a trail of sorts from Austin through Tucson to Denver and into Iowa. He seems to slowly be heading east. His ex-wife is being interviewed tomorrow."

"Dead-end leads do not make a trail! He could be anywhere now. Local police probably know more than we do! Where the hell is Kearns?"

"Checked into his hotel for the night."

"Have him here first thing in the morning for a strategy session. And bring some fresh ideas with you, Stewart."

"Yes, sir."

"We need that drug--and we need Sizemore at Otter One!"

Stewart backed out of the office as Solomon rocked back in his desk chair.

Solomon reached across his desk and drank what was left of Stewart's port, then stood up and threw the glass hard into the fireplace, hurting his arm in the process.

55

DAY 139 – Cincinnati, OH

The nerdy waiter with big ears, sporting a necktie with a Cincinnati Reds logo, approached the round table and poured Erin a second cup of coffee. She glanced up from her laptop and looked around the upscale lobby restaurant for Kevin before acknowledging the waiter.

"Thank you."

"Would you like to order breakfast now?"

"Not quite yet. Thanks."

The young man nodded and moved on to another table. She wondered why Kevin was taking so long to check out of the hotel.

Erin looked down at the *Washington Post* article on her screen. The news item from a year ago chronicled the relationship between Kevin and Neta Eichler, the same woman she'd seen on the TV at the gym, the Israeli spy Kevin had been involved with while working at the FBI.

She hadn't found the courage to ask him about it last night as they shared some overpriced wine from the minibar. They talked about many things while enjoying the balcony of their ornate two-bedroom suite overlooking downtown Cincinnati. Kevin was in such a good mood, she didn't want to ruin it. He relished sticking Wade with a fat hotel bill for the trip to Cincinnati. When they finally parted for bed, Erin locked the door to her room but arose an hour later to quietly unlock it, just in case. She chuckled to herself about that.

What was she, sixteen all over again?

Kevin entered the dining room and made his way between the tables to Erin.

"Order yet?"

"Waiting for you."

"How's the buffet look?"

"Looks like twenty-five-ninety-nine on the menu, so it better be good."

Kevin motioned to the waiter for coffee. He arrived and filled both cups. Kevin flashed the room key.

"Put us down for two buffets. Charge the room."

"I can't eat that much," Erin said.

"Don't worry. Wade's the one eating it. How much time have we got?"

Erin pulled out her cellphone and looked at the screen.

"Appointment's at eleven a.m., so a little over an hour or so before we have to leave."

"Well then, if I'm driving, care for a mimosa with your breakfast?"

56

DAY 139 – Memphis, TN

Amanda Chu finished her over-easy eggs by dipping gluten-free toast in the remaining yolk. Her morning workout had been vigorous as usual for an Olympic athlete, and she was tempted to prepare another egg. She picked up her cup of coffee and walked around the large center island with the colorful granite top.

She would miss everything about the house--the indoor pool, the gym, the peace and quiet--all of it more than the average mansion in Taiwan offered. She would miss it all except for the dead man in the basement.

Her flight to Vancouver was at noon, and she decided there wasn't enough time for more food if she was going to shower and change out of her spandex workout attire. She was excited to be headed home and back to her national volleyball teammates. Preparations for the Olympics were already underway, and she wasn't happy that her father had made her stay this long. Amanda poured another cup of coffee and decided to walk around the house one last time.

The living-room couch brought back memories of a tryst with Sam Asrani. The week-long romance had served its purpose, and she didn't know why he hadn't showed up this time with the man called Sizemore. Hoffman said he would come, but she wondered if Sam knew Hoffman was dead. The accident had just happened yesterday and had spurred her father's decision to bring her home. There were way too many risks to stay and finish the clean-up job.

Amanda remembered hating Hoffman since she was a young child. Her father loved the money Hoffman made for him over the years, but she loathed his presence whenever he was around. The older and more attractive she became, the more he tried to engage her in conversation that masked an ulterior motive.

She passed through the formal dining room and into the wide foyer with the circular staircase. She always felt like a princess coming down those stairs each morning.

In the hallway leading back to the kitchen she passed the locked door to the basement. Jonathan Shelby lay dead down there, after taking his own life the day before Hoffman's car accident. She actually respected the doctor's decision not to cooperate with her father--something she personally struggled with herself.

She would not miss the daily trips into the basement wearing a ski mask and carrying a stun gun just to bring Shelby food and push him to reveal "the source plant material" that her father wanted. Showing him the picture of his dead brother didn't have the desired effect. He chose to protect the rest of his family by downing all of the remaining Cecilimate pills and trying to start a fire.

His brain must have exploded from the drug, and with it went the knowledge of the location of the one ingredient needed for the efficacy of the compound. Essential oils derived from other members of the same plant family had shown no similar benefit. Only the one strain that Shelby had found had worked at all. Notes recovered from the grad student's apartment at Berkeley proved it worked. The student had predicted two future events in his notes, but no other test subject had survived very long after taking the drug, until this Sizemore.

Amanda arrived in the kitchen, ran water in the sink, and collected the dishes. Hoffman gone. The doctor gone. Sam was who knows where. Within hours she would be out of the country and happy to leave her father's mess behind.

57

DAY 139 – Cincinnati, OH

Matt stared out the windshield of his idling motorhome across the street from the old brick building that he hoped would somehow yield clues to the whereabouts of Dr. Cecil Ross. He drained his third Red Bull of the morning and then double-checked the scrawled address on the wrinkled scrap of paper in his hand.

The two-story building near the CSX railroad yard north of downtown appeared to be a former warehouse, a structure ultimately converted in a slipshod manner over time, that now held a series of interesting tenants of all types.

A crowded fenced-in parking lot out front contained half a dozen school buses and shuttle-type buses waiting for repairs. A large electronic recycling company sign above a roll-up door overlooked a series of dark-blue drop-off bins. A sizable yellow arrow painted on the old brick wall pointed to offices on the second floor that were reached via a rusted exterior metal stairway.

Matt squirmed out of the driver's seat. Everything ached after the tough nighttime drive. He moved slowly to the dinette booth and sat down. He picked up the remote and turned on the TV before Bob could even ask. The cat climbed down off the bunk above the cab and onto the table, sitting directly on Matt's notebook.

"Off," Matt grumbled as he slid Bob to the side.

Matt scrolled through the available broadcast channels. He found a local cooking show and hoped it was good enough to entertain Bob for a while.

He opened the notebook and reread his notes made late last night. There was the day-long drive across Illinois that he barely remembered, and then his leaving the waitress Nikki in Evansville to find her sister. He wondered if she had made it to her side by now. The overnight parking spot he stopped at outside of Louisville for a few hours was quiet enough, but the disruptive dreams still plagued him.

A man tumbling down a tall pile of coal. Snowmobiles racing across a frozen lake. Someone crawling through thick wet mud amid the sounds of distressed horses.

When would it stop?

He flipped through the pages of dreams looking for anything that remotely applied to the scene in front of him, the grungy headquarters of the Cecilimate empire. Nothing seemed to fit.

He turned to a fresh page and wrote "Day 139" at the top. He wrote down the doctor's name and described the building across the street.

Bob looked back at Matt, apparently disappointed in the choice of TV program. Matt changed channels and found a travel program profiling Hawaii and hosted by a young Polynesian woman wearing a grass skirt. Perfect, given Bob's predilection for the ladies.

Matt closed the notebook and stood up at the sink. He splashed some water on his face and ran fingers through his scraggly hair. He toweled off and tucked in his shirt. He retrieved his father's gun out of the backpack and tucked it into his sling. He opened the fridge and plucked the plastic wrap off a half-eaten can of tuna and set it on the dinette for Bob. He took another Red Bull for the road. He checked his watch as he stepped out the rear door of his motorhome. Fifteen minutes to eleven.

There was plenty of activity at the building. A shuttle bus was being moved into a repair bay, and other companies operating behind roll-up doors were open for business. Matt opened the Red Bull and knocked half of it back before walking across the street towards the open gate of the parking lot.

Below the painted arrow on the building, a list of company names on a wood panel did not show Ross Medical Enterprises occupying space on the second floor. An old leasing sign posted below the list of tenants was askew, and Matt tried to make a mental note of the faded phone number. He checked his wad of paper with the address and then headed up the metal stairs to find Suite 225.

The dented metal door to the suite was littered with rust spots. Affixed to the door was a bright-red legal notice courtesy of the FBI. The notice warned individuals that this crime scene remained active and instructed all persons not to enter without explicit permission. Broken mini-blinds obstructed most of the view to the interior from windows on either side of the door. What Matt could see of the inside was dingy and unoccupied. He held the rickety handrail as he worked his way back down the stairs to reread the leasing phone number that his foggy mind had already forgotten.

Matt was halfway down when a four-door Lexus pulled into the lot and parked close to the stairway landing. A sweaty middle-aged man in a poorly fitting suit jumped out and adjusted his loud tie in the car's side mirror. He looked up and saw Matt on the stairs.

"Mister Sharpe?" the man asked.

Matt looked over his shoulder, assuming there was someone behind him. The man climbed the stairs towards him.

"Kevin Sharpe, correct?" the man asked again as he arrived in front of Matt.

"No, not me."

"Ah, sorry about that. I thought you might be my eleven o'clock."

"Afraid not."

"Well, the sling and all had me wondering if you were this Sharpe character. Figured a scrape with a perp had not gone well. Occupational hazard of being a federal agent, eh? Do you work here somewhere?"

Federal agents?

"No, just looking at--maybe renting an office," Matt said.

"You're in luck, then. I'm the man to see, Carter Knowles, at your service. Which space are you interested in?"

"Top of the stairs vacant?"

"Can't show that to you. Off limits, even to me. I'm letting the feds in there again in a few minutes. I open the door and then just step aside. Wish they'd let me put it back on the market."

"A murder happen in there or something?"

"No sir, nothing like that. Medical billing company. Medicare scam from what I've heard."

"They caught them yet?"

"Don't know. Guy I remember was Eastern European I think. Paid a year's rent up front in cash. Boy, would I like more of those."

"No idea where they went?"

"Nah, on the run, I imagine, with the feds on their heels."

Matt moved sideways to step around the man.

"Thanks anyway."

"Hey, there's another space I can show you once I'm done with this guy. Stick around!"

"I might do that."

***

Erin pointed at the overhead sign as Kevin sped down the fast lane of the I-75 heading north from downtown Cincinnati.

"Better get over, only a half mile," she said.

Kevin braked and weaved across four lanes of traffic to just make the Hopple Street exit into the industrial area. He made a left at the bottom of the ramp and entered the zone of the mishmashed collection of buildings crammed between the freeway and the railyard. He turned onto a side street and slowed down. They both looked for addresses on the passing structures.

"Ironic, isn't it?" Erin said.

"What is?"

"That our scam artists would rent offices on Straight Street."

"And, yes, here it is, just in time."

Kevin turned into the fenced parking lot. A parked car by a stairway landing partially blocked the drive. A tired-looking man with his arm in a sling leaned against a wall near the stairway. Another man in grey overalls walked out of a doorway, climbed into a small school bus, and backed it out of a parking spot into a repair shop. Kevin angled the rental car into the space vacated by the bus. The tight quarters between two buses left Erin sliding over to the driver's door to get out of the car after Kevin.

"Mister Sharpe!" Carter Knowles barked from above.

Kevin looked up and waved at the man at the top of the stairs.

"This way. The suite is up here."

"Ladies first," Kevin said.

Kevin ushered Erin up the stairs while carrying a rigid silver briefcase. He exchanged a compulsory nod with the odd man with his arm in a sling. Erin reached the top of the stairway.

"And you are, my dear?" asked Carter extending a hand.

"Erin Owens," she said as Kevin joined them.

"And Mister Sharpe. I'm Carter Knowles. Thanks for being on time. Any trouble finding our little slice of paradise?"

"Thankfully no."

"Very good. We're right over here. Number two-twenty-five."

Carter unlocked the door and pushed it open wide.

"This is where I get off," Carter said. "I'll be downstairs trying to talk someone into renting space if you need me."

"Thank you. We shouldn't be too long."

Carter left them and started down the stairs. Kevin opened the briefcase and retrieved rubber gloves and cotton booties for their shoes. He handed Erin a set of each.

"Here. Try not to touch anything."

They both put the gloves and booties on and entered the office. Kevin flipped the light switch on, and banks of fluorescent lights suspended from the open-beam ceiling began to hum. The windows on either side of the door provided the only natural light to the 15X30' room. An exposed brick wall covered the length of the back wall. Stained forest green carpet with wear patterns around a handful of desks filled out the room. Behind a low wall on the right, a small kitchenette area was outlined with a checkerboard linoleum floor. A short countertop with a small sink butted up against a full-sized refrigerator.

"Looks like the FBI swabbed the place pretty good," Kevin observed. "See all the numbered tags?"

"Yeah."

"All these locations were checked for fingerprints or forensic evidence."

Erin looked around the room at all the numbered stickers on the walls, the furniture, the carpet, and the appliances. She guessed there were at least fifty of them.

"Is this normal?"

"Nah, they probably came back a second time after the first results were negative. This is one impressive clean-up job. No amateurs here."

Kevin walked over to the kitchenette and opened the refrigerator door. He turned away from the warm, musty air escaping from the empty interior. He closed the fridge door and inadvertently touched the black plastic kickplate on the bottom of the fridge with the toe of his shoe. He looked down and watched it flop forward onto the linoleum. He bent down to put in back in place.

Erin watched as Kevin paused in the middle of fixing the kickplate. He dropped onto his knees and looked underneath the refrigerator.

"What are you doing?"

"There's always something to find," Kevin said.

"What?" Erin said as she walked up behind him.

"See there. Under the foot."

"Looks like cardboard."

"Pull it out when I lift this up."

Kevin cradled his hands under the corner of the refrigerator and lifted it up. Erin spun the square piece out from under the little metal foot with a flick of her index finger. She opened the folded fragment.

"It's an empty matchbook for some restaurant," Erin said as he handed it to Kevin.

He stood up and looked it over. The logo on the matchbook was faded, but he could make out a place called The Honey Creek Inn in Cannonsburg, Michigan.

"Looks like we just might miss our flight back to D.C."

***

It took a couple minutes' awkward convincing before Matt got Carter, the pushy real-estate broker, to leave him alone. He had escaped into the recycling company office and lobbed a quick question at the woman manning the front desk. She couldn't add anything new about the former tenant upstairs. She had hardly seen anyone up go up there during the day. She guessed they mostly worked odd hours, and her descriptions of the few men she thought worked there were lacking any helpful details.

After walking back outside, Matt left the parking lot and returned to his motorhome. He opened the driver's door and climbed into the seat. He looked back at Bob who seemed to still be enjoying the TV show.

He draped his good arm over the steering wheel and thought about his next step. He could talk to more tenants in the neighborhood to see if anyone knew anything about this Dr. Cecil Ross or his company. It felt all too tiring to even think about. He could really use help, but Nikki was gone now.

The FBI seemed to be after the doctor too, and he had to be careful. Asking them for help would be problematic, opening up his own recent history for inspection and likely leading to jail time or a mental institution. Just the thing Lisa and Kyle would like to happen.

Without help and running out of time, Matt's cluttered mind decided there was only one reasonable thing to do. Let the feds to the legwork and try to follow their trail of breadcrumbs. The tall black agent had a name. The sweaty broker had said it, had called out to him. Was it Scott? Shapell? Sharpe! Sharpe, like a knife.

What was his first name?

Kurt. Something like that. No. Kevin. Yes. Kevin Sharpe.

Matt turned the ignition key, and the motorhome sputtered to life. He would follow this Kevin as best he could, let him collect the clues and lead the way to the infamous doctor.

Matt looked down at the dashboard instruments. Gas. He needed gas. There wasn't much time to fill up at the corner station and get back to the building before Federal Agent Kevin Sharpe and the woman with him made their next move.

58

DAY 139 – Evansville, IN

Two hours had passed since the last group of puddle-jumping children walked past Sam's rental car on their way to school. The mailman had finished wheeling his cart of mail up and down both sides of Taylor Street within the last thirty minutes. The relatively busy morning in the Goosetown neighborhood transitioned into a gray midday slumber under a light rain.

Sam Asrani had observed zero activity at the house since he arrived at 3 a.m. No one came in or out of the address where the cellphone had been pinpointed by Hoffman's hacker team--the same cellphone the waitress had attempted to call from that dumpy store back in Iowa. No motorhome sat nearby, on the street or in a back alley. Most importantly, there was no sign of the man Sizemore. At least Hoffman wasn't calling and swearing at him every ten minutes asking when he would be bringing the man to Memphis.

Sam stepped out of his car and lit a cigarette. He turned up the collar on his raincoat and sauntered across the street. He tossed his cigarette butt against the wet curb before following the sidewalk a few doors down to the targeted house.

He stopped before starting up the front steps at the sight of torn yellow police tape tangled around the porch railing. Not good news. He continued past the house and looked over the street scene again for any police presence. On the side of the house he saw a wire gate propped open between overgrown bushes. A few agile jumps across the lawn and he was out of sight.

A wooden deck in the backyard overlooked a neglected vegetable garden and a weed-infested patch of grass. An old detached garage was further back and faced the rutted dirt of the back alley.

Sam climbed the few steps up onto the deck. He peered through an open sliver of a curtained window on the back door. The vintage kitchen immediately inside had no lights on. A coffee cup sat on its side in a saucer on a small table in the center of the room. A broken dinner plate and pieces of silverware littered the floor.

He pulled the police tape off the door frame and tossed it onto the deck. The old lockset looked like an easy pick. After a few deft movements with his Swiss Army knife, the door fell open only two inches. A chain drew tight across the opening.

He listened for any noise coming from inside. He reached inside the door, fingered the small bracket holding the chain, and realized it was no match for him. He placed his palm on the door and threw his shoulder into it at the level of the chain. The bracket popped off the frame flinging screws across the kitchen floor, and leaving the chain swinging wildly against the inside of the door.

Sam quickly stepped in and drew his silenced Glock from his deep coat pocket. He waited ten seconds for any sounds from upstairs, but there was nothing. He walked through the kitchen and into the living area.

Tumbled furniture greeted him--chairs turned over, a ratty couch with two broken legs on one side. A bent floor lamp leaned against a table with papers on top that included an open checkbook. The broken screen of a laptop computer stared at him from the floor. A large flatscreen TV on the wall was untouched. If this had been a robbery, the culprits were idiots.

He moved to the table and looked down at the strewn papers. They were mostly unpaid bills. A black power cord came out from under some of the papers and curled over the edge of the desk. He looked under the desk and found the end of the cord plugged into a wall socket. On the desktop, Sam pushed the papers off the cord and found a cellphone. He flipped it open and checked the number. It matched the one he was looking for.

He scrolled through the recent calls and saw that there was one voicemail, likely from the waitress. He decided to pocket the cellphone instead and try to access the voicemail later.

Sam worried that Hoffman would call any time now for an update. He silenced his own phone before exploring the house further. He tiptoed up the stairs and checked the bedrooms. The house was empty.

He appeared to be at a dead end. Failure, pure and simple. No Sizemore and nowhere to look for him next unless the cellphone offered some clues. Sam reckoned it would be better to call Hoffman first.

What would he say? What could he say?

He retreated down the stairs, through the kitchen, and out onto the back porch for a smoke before dialing Hoffman.

***

Travis turned the minivan off Taylor Street and slowly rolled down the back alley behind Nikki's sister's house. He stopped near the neighbor's garage and peered through the wet windshield at a man on the back porch smoking a cigarette.

The rain intensified, and he watched the pacing man flick the cigarette butt into the wet grass before opening the back door and disappearing inside. Curiosity quickly bubbled into anger as something clicked in Travis's head.

The coat! He had seen him before!

The goofy diner in Iowa, talking to Nikki! He had watched them interact through his binoculars, and he could tell she wanted him. The man had walked right by his truck!

Seeing the tall man in the coat at this house meant only one thing to Travis.

Nikki was here too.

***

Sam dialed Neil Hoffman on his cellphone as he walked through the kitchen and back into the messy living room. He decided to leave a short message for the fisherman. Better to be in front of Hoffman's wrath if at all possible.

"Call me. Problems here. No Sizemore."

He ended the call and decided to dial Randy Knox one last time. Sam was fed up with both of them. The house was a crime scene, and he wasn't going to hang out there for long. He decided that if he couldn't get through to a live person in the next five minutes, he'd drive to the airport and head home to Miami.

***

Travis slowly pushed open the back door into the kitchen with the policemen's gun at the ready. He crouched behind the center table and looked toward sounds coming from the front room. The man in the living room walked by the doorway a few times, pacing back and forth with a cell-phone to his ear.

"Goddamn voicemail! Knox, this is shit! Is Hoffman with you? Problems here," the man said.

He ended the call and started dialing again.

Travis inched closer to the living room and saw nothing had changed inside the house since he'd forcibly extracted information from Jill on Nikki's whereabouts. Everything in the room same as when he'd left. Something was wrong, and this guy had to be in the middle of it.

"Yes, thank you, please. You have flight Cincinnati to Miami today?"

The man's return route brought him close to the open doorway to the kitchen. Travis slowly rotated the gun in his hand, gripping it by the barrel instead. He waited as the man turned and worked his path on the carpet back and forth.

"No, Orlando no good. Only Miami."

The man turned away from the doorway again, and Travis sprang through the opening. He leveled a vicious swing at the side of the man's head with the butt of the gun. The man in the coat somersaulted sideways over the broken couch and crumpled to the floor. From where it landed across the room, elevator music emanated from the man's cellphone. Travis found the phone and closed it just as a female voice started to speak.

He returned to the man on the floor. The victim was out cold from the heavy blow to the temple. Travis rummaged through the man's coat and pockets. He was surprised to find a Glock with a silencer and happy to add it to his personal arsenal. Another cellphone was in his pocket, and he scrolled through the recent calls but none looked familiar. In the tanned man's pockets were keys for a rental car with a tag showing Denver's airport.

The man's wallet was sparse. A credit card from a bank he'd never heard of, plus eight hundred or so in cash. The South Carolina driver's license showed an address in Myrtle Beach for a Brian Allen Baker. Travis pocketed the items. He was sure this was the man at the diner in Swisher, but there was nothing about Nikki on him.

Travis looked around the room. He flipped through the unpaid bills on the table and then walked back into the kitchen to see if there was anything that could help him track down Nikki or her sister. Nothing. Maybe upstairs.

He held the man's Glock at the ready as he walked up the creaky stairway to the upstairs bedrooms. There was a combo office and workout room with a treadmill in the corner, left just as he remembered. Jill's bedroom seemed untouched, the bed still unmade. But dresser drawers were open, and there were very few items hanging in the closet. This was new. She must have survived the beating and simply taken off.

He resumed scouring the bedroom for any clue to her whereabouts. Jill was the only link he had to Nikki, besides the man on the floor downstairs. Travis flipped a bedside table over with one hand and yanked the small drawer open. Nothing. He looked under the bed and pulled a few shoe boxes out, but there were only shoes to be found.

He sat down at Jill's dressing table, an old-fashioned one with a mirror directly in front. He pawed through the drawers finding only small jewelry items, stretchy hairbands, and various lipsticks. He threw a plastic makeup case across the room and then stared into the mirror, his face red with anger.

Where was she?

Wedged into the frame around the mirror was a picture of Nikki sitting atop a horse. Travis admired it for a minute. He took it out and read the description on the back. She was fifteen when it was taken somewhere in Kentucky. There were other pictures of Jill and Nikki together stuck around the edge of the mirror, even one from an amusement-park photo booth when they were little. He took a few postcards off the mirror and read each one. Nikki had sent one from the riverboat casino in Tunica, Mississippi. Travis reminisced about meeting Nikki there. One postcard was from their estranged mother in Maine, a pretty coastal scene of fishing boats in a harbor.

The last postcard he lifted off the mirror showed a series of small pictures of a beautifully restored, turn-of-the-century hotel and casino on the front with the words "French Lick Resort" at the top. On the back, some-one named Glenn implored Jill to come visit him as jobs were plentiful there.

Travis heard a thud downstairs and quickly pointed the man's gun at the doorway. He folded the postcard and pocketed it. He slowly walked into the hallway and down the stairs, his ears straining for more and with the Glock pointed straight ahead. As he entered the living room, Travis heard more thumping behind the couch, and he watched the floor lamp fall over and the light bulb burst. He trained the gun on the couch and slowly moved around the end of it.

The injured man was having a seizure on the floor. The rapidly growing hematoma behind the man's temple was doing its dirty little work.

Travis looked down at the twisting man and wondered if he had been the one that shot him in Iowa. The thought of this man actually being with Nikki had his stomach in knots. There was nothing more to learn here.

He stood and pointed the gun at the man's forehead and casually squeezed off two muffled shots. The jerking stopped.

He lifted the dead man's car keys and walked up to the front window. He pushed the curtain aside and pushed the unlock button. The rented SUV's lights flickered down the block, and Travis smiled.

Good riddance to that gutless minivan.

59

DAY 139 – French Lick, IN

"I look like dried-up frosting on a cake," Jill said.

"It's not covering up."

"It's all right, Nikki. I'm in the cash room again tonight. They won't let me deal blackjack if I still look like a prizefighter."

Nikki put down the makeup and looked at her older sister in the bathroom mirror. The bruising inflicted by Travis was still prominent. One eye socket was black and blue nearly all the way around, and there was a purple patch at the corner of her mouth. Larger bruises on her shoulder and neck were hidden by the standard-issue collared shirt embroidered with the logo of the French Lick Resort and Casino.

Nikki gingerly put her arms around Jill's neck. They both looked into the mirror.

"You could use some makeup too," Jill said.

Nikki touched the thin rows of scabs forming on one side of her own face.

"I hope I don't have scars."

"Should be okay."

Beyond the mementos from Travis, Nikki noticed the resemblance was still clearly there, even with Jill's longer black hair and the first few wrinkles around her eyes setting in.

"Wish you weren't working swing shift today," Nikki said.

"I know, sweetie, but I just got the job. You'll be fine here. Glenn's off work at eight, and he can show you around until I'm done at midnight. Then we'll have a few drinks."

Nikki released Jill and started to brush her hair.

"Sounds like fun."

"You'll love it here. A much nicer place to work than the riverboat back home. Both the hotels are high class and fixed up beautiful inside. You'd never guess they were over a hundred years old."

Jill stood up, and they walked back into the living room of the small apartment. Nikki followed and picked up the pre-paid cellphone Matt had given her. She flipped it open. There were no missed calls, but the phone needed charging and Matt hadn't given her a cord to charge it.

"Expecting a call?" Jill said as she slipped a maroon blazer on.

"Yes and no."

"Well, just relax and get some rest. You've been through the wringer too."

"He's behind bars by now. I am finally free of him."

"Amen to that."

Jill hugged Nikki before handing her a key.

"Take this. I'll see you later. Feel free to raid the fridge. Sorry about the slim pickins."

"I'll grab a shower first. Gotta clean up to party later!"

Jill rolled her eyes and opened the front door.

"Glenn's working roulette under the dome in the other hotel. Just meet him there, and don't get too wild without me."

"Where's the dome?"

"Take the path down the hill to the street, then look left. You can't miss the eighth wonder of the world. It's pretty spectacular. See you later."

Nikki closed the door behind Jill. She circled the living room wondering what she would do after a shower. Her sister's shift was eight hours, but Glenn was free in about four. A nap sounded good, but she felt awfully wound up at the same time. The rush to drive to French Lick that morning had jacked her up, but now, after reuniting with Jill, she was more tired than she knew. She yawned and thought about the last few days. The nine months working at Maybelle's seemed like ancient history. She'd call Donna once things settled down, and she wondered if the man that called himself Matt Sizemore had found what he was looking for.

Nikki picked up the cellphone and checked it again. Maybe he'll call tomorrow. She powered down the phone to save the battery.

She walked out onto the narrow back deck of the employee apartment complex and looked down the steep wooded hill towards the backside of the impressive resort. The trees obscured the view of the twin hotels, but the sound of a gentle breeze through the leaves was relaxing enough. She decided a nice cup of tea on the back deck before showering might just calm her down.

60

DAY 139 – Cincinnati, OH

The scraggly-bearded gas-station attendant looked puzzled as Matt poured a small pile of items out of his sling and onto the checkout counter. There were sleeping pills, candy bars, a can of tuna, and four Drumstick ice-cream cones. He lifted a six-pack of Red Bulls onto the counter with his good hand.

"Any maps?" Matt asked.

"Over there, by the magazines."

The attendant started sliding the items over the barcode reader as Matt walked over to a large display rack, one end of it dedicated to maps and tourist flyers highlighting local attractions. He fingered through the selection of maps and found the ones he needed-- Ohio, Indiana, and Kentucky, plus one for the whole USA. He was covered now no matter which direction the federal agents led him, unless they simply returned to the airport to catch a flight.

One of the tourist flyers caught his eye, with the words "French Lick Resort and Casino" in bold type on top of the folded brochure. Nikki was there right now.

He wished she had come with him. The long drive to Cincinnati had worn him out. Few new clues had surfaced on the whereabouts of Dr. Cecil Ross. And with the one path he could follow, he could really use her driving help to keep up with the federal agents as they pursued the doctor.

Matt turned his attention to the flyer in his hand and opened the colorful brochure. Golf, horseback riding, gambling, all of it at huge restored hotels nestled around underground springs that were once bottled as healing waters in Victorian times.

One picture of the vintage resort complex jumped off the page and straight into his brain. A sharp pain shot behind his right eye. He felt faint, and grabbed onto the magazine rack to steady himself.

A massive dome on one hotel sported a series of large glass skylights.

Nikki! The vision. The recurring dream! Black-and-pink hair whipping around and exposing the snake tattoo, then more, the glass, shattered glass flying everywhere! He had to warn her!

Matt fumbled for a prepaid phone tucked in his sling as he staggered to the counter. He knew it hadn't happened yet, Nikki's encounter with broken glass, but not this! Not this big! The attendant rang up the maps while Matt dialed Nikki's phone. He started to sweat.

"You okay, buddy?"

"Yeah, fine."

"Eight-seven-forty, with the gas."

Matt dug a wad of $20 bills out of his pocket and flopped them on the counter. He walked over to the glass doors and peered out at the street as he waited for Nikki to pick up.

The surprised attendant took five of the twenties and made change. He looked at the dazed man staring out the door and then simply put the change and extra twenties in the paper bag. He held out it out for Matt.

"Here you go. Change is in there."

Matt slapped the phone closed after six rings. He lurched over to the counter and took the bag.

"How far to French Lick, Indiana?" he said.

The attendant shrugged.

"I dunno exactly."

"Guess, damnit!"

"Maybe three hours?"

Matt stumbled out the door to his motorhome, opened the side door and dumped the bag on the floor, spilling the contents. He went around to the other side and put the nozzle back on the pump and quickly screwed the gas cap back on.

As Matt gingerly pulled himself into the driver's seat, he saw a sedan pull up to the stop sign next to the gas station. The woman in the passenger seat was clearly visible, the same one he'd seen climb the stairs with the federal agent named Kevin Sharpe.

"Goddamnit!"

He started the engine, hit redial on his phone, and then wedged the phone between his neck and ear.

The sedan started down Straight Street, and Matt winced as he one-handed the steering wheel hard right to turn out of the gas station and follow the car.

More rings and no answer. He tossed the phone onto the dashboard, bouncing it around before it settled against the windshield. A blossoming headache added to his confused thoughts. Nikki was in real danger now, yet his one real lead was directly in front of him and on the move.

Why didn't he go with her? Why couldn't she have just come with him?

The sedan turned onto Hopple, and Matt watched closely as it approached the I-75 freeway interchange. He knew a merge southbound could mean the airport and would also put him on the quickest path to French Lick. Northbound meant they were headed who knows where. South might let him save her life. North might help him save his own.

The agent's car merged on to Interstate 75 heading north towards Detroit.

Matt punched the accelerator to catch up.

***

Erin yawned while looking down at her cellphone.

"Take a nap if you want to," Kevin said.

"I know. That mimosa wasn't the best idea."

"How far does it say?"

"Looks like six hours or so. Cannonsburg is a small town just outside Grand Rapids."

"Could be nothing there, but I'm in no rush to head back to D.C. and see Wade. Okay with you?"

"I'm unemployed, remember?"

"Ever been in Ohio before?"

"Nope."

"Then technically you're on vacation from your vacation."

Erin smiled.

"I think I'll take that nap. Wake me if Ohio is interesting."

***

Matt stared at the cellphone up against the windshield and tried to figure out how to reach for it and not lose control of the motorhome. The sedan a few cars ahead was pushing eighty miles an hour. It had only been twelve miles, and he was already fighting a nasty headache and squirming with mental and physical discomfort. Every mile north was further away from Nikki and the glass of the hotel's dome. And every mile north was closer to the truth of what had happened to him, if he could keep up with the sedan's pace.

The suburbs were gone, and fields of young corn whizzed by. Overpasses zoomed by at regular intervals. Bob meowed a guttural disapproval of Matt's jerky driving.

"What do you want me to do?" Matt said. "He's driving like a mad man!"

He stepped on the accelerator to pass a big truck. His old motorhome struggled to respond. The sedan was even further ahead, barely visible as it weaved in and out of traffic. He gripped the steering wheel and quietly cursed Cecilimate and what it had done to him. He also cursed Nikki for what she had done to him.

Matt pushed the motorhome to pass the big rig. He was losing sight of Kevin's car. He cleared the big rig's bumper, clenched his teeth, and closed his eyes.

He yanked the steering wheel hard right and shot the motorhome across the lane, barely in front of the big truck, and just making it onto an off-ramp. Matt braked hard, coming to a skidding stop on the gravel on the side of the rural ramp. He winced as a jolt of pain coursed through his shoulder and neck from the whiplash. Bob flopped out of the bunk and down onto the floor.

She mattered. Right now, she mattered more.

Matt worked himself out of the driver's seat. He picked up Bob and returned him to the bunk, receiving a nice bite mark on the hand in the process. He picked up the strewn items purchased at the gas station off the floor. He unwrapped one of the Drumstick cones and put the rest in the small freezer before sitting down in the dinette booth. He opened the notebook on the table and wrote "Kevin Sharpe"' on the page headed "Day 139" so he wouldn't forget it.

Matt stuffed the ice-cream cone in his mouth, then fumbled with the map of Indiana with one hand. He hoped he could get there in time. He carried the open map up to the front and placed it on the dashboard.

Seconds later, the motorhome plowed down the on-ramp onto the I-75 headed south.

61

DAY 139 – French Lick, IN

Travis Whitacre enjoyed his last bite of fried cheese sticks and tried to avoid the temptation to wipe greasy fingers on his new pants. He licked them instead and then drained the last of a bottle of beer just as the young waiter arrived.

"Burger will be up in a minute. Another beer for you, sir?"

"Yeah, same thing."

The waiter cleared the appetizer plate revealing the plastic Denny's Restaurant placemat highlighting the French Lick area. Pictures of local basketball legend Larry Bird figured prominently, along with the historic hotels and resort that dominated the small southern Indiana town.

Travis flipped the placemat over and found a helpful local area map. The colorful map and pictures on the place-mat didn't do the French Lick Springs Hotel and Resort complex justice. He could see one of the hotels out the window of the restaurant and directly across the street. He admired the photos of the beautifully restored hotels, one of them built around an impressive dome that was once the largest in the world.

The two historic hotels were less than a mile apart with a golf course in between. The task of finding Nikki's sister Jill and this Glenn person wasn't going to be easy. The resort totaled 3,000 acres. Travis read on about the hotels and tried to formulate a plan to search for the pair and, with any luck, turn up Nikki too.

The West Baden Springs Hotel just down the road boasted the engineering marvel of a self-supporting dome, the largest of its kind in the world for sixty-some years until the Astrodome in Houston had been built. Mineral springs had been discovered here before the Civil War and were the original reason the hotels even existed. The potential of the so-called "healing waters" drew politicians and celebrities alike. Clark Gable to Roosevelt and Liz Taylor to the Reagans, all had stayed and played at one of the sublime French Lick hotels.

At least he was dressed for some mingling with the upscale clientele during his search for Jill. A stop at a Salvation Army store outside Evansville had yielded decent slacks to replace his bloodied jeans, along with a collared dress shirt that mostly covered the stained bandages covering his neck wound.

The burger and beer arrived, and the waiter covered up the area map with the plate. Finding Nikki's sister Jill or this Glenn character at the large resort wasn't going to be as simple as he had hoped.

***

The walkway down the steep hill from the nondescript employee apartments dropped Nikki out of the woods and onto a red-brick street with old-fashioned streetlights. It was a literal step back in time.

Across the street, hotel guests walked through formal gardens of trimmed hedges and colorful rosebushes. She imagined the same scene unfolding over a hundred years before, complete with women in hoop skirts and carrying parasols, their arms intertwined with men in formal suits and top hats.

Nikki made it to the other side of the street between passing cars bumping over the uneven brick pavement. She arrived on a bike path bordering the gardens and looked left. The massive round façade of West Baden Springs Hotel rose above the trees just 100 yards ahead. The hotel was butter-cream in color, with a red-painted dome roof punctuated with large skylights. The old brick street divided around the hotel.

A portico at the rear of the domed building had impeccably dressed valets parking mostly expensive cars. A lighted sign overhead directed patrons to the casino and a steakhouse. An ornate covered veranda wrapped around the front of the hotel and overlooked more gardens and a creek at the valley bottom. At the main entrance guests were directed up a wide staircase onto the expansive veranda and into the hotel lobby.

Nikki slowly ascended the staircase and tried to take in all the vintage decoration. Jill was right, this place was way better than any other casino she had ever seen. A friendly doorman dressed like a Vatican guard opened the lobby door for her. She walked past the large reception desk and refined sitting area. She looked down a curving hallway to the right and saw a sign in the shape of an ice-cream cone. A gift shop was off the hallway curving to the left and straight ahead was a twenty-foot-wide opening to the hotel interior under the dome. The noises of a casino drew her to the doorway.

Five steps across the threshold and Nikki had to stop in her tracks. She had never seen anything like it. The monstrous round atrium space was majestic and large enough to hold a football field. At her feet, the floor was covered with millions of tiny one-inch Italian tiles making an ornate, serpentine pattern around the perimeter.

One quadrant of the room had a bar and restaurant adjacent to a fifteen-foot-tall, exquisitely tiled fireplace that a dozen men could easily stand in side by side. A series of gaming tables filled another quadrant, the muffled sounds of roulette wheels and cards being shuffled filled her ears. A stage was being set up by workers for a concert in another area for a big-band performance.

Nikki was enthralled with the beauty of it all until she glanced overhead. Six stories of hotel rooms with balconies overlooking the atrium drew her eyes up 150 feet above the floor to intricate steel girders supporting the big dome, perforated by a ring of sixteen large glass skylights. She felt a little dizzy, and her breath quickened.

Glass. She's supposed to avoid glass.

That's what he'd told her, but could she believe him? How could he know? He had been awfully sure of himself, and he'd been right so far. She decided not to go in any further.

Nikki retreated out the doorway and headed to the ice-cream parlor. A relaxing double scoop of chocolate on the veranda was needed before she attempted to reenter the overwhelming atrium and find Glenn.

62

DAY 139 – Cannonsburg, MI

Kevin rubbed his eyes while waiting at a stoplight. The six-hour drive north from Cincinnati had left him less than perky. They were close now, not far from Cannonsburg, passing through a village named Ada at the confluence of the Thornapple and Grand rivers. The traffic light turned green.

"Over the bridge, then left," Erin said.

He followed her instructions, and within a mile they reached the turnoff to Cannonsburg.

"Now right. That's the one."

"Thanks. You're quite the navigatrix," Kevin said.

"I assume that's a compliment."

"Correct."

The undulating five-mile drive up Honey Creek Road from the Grand River Valley seemed to take forever. The fading summer daylight alternated between bright-orange rays of the setting sun cascading across open farm fields to a filtered muddy-brown obscurity when they passed through stands of hardwood forest that hugged the road.

"Not much out here," Kevin observed.

"Pretty, though."

"How much further?"

"This dead-ends into Cannonsburg. We can't miss it."

"Sure feels like we might."

Kevin braked on the final downgrade into the small hamlet as a few houses appeared on wooded lots on either side of the road. He rolled up to the stop sign at the T intersection.

Cannonsburg consisted of a collection of vintage buildings huddled around the lone stop sign. A newer gas station and market combo was on one corner. A large bronze giraffe stood front and center on the grass by the gas station. The odd monument distracted Kevin for a second.

Erin pointed to the illuminated Honey Creek Inn located between two vintage buildings across Cannonsburg Road. A few people stood smoking on the front porch of the restaurant, a converted Victorian house.

Kevin pulled the car into the dirt parking lot. He found an open space halfway back and parked under some low-hanging tree branches. He turned to Erin.

"Here's the game plan. I don't know what we'll find here, but I'll go in first just in case. I want you to sit here, behind the wheel. I'll call you in five minutes if I don't perceive any threats. Then you can come in, and we'll have some dinner while we mostly listen and observe."

"Okay."

"If you don't hear from me after those five minutes, I want you to drive out of here, back to Ada, and call Wade Kearns for some back-up."

"Just leave you?"

Kevin reached into the back seat and pulled a plastic bag out of his suit jacket.

"Yes, and keep these safe."

"Is this what I think it is?"

"Remember the mother in Albany? She found a few pills and sent them in. I don't want them on me when I go in there."

"What do I do with them?"

"Hide 'em, keep 'em safe. Just in case I don't call you."

"I don't like this, you going in there alone."

"If I find trouble in there, I'm not going to bring it outside to you. I'll simply stay and play it cool. You just call me after you've made the call to Wade. I'll know help is on the way."

"You're scaring me."

"Nothing to worry about. Normal procedure. Let's hope the food is good."

Kevin opened the car door. Erin reached across the seat and grabbed his arm.

"Be careful."

He put his hand over hers and smiled.

"I have to be. I'm unarmed. Remember, five minutes."

Kevin closed the door and watched Erin slide behind the steering wheel before giving her a thumbs-up. He turned to the dirt parking lot and headed to the back of the building first, checking behind the old structure for other exits. He saw a tall thin man in a suit slam the door of a parked car and hurry past a waitress taking a smoke break on a plastic chair. The man entered a lower-level door underneath the main floor carrying a folder of papers.

He casually walked back through the parking lot towards the front of the tavern. None of the cars in the parking lot looked suspicious. Then he came upon a weird Volkswagen bug parked against the curb below the front entrance. Cars shouldn't have hair, he thought.

Kevin took the steps up to the vestibule two at a time and disappeared into The Honey Creek Inn.

***

Stewart Crites arrived at the high-backed wooden booth with a folder of papers just before a strawberry-blonde waitress arrived with dinner plates for two men already seated there.

"Progress," Stewart said.

He stood out of the way as the waitress placed two identical orders of half-chickens directly in front of Solomon Carr and Wade Kearns. Stewart sat down with the men after the waitress finished.

"Anything for you, sir?" she asked Stewart.

"No, no thanks."

"Another beer for me, thanks," Wade said.

Stewart waited for her to collect Wade's empty bottle and move away into the loud bar. He leaned over the table.

"Got the cell number Hoffman was using at the cabin. He called someone right after you left. The carrier was quick in getting us the records."

Solomon finished a bite of mashed potatoes before responding.

"I do love the Patriot Act," Solomon said. "What else?"

"A company we traced back to one of Hoffman's investors bought an estate in Memphis last fall. The investor's daughter, Amanda Chu, has been living there."

"Was that where he was heading?" Wade asked.

"Very likely," Stewart said.

"Get Twig up to speed on that location, and have him prep a team. I need to know what's there," Solomon said.

"Yes, sir."

"Who did Hoffman call?"

"No name yet, but Hoffman called a cellphone that was located in Iowa at the time. It since moved on to Evansville and is in French Lick, Indiana, at the moment."

"Any resources nearby?"

"None, sir, but FBI agents from Louisville can be there in about an hour."

"I don't want low-level feds asking this person questions. This is too sensitive," Solomon said. "Where's your man, Wade? Isn't he in Cincinnati?"

Before Wade could respond he was distracted by a tall black man arriving at the bar.

"That's further away, sir, maybe three hours," Stewart injected.

"We need to be discreet, use our own people. Wade? Where is your man?"

Wade cleared his throat before responding.

"I'm afraid he's at the bar."

63

DAY 139 – French Lick, IN

Bob knew something was up on the drive to French Lick. He sat in the empty seat opposite Matt most of the way, occasionally putting his front paws on the dashboard to see the countryside.

Matt paid little attention to the view. It was hard enough to focus on driving with one arm on the curvy back roads of southern Indiana. He had pushed through the arm fatigue and shoulder pain to get to French Lick before nightfall and hoped to find Nikki safe.

The large dome of the West Baden Springs Hotel was easy enough to spot, once he reached the town of French Lick. He drove under the elaborate arched entry and up the wide red-brick driveway to the famous round hotel. He passed by the hotel lobby drop-off area at the foot of the veranda and circled around the back. He continued on beyond the valet staff and security guards stationed at the casino entrance. He wrapped around the building further and found two spaces to straddle in the self-park lot near other RVs and tour buses.

Matt started fishing through the backpack for the old sweatshirt cradling the revolver. He was nearly out the back door of the motorhome when he paused. The gun. Taking it with him was a big risk. There would be plenty of security at a casino like this, and not just cameras. He rolled the gun back up in the sweatshirt and returned it to the backpack.

He opened a cabinet and found the bottle of painkillers for his achy shoulder. He popped four pills and swallowed them with the warm remnants of a Red Bull. He tossed the empty can in the sink and left.

Bob jumped up onto the bunk and watched out the window as Matt hobbled across the parking lot.

***

Nikki strolled with her ice cream in front of long rows of lounge chairs on the curving veranda dotted with people and families enjoying a variety of drinks or ice-cream cones. A few smokers holding beers congregated at the railing while cursing their losses in the casino.

Most of the wide veranda looked out over a lush green lawn sprinkled with large trees with French Lick Creek wandering through it. An ornate lamppost with a rotating four-sided clock defined the midpoint of her walk. She still had a half hour before Glenn got off work.

The complete arc of the veranda took Nikki around to where it dead-ended into the side of the posh steakhouse. Double doors at the end turned back into the curving corridor encircling the atrium of the hotel.

The last few yards of her veranda walk had no view of the pretty lawn, only the beginnings of a sizable parking lot extending from the backside of the hotel.

***

Matt paused by the valet station outside the rear entrance to the hotel. He felt exhausted from the drive and now faced the climb up a canopied staircase. He leaned on a sturdy railing at the bottom of the stairs. A concerned valet runner returned from the parking lot.

"Can I help you, sir?"

"Any elevator around here?"

"Yes. Around to the right and duck under the staircase. Will take you up to the main level. Do you need assistance?"

"No, I think I can make it just fine."

Matt slowly made his way down a side path beside the staircase and through a doorway to an elevator lobby. The doors opened, and a woman in a powered wheelchair darted off and nearly ran over his toes. He stepped inside and touched the button. The elevator walls were covered with pictures of the many famous people that had stayed and played at the hotel.

The doors parted, and Matt found himself in a hallway across from the main entrance to a steakhouse. Sounds from the casino filled his ears from another direction, and he headed that way. The curving corridor was full of people, and he hugged the railing along the wall to keep his shoulder from being knocked into. He could hear the casino getting closer. He came upon a large opening into the center of the round hotel.

This was it. The huge dome, from the brochure, set high off the floor and punctuated by large glass sky-lights. He had to find Nikki, and soon.

Matt didn't notice any of the magnificence of the massive atrium, his eyes were solely focused on searching the casino crowd for Nikki. He meandered through the various gaming tables, scanning the faces of each dealer, hoping Nikki's sister Jill bore a resemblance.

He caught a glimpse of a waitress weaving through the players with black hair, and he rushed up behind her. He grabbed her arm and spun her around, nearly spilling the drinks off her tray.

"Nikki?"

"Hey! Watch it!"

It wasn't her. She was mid-forties, and her name badge read "Sylvia." She tried to twist out of his grip.

"I need to find Jill, she works here."

"Let go!"

Matt held her arm tight.

"Please help me."

She stared him in the eye.

"You better let go, mister."

"Jill. Just point her out, please."

"I don't know a Jill."

She broke out of his grip, leaving him standing there alone. Matt noticed customers at the tables looking at him, the desperate, disheveled man with one arm in a sling.

***

Travis Whitacre walked into the hotel atrium and tried not to look up at the dome overhead. His neck wound wasn't quite ready for the required movement. This was his last place to look. His questioning of valets and busboys at the other hotel hadn't turned up the Glenn person he was eager to find.

The floor area covered by the massive dome stunned him. There seemed to be a thousand people. Staff members were everywhere with waitresses, dealers, pit bosses, and security, all on the move. He realized walking around and checking individual name badges would take too much time. Better cut to the chase. He approached a security guard walking the perimeter of the gaming tables.

"Excuse me?"

"Yes, sir?"

"I'm looking for an employee who helped me last night at the tables. Name was Glenn. I'd like to give him a tip."

Before the guard could answer, a waitress carrying a tray walked up and patted the guard's shoulder. She pointed into the center of the tables.

"Nut job over there, baseball cap with the sling, grabbed my arm plenty rough."

"Just a minute, sir," the security guard said as he followed the waitress.

Travis watched the waitress point to a man in the crowd. He clenched his fists tight.

It was the man who had stood up for Nikki at the diner.

***

Nikki leaned on the white railing of the veranda and looked down at the flowers poking up out of the grass by the creek. She sucked the last of the melted ice cream from the bottom of the sugar cone before biting off a chunk of it. It had to be close to eight by now.

She walked further down the veranda while finishing the cone. She approached the end of the line and was about to enter the double doors back inside when something familiar caught her eye from the end of the veranda.

The section of parking lot visible in the distance was largely full and contained a mix of vehicles including tour buses and RVs parked together. One familiar motorhome faced her direction. It had a bunk above a van cab. It had a cat staring out from a small window.

Nikki walked up closer to the thick railing and squeezed it tight. She squinted at the motorhome.

He's here! He didn't call, he came!

She spun around and pushed though the double doors into the interior hallway circling the hotel. She raced past the administrative offices and a gift shop before arriving back at the ice-cream parlor. A quick turn and she was through a wide entryway and under the dome once again.

She stopped and leaned on the end of a roulette table to catch her breath. Her excitement bubbled over into a wide smile in anticipation of finding Matt.

Nikki stood on her tiptoes and scanned the casino area for Matt until her eyes landed on the one man she never wanted to see again.

64

DAY 139 – Cannonsburg, MI

Kevin squeezed between the tightly packed dining tables on his way to an open barstool. The tavern seemed to be a family place, not the lowbrow establishment he'd expected. There was a wide age range of customers sitting at tables and at the bar, everything from elderly couples to college students to young parents struggling to control kids.

He plopped down on a barstool. It had been a long drive to get there, and he wondered if coming to Cannonsburg was a wild-goose chase. The matchbook he'd found under the refrigerator in Cincy could have been there for some time, maybe even long before Cecilimate had been sold out of that office.

He cracked a peanut open as an animated bartender with a handlebar moustache headed his way.

"Welcome, my friend. Harry's the name and beer is my game."

"I can see that," Kevin said.

The large selection beckoned from the shelf behind the bar. He spied his favorite just as Harry tossed a coaster on the bar.

"What can I getcha?"

"You know, a bottle of Grolsch sounds good."

"Solid choice."

Stewart Crites approached from across the room and snapped his fingers. He arrived behind Kevin just as two plainclothes Navy Seals rose from a corner table and walked towards the bar. Stewart sat down on the empty stool next to Kevin.

"Harry, I'll have what he's having," Stewart said.

Harry pointed a finger at Kevin.

"This here is a man I can respect, Stewie. He went with Grolsch," Harry said.

He bounded away to retrieve the beers, and Kevin turned to the man the bartender called Stewie. He was lanky and looked almost frail, but Kevin could tell he knew how to handle himself.

"Someone would like to buy you that beer," Stewart said.

"I hope she's single," Kevin said.

"Not unless Doctor Kearns has a daughter to spare."

The Navy Seals inched closer on each side of Kevin. Stewart looked back to the booth. Kevin followed the man's eyes to find Wade Kearns standing across the room beside an older man. Both stared directly at him.

Harry hummed a tune and dropped off the bottles of beer.

Kevin turned back to face his beer and rubbed his hands together. His mind raced.

So much for a wild-goose chase. Wade was in on it all along! And I told Erin to call Wade!

He felt hands rummaging across his torso. The Navy Seals were quietly patting him down, and he let them. He needed to buy whatever time he could for Erin's sake. One of the men nodded at Stewart.

"Not armed. I'm impressed."

"I'm on vacation."

Stewart pointed at the beer bottle.

"Pick it up."

"Sorry, I have a drinking problem. I'm slow."

"Pick it up. Doctor Kearns wants to talk outside."

Kevin remained completely still on the barstool until a knifepoint in his side prodded him. He picked up the beer and swallowed half of it.

"Maybe I should stay and have another."

Stewart slapped cash on the bar.

"Next time. Get up."

Another upward jab with the knife had Kevin standing. He took another swig. Stewart motioned towards the back of the dining room. One Navy Seal draped an arm around Kevin's shoulders, while the other poked the knife in his side again. Kevin moved carefully forward following Stewart. Wade came across the room and stood in front of the swinging doors to the kitchen.

Kevin kept his eyes fixed ahead, ignoring Wade's immediate presence. He drained the rest of the beer right in front of Wade and handed him the empty bottle without looking him in the face.

***

Erin fidgeted in the front seat. She stared at her cellphone, watching the time closely as the four-minute mark approached. She looked over her shoulder towards the front door hoping Kevin would emerge.

A leafy branch pushed by a breeze tickled the windshield, startling her. Her fingers nervously played with the dangling car keys. Four minutes and thirty seconds since Kevin went in. She turned the key and the engine idled.

Did he lose track of time?

His instructions were perfectly clear. Leave after five minutes.

"Damnit!"

Erin stuffed her phone back in her purse and switched the ignition off. She got out of the car and slammed the door shut. She looped her purse over her shoulder. Her heart pounded in her chest, and her stomach was in knots. She wasn't trained for this sort of thing. He had instructed her to leave to protect her. But it just didn't feel right to simply drive off without him, without Kevin.

Outside lights came on behind the tavern, illuminating the rear of the gravel parking lot. Erin reacted to the glow and turned in time to view two men pushing Kevin into a windowless van with Wade Kearns following close behind.

Wade Kearns? Here? Oh, no, please no!

She quickly crouched down, pressed her back hard against the car door, and tried not to hyperventilate. Erin closed her eyes and clasped both hands over her mouth as the van crunched past her and out onto Cannonsburg Road.

65

DAY 139 – French Lick, IN

Matt wandered through the middle of the gaming area trying to decide whom to ask next about Jill or her boyfriend. He approached the side of a blackjack table where a stern-faced woman dealt cards to a full table.

"Excuse me, miss."

"You can't stand there, sir," the dealer said.

Her eyes remained focused on her players.

"I have a quick question."

"Sir, you have to move around and wait for a seat. I can't have you there."

A hand landed on Matt's shoulder. He turned to find a solid security guard standing behind him.

"Please step over here, sir," the guard said.

"It's okay, I'm just looking for someone."

The guard directed him away from the table to an open area.

"It's not okay. You can ask me whatever you want, but it has to be outside."

"She works here. Jill somebody."

"This way, please," the guard said while placing a hand on Matt's back.

"I need to find her--"

The guard's hand moved from Matt's back to grasp his upper arm. He pulled Matt forward.

"Let's go, sir."

"Glenn! He's her boyfriend."

"Wait till we're outside, please."

Matt tried to scan the casino area for any clue before being ushered all the way outside.

The ornate light fixtures on the walls suddenly came on. The fading glow of a spectacular sunset was all that remained of the day's natural light filtering through the sixteen arching skylights overhead.

***

Nikki quivered as she hid behind an overweight elderly couple playing roulette. When the wall lights came on it became perfectly clear who the man was.

Travis!

Her eyes searched the crowded casino for Matt but found Glenn first. He noticed her and waved, motioning her to come over to his table. Nikki didn't respond in kind.

She stayed focused on Travis. He was staring at something, but she couldn't see what. Nikki moved around the roulette table to get a better view.

A security guard pushing on Matt!

She had to help him and stood up. A deep popping sound echoed in the atrium just as Nikki moved out into the open.

***

At first Glenn wasn't distracted by the odd sound and assumed that it likely came from a tipped-over barstool bouncing on the tiled floor at the café across the atrium. Additional popping sounds grew louder, and Glenn realized they weren't emanating from a horizontal location but a vertical one, above.

He followed the sound overhead and looked up at the dome but could barely see the growing deflection between two of the old trusses straining to hold the weight of a newly installed concert lighting bar. A half-inch gap between brackets was all that was needed to release the first section of glass from a large skylight.

He watched as waitresses stopped in their tracks, gamblers looked up from their cards, and dealers shrugged at each other, all wondering where the sound was coming from. Above them, the first 10X3' pane of glass from a skylight fell free, hitting the concert lighting bar and shattering. Those who saw it happen had scant time to cower or dive under a table. Everyone else froze.

"Look out!" someone yelled.

Glass chunks of varying sizes rained down on three tables at the edge of the gaming area opposite Glenn. People were knocked off chairs and onto the floor. Pieces of glass bounced high off the tables before landing on the injured scattered about the floor. Women screamed as blood oozed from sliced arms and legs. Those unaffected by the initial carnage scrambled to run for the exits as additional screeching of metal vibrated in the dome. Some patrons tempted fate and stayed put, plucking chips off the floor rather than flee.

Glenn rushed up to Nikki and grabbed her arm.

"This way!"

Nikki fought off his grasp as she watched a red-faced Travis deliberately walk across the chaotic area towards Matt and the security guard, hunkering on their knees together beside a table.

Glenn looked up as the metal frame holding the concert light bar squealed for the last time and snapped a soldered joint at one end. The end of the long lighting bar swung through a full 180 degrees and slammed into an adjacent skylight. Glass exploded above him.

He pulled on Nikki, but she scrambled away from him as large pieces of broken glass landed hard on nearby tables, forcing him to take cover. He shielded his eyes as he watched her head directly for a large man running between the tables.

66

DAY 139 – Cannonsburg, MI

Erin cowered between the parked cars for another minute after the van passed by. Her swirling mind slowly calmed down enough to think strategically again. She knew she had to act, and fast. Saving herself first gave her the only chance to find Kevin.

But how? Do what?

Hide. She had to get somewhere safe and think.

Wade! He's been the internal problem all along!

Her thoughts jumped between intense anger and fear for her own life. She quickly peeked above the car door and didn't see anyone in the parking lot. She prayed Wade and his men didn't know she was there with Kevin and wouldn't be looking for her. With luck, her recent resignation from the law judge office would keep her off their radar.

Her eyes searched the shadows of the parking lot again. A father corralled two small boys down the front steps and into the back seat of a car near the entrance.

She knew Wade and his sinister team would be back. They would search the car, Kevin's rental car. Her fingerprints were all over it. Erin opened the door and climbed back into the car. She unwrapped the scarf from around her neck and wiped down the interior as best she could. There wasn't time to do a perfect job. She found the button to pop the trunk open, then wiped off the keys hanging from the steering column.

Erin jumped out of the car and opened the trunk with the scarf. She lifted her small suitcase out and closed the lid with her elbow. She jogged out to the curb, bouncing the roller bag across the rough gravel. Diagonally across the street stood a large bronze giraffe in front of the Grist Mill Gas Station and Mini-Mart.

She dashed across empty Cannonsburg Road, watching over her shoulder for movement at the Honey Creek Inn. She pushed through the door of the mini-mart to find the cashier, a white-haired woman, holding a book of crossword puzzles.

"Can I get a cab around here?" Erin blurted out.

"Yes, but might take a little bit."

"I'm in a hurry. Is there a bus or something?"

"Nope. Not out here," the woman said, noticing Erin's suitcase. "Trouble at home?"

Erin followed the woman's lead.

"I need to leave, get to Chicago, as cheaply as I can."

The woman picked up the phone and dialed a taxi company from a handwritten list of numbers on the wall.

"Best way to go, bus or Amtrak from downtown Grand Rapids," she said.

Erin grabbed a few comfort-food items displayed on the counter. A dinner of mixed nuts, Twinkies, and a Diet Coke would have to do. She dug cash out of her purse, but the woman waved her off from paying.

"Yes. The Grist Mill. Cannonsburg. I'm the owner. First driver to get here gets a free deli sandwich, a soda, and six-pack for later. No, no joke. Seven minutes? Yes. Get 'em rolling! Thank you."

"Thanks so much," Erin said.

"Glad to help, my dear."

Erin pulled her suitcase out the door and looked around the corner of the mini-mart towards The Honey Creek Inn. There were folks on the front porch smoking and an ugly car out front but otherwise calm. She turned and sat on a bench facing the gas pumps.

She opened the Twinkies package and put one in her mouth. She then checked the supply of cash in her purse. A little over a hundred bucks. One last look at her cell-phone for messages confirmed no calls from Kevin. She powered it off and decided to dispose of it later.

Erin stared at the small bag of Cecilimate pills Kevin had given her. Plenty of people had died actually taking the drug, others by just being associated with it. She prayed Kevin hadn't joined the list.

They would hold Kevin, wouldn't they? Learn what he knew. He was valuable.

She started on the second Twinkie and enjoyed washing it down with the soda. A plan came together in her mind. She knew where she could go and be safe for a while.

Erin jumped to her feet as a cab suddenly screeched into the parking lot, just missing the gas pumps. An elderly man opened the door and got out. He stood proudly by his rusty sedan. The cashier emerged holding a grocery bag.

"Am I the first?" the driver asked.

"Yes, you are. Take her downtown," the cashier said.

The driver put the grocery bag on the front seat and then opened the trunk. Erin turned to the cashier. She didn't expect the hug.

"Good luck to you, and stay safe."

"I will, and thank you."

67

DAY 139 – French Lick, IN

Nikki watched the security guard stand in horror at the scene unfolding on the casino floor. The guard looked up at the ceiling just as Travis barreled into him, knocking the man backwards over a blackjack table with one swat of a massive arm. Travis smiled as he looked down on Matt.

Nikki scrambled forward against the screaming tide of people racing for an exit. She fought through the masses, catching momentary sight of Travis bending down and pulling Matt up from under a table by his collar. She was ten feet away.

Travis reared back to strike Matt with his thick fist.

"REMEMBER ME, COP?"

"TRAVIS!" Nikki yelled.

Travis stopped his backswing and turned towards Nikki. A large pane of glass fell to shatter atop a gaming table separating them.

Matt turned his face away as the glass exploded. He reached for a stick with a metal head lying across a craps table. Matt feebly swung the craps rake at Travis's head, only to have the big man block the attempt, snapping the stick in two.

There was no defending himself against the coming punch. Matt took a full uppercut into his stomach, knocking him backwards and voiding his lungs of air. He skidded across broken glass as shards poked through his clothing. Travis walked towards a gasping Matt.

Nikki flung herself at him.

"You asshole!"

He swatted her away like a fly. She tumbled to a stop near a roulette table. Her hand found the splintered end of the broken craps rake on the ground.

The roof truss holding the end of the lighting bar groaned with the swinging movement. A large can light with a red lens dropped free, smashing onto a table not far away. More glass panels popped free of their frames. Matt struggled for air and tried to crawl under a table away from the madman coming at him.

Nikki appeared behind Travis holding the jagged stick. She thrust it as hard as she could between Travis's shoulder blades. He turned around, his hands grasping behind his back at the protruding stick. Travis finally found it and pulled it free, flinging it away. Nikki barely ducked under a swinging fist from Travis and dove under the table with Matt.

As she spun around next to him, her black hair flung wildly, exposing the snakehead tattoo on the back of her neck. A flash of light filled Matt's blinking eyes as the mirror-image from his recurring dream unfolded in front him. Nikki clung to him as they watched Travis growl and turn towards them.

Matt and Nikki cringed as the screeching squeal of metal tearing apart overhead roared through the atrium. They closed their eyes.

Travis lunged at them as the ceiling debris arrived from above, accompanied by a thunderstorm of glass. The concert lighting bar landed hard between them. Metal racking and glass pounded the table protecting Matt and Nikki, collapsing two legs on one end. A bloody hand reached under the table and grabbed at Nikki's leg.

"Go! Now!" Nikki said as she kicked at Travis's hand.

Matt squirmed out first, pushed by Nikki. They sprang to their feet and stumbled with the screaming masses towards an exit.

***

Nikki did her best to hold Matt upright as they were jostled along by the crowd flooding out through the lobby and onto the veranda. Her eyes met Glenn's, and he pushed through the stream of people to reach them.

"Jesus, Nikki!"

Glenn put his arm around Matt and helped steer them both to the railing lined with the injured being tended to by frantic hotel staff.

"Sit him over here. I'll get help!"

"NO!" Matt blurted out. "No help."

"Come on! He's coming! Hang onto me," Nikki said.

She ducked her shoulder under Matt's good arm.

"He's hurt, Nikki. Stay here!" Glenn implored.

Glenn took off and disappeared into the crowd. Sirens wailed in the distance. Uninjured patrons streamed off the veranda and down the front steps. People twirled in disbelief on the red-brick road in front of the hotel.

"This way. The RV. Quick!" Nikki said.

"I don't know. I can't--"

"Come on!"

Nikki watched over her shoulder for Travis as she fought to keep Matt upright and moving forward across the veranda. Nikki guided him down the wide front steps. The sidewalk and brick street were covered with stunned people, some sitting on the ground, while others circulated through the crowd looking for loved ones.

They made a sharp left at the bottom of the staircase as the first police cars and ambulances arrived. Nikki pulled Matt into the undergrowth at the base of the veranda. His legs were failing him, and she worked hard to keep him moving, weaving them in between bushes and trees of the planter bed and towards the parking lot.

She checked Matt over with her hand. He winced when she touched his side.

"Ribs maybe," she said.

"I can't make it."

"Not much further, you can do it!"

"I don't--"

Matt stumbled to his knees, and Nikki yanked him back to his feet.

"Don't gimme that! Just one foot in front of the other. That's it. We'll make it."

68

DAY 139 – Rockford, MI

Solomon Carr walked down the narrow concrete hallway with Twig by his side. He didn't much like being underground in the guts of the myriad research departments and labs that made up the heart of the Office of Terminal Resonance known as Otter One. The thought of sixty feet of earth and concrete overhead bothered him on occasion. He preferred to remain in his farmhouse and hold any necessary meetings there if at all possible.

This evening was different. Wade's man who had casually walked into The Honey Creek Inn had to be dealt with in a timely manner. Wade had clearly underestimated Kevin Sharpe, and Erin Owens was still at large. It was a serious breach of faith to allow any unclassified subordinate to get this close to Otter One without proper controls in place, a situation that needed to be quickly remedied.

"The failsafe is operational?" Solomon asked.

"Yes, sir."

"Is he awake?"

"Coming out of it. Anesthesia should wear off completely in fifteen minutes."

At the end of the hall, Stewart Crites stood with crossed arms next to a metal door.

"He's ready, sir." Stewart said.

"Any news on the girl?" Solomon said.

"Nothing yet. She was with him there, at the tavern, and definitely on the flight from Dulles with Sharpe."

"I have assets quietly searching Cannonsburg," Twig said.

"I want the loop closed on this mess before midnight. She knows too much. Use all available resources to find her."

Stewart nodded and walked away with phone in hand.

***

Kevin leaned forward on the recovery-room table and stared at the pattern of the floor tile. He was having a hard time focusing. The gridlines on the floor looked blurry. His shirt was off, and he didn't know why. Wade Kearns stood nearby next to a man in a white coat, a doctor in his fifties. Both Wade and the doctor stood stoic. A younger male nurse in blue scrubs approached and wrapped something around Kevin's arm. His blood pressure was being checked. He squinted at the wall clock to read the time.

A missing hour I don't remember.

The heavy door pushed open. An old man in glasses lumbered in, followed by a thick man dressed in black and holding a gun by his side. The man in black closed the door and locked it. The sound reverberated in the room, jostling Kevin to lift his groggy head.

"Mister Sharpe?" the old man said.

Kevin didn't respond. His glazed-over eyes tried to focus on the man's large nose. The doctor stepped forward and checked Kevin's pulse with cold fingers.

"Mister Sharpe?"

"I hear you," Kevin whispered.

"Good, very good. You are a special man, Mister Sharpe. The first non-volunteer to join our ranks. My name is Solomon Carr. I'm the one in charge of this private sandbox of an agency. My associate Twig here will soon become your best friend."

"I'm not joining anything."

"Ah, but you already have, and your friend will too."

"What?"

"He means Erin Owens," Wade said.

"Miz Owens will be found, and you can help her greatly by telling us where she is."

They don't have her. Thank God she didn't call Wade!

Kevin sat up straight and rubbed a sore spot he found at the base of his neck above his sternum. A round Band-Aid covered the area.

"She's in Washington," Kevin said.

"Kevin, we know Erin was with you just a couple hours ago," Wade said. "She'll survive the night if you help us bring her in."

"You'd go that far, Wade?"

"He has no choice, and neither do you," Solomon said. "That tender spot you're touching? Yes, there, that one on your neck. That means you're mine now. I control your life."

Kevin slowly lowered himself off the table and stood upright while holding onto the edge.

"Bullshit. You'd have to kill me before I work for you."

"If it comes to that, I will oblige you. It would be a shame. You do have talents I'd like to utilize but--"

Solomon looked down at his wristwatch before facing the dial towards Kevin. He pushed a button on the side, and the dial changed into a screen. Kevin watched him push his thumbprint onto the screen. He then scrolled though the listed names, stopping on the newest addition to the list, Kevin Sharpe.

"You see, Mister Sharpe, all of my team members have what you now have, an implanted failsafe device that allows me to track any individual's movements under my employ. It also has the ability to terminate any team member within roughly thirty seconds or so."

Kevin held tight onto the table edge. His legs still felt like rubber. The man called Twig raised his gun and pointed it at him.

"You're bluffing."

"I don't bluff, Mister Sharpe. Not with the future of our country and the civilized world on the line. What you've stumbled into has vast consequences for humanity that demands secrecy at the highest levels. I myself have a failsafe device inside me that only the President of the United States controls."

Wade reached out and touched Kevin's arm.

"This is bigger than all of us," Wade said. "I didn't know these drug cases would be tied to this. But they are, and you're in it now, deep. You have to help us find this Cecilimate drug and continue your investigation."

What the hell is going on? This can't be real!

"I don't know what kind of game this is, but I'm not playing. I'm calling your bluff, whoever you are. I'm going out that door. Have your man shoot me down if you must."

Kevin took a wobbly step before grabbing the table again.

"Just a minute, Mister Sharpe."

Solomon started fiddling with his watch. Twig kept his gun trained on Kevin's chest.

"Wade, I believe your Mister Sharpe will fully appreciate this demonstration."

Solomon scrolled down the list of names on his watch. He pressed a button.

"There," Solomon said.

Kevin watched as the doctor and the male nurse exchanged worried glances. Twig's aim remained fixed on Kevin.

"I'm sorry," Solomon said to the group, "but Mister Sharpe needs to understand the seriousness of this matter to his country. He is a vital link to our ultimate goal."

Wade stepped forward and pointed at the two medical staff members.

"Solomon, this, this is not necessary," Wade said.

The doctor calmly sat down in a chair and lowered his head.

"I understand," said the doctor.

The young male nurse jumped forward.

"Sir, I've done nothing wrong! Please!"

Solomon did not acknowledge the nurse. No one in the room spoke further. Kevin wondered what was happening. He ran his fingers over the Band-Aid on his neck.

He looked at Twig by the door. The man in black cocked the handgun.

Without a sound, a flash of panic spread across the face of Doctor Wade Kearns. His eyes grew wide and his eyelids began to flutter. He stumbled backwards against the wall.

"Solomon!" Wade gasped.

Solomon approached Wade and placed a hand on his shoulder.

"I'm sorry, my friend, but you brought this problem to our doorstep, and you know the rules."

The doctor stood up and helped sit Wade down on the floor. Kevin slumped to the floor opposite Wade in disbelief.

This can't be!

Wade's empty eyes stared at Kevin. He managed a few last words.

"Do what he says--"

Wade Kearns closed his eyes. The doctor helped him slide sideways down the wall and onto his shoulder as a last breath left his lips. Kevin turned away.

"Sharpe! Look at me!" Solomon boomed, his face flushing red. Kevin slowly looked up at Solomon.

"You *will* find what I need. You will get me some of the drug, and you will bring me this Matt Sizemore!"

69

DAY 139 – French Lick, IN

Nikki held Matt around his waist as she eyed the parking lot up ahead. He was breathing heavily, leaning on her hard. The sun had gone down, and the tall lights in the lot were on. Twenty yards of open grass separated them from their spot in the bushes and the big parking lot.

"You ready?" Nikki said.

"No."

"Too bad."

Nikki pulled Matt along and out into the open. He struggled to keep his feet moving. She looked over her shoulder at the flashing lights of emergency vehicles in the distance, all crowded around the front of the hotel. The veranda was bright, and she saw paramedics working through the congregating mass of people.

They arrived at the edge of the parking lot. Matt braced himself against a car. All that remained were six double rows of parked cars to get past to reach his motorhome. Nikki pushed him upright.

"Come on. We're close."

Nikki helped Matt hobble between the parked cars. He banged his sling on a side mirror and twisted his face in pain.

"Jesus!"

They reached the third row in, and Nikki could see Bob's face in the window above the cab. She looked back towards the hotel. A flash of fear brought tears to her eyes before she pushed Matt hard on the back.

"Go, go, go!"

***

One eye was all Travis needed to see what he was doing. The other was swollen shut. He forced his way through the crowd on the porch and stumbled across the veranda to an open spot at the railing. He could make out two figures in the distance squeezing between parked cars.

Travis hurdled the railing and landed awkwardly in the planter bed eight feet below. His ankle gave way, and he fell into a prickly bush. The sprain didn't stop him from getting up and limping across the grass towards the parking lot.

***

Nikki panicked as she pushed on Matt from behind. Travis was at the edge of the parking lot and gaining fast.

Keys! She needed the keys!

Matt staggered out from between the last set of cars and into the wide drive aisle in front of the oversize vehicles. He couldn't catch himself and collapsed onto the pavement.

Nikki jumped on him and dug in his pockets.

"The gun! Where is it!"

"Backpack."

She found the keys. Nikki grabbed the back of Matt's collar and tried to drag him across the ground towards the motorhome. A bloodied Travis emerged from between the cars. Nikki sobbed while pulling on Matt.

"Travis! Stop!"

He was upon her before she could move away. Travis grabbed her arm, turned, and kicked Matt in the stomach, rolling him closer to the motorhome. Nikki flipped the keys onto the ground near Matt. Matt pushed the keys forward on the ground as he crawled alongside the motorhome.

Travis spun Nikki around and raised his fist. His hand wobbled and he lowered it by his side. He clutched her shoulders and shook her violently.

"Why! Nikki? Why?"

Travis pushed her hard into the grille of Matt's motorhome. Nikki groaned and held her elbow as she watched Travis lean to the side and look at a feeble Matt reaching up from the ground for the RV door handle. He turned his attention back to Nikki.

"It didn't have to be this way! You ruined everything!"

Nikki cowered against the bumper.

"Travis, no! Please! No!"

As Travis stepped back and prepared to strike Nikki, the sound of an accelerating engine filled the drive aisle. The speeding front end of a pickup truck came into view and slammed into Travis. The impact slapped the side of his head hard on the hood, and his body spun sideways, pitching him directly into the grille of a parked tour bus. He crumpled face down to the pavement and didn't move.

The pickup truck pulling a travel trailer continued past before braking hard to a stop further down the drive aisle.

Nikki saw Donna jump out of the pickup and run towards her. Tears filled her eyes.

"Oh, God! Donna!"

"Baby, baby. It's okay now."

Donna lifted her off the ground, and they hugged each other tight. Nikki watched over Donna's shoulder at Travis. Blood was pooling by his neck. Nikki broke free and ran to Matt. Donna followed her.

"I saw him, and I just snapped," Donna said.

"Thank God you showed up!"

"Is the man okay?"

"Not really. Help me get him inside," Nikki said.

Nikki took the keys from Matt and tried to help him up.

"We need to get to D.C.," Matt mumbled.

"Right now, we gotta get out of here."

Nikki unlocked the door, and Donna helped lift Matt into the motorhome. They laid him out on the floor. Bob jumped down onto the table.

"The man. We need to find him. He knows," Matt said.

"We will, we will. Just rest."

Matt pointed at the backpack.

"His name is in there, in the notebook."

Nikki reached for the backpack and tossed the notebooks on the dinette table as Bob scurried away. Donna wedged a cushion under Matt's head. Nikki unrolled the gun out of the old sweatshirt. Donna quickly swiped the gun out of her hand and rushed out the door. Nikki chased her outside.

"Donna!"

She watched as Donna slowly walked up to Travis's immobile body. His right leg pointed in an awkward direction below the knee. She aimed the gun at the back of his head.

"I want to so bad," Donna said.

Nikki put her hand on Donna's arm.

"There's no time!"

Donna didn't put the gun down.

"I was so scared for you. The voicemail message at Maybelle's said your sister was here. He beat her up to find you. Did you know that?"

"Yes, Yes. It's over now! We need to go! Follow me south out of town. We'll sort this out somewhere."

Donna let her wrist go limp, and she handed the gun to Nikki. They both turned and ran a few paces towards the motorhome.

Nikki stopped.

This is Travis, remember? It ends here.

She turned and pointed the gun at Travis's back from fifteen feet away. Nikki turned her head as she pulled the trigger.

70

DAY 143 – Natchez, MS

The photo of the platinum-blonde with too much eye makeup stared back at him from the colorful real-estate flyer open on his lap. He looked out over the steering wheel of his mint condition 1967 Camaro SS and then checked the rearview mirror. No cars were in sight. He settled back into the bucket seat. She was late for the tour, but it didn't really matter. He had nowhere else to be anyway.

He tossed the flyer onto the passenger seat. There was no getting into the property without her. He turned on the car radio and found a southern rock station. He rolled down the car window and peered at the place for sale.

The online pictures had oversold the situation. The clearly vacant brick box of a bar and small restaurant had been marginally added to the front corner of an old colonial home, a former bed and breakfast, that was in need of some serious restoration.

The setting provided the real value. The nice spot, a tree-filled corner lot on the bluff north of Natchez, faced west across the Mississippi River. He figured he was paying for the view. The pictures of amazing sunsets on the internet listing had sold him.

Randy Knox needed the extra time before the realtor lady arrived. He opened his leather briefcase and sifted through the half-dozen available passports and support documents in a manila envelope. Four were United States passports, plus one Canadian and one British. He had to pick a new identity before formally introducing himself to the realtor and going through the business steps of making an offer. He'd need to open a bank account, rent a temporary place to live, and fully set up shop in his newly chosen locale.

Randy opted to avoid keeping up an accent and picked a U.S. passport. If a David Carlson from Cleveland could ultimately make a go of it here, maybe someday the locals would call him Mayor.

71

DAY 143 – Rockville, MD

Kevin Sharpe stood alone in a corner of the vast employee cafeteria, soaking up the midday view of the Maryland hills. He rolled a toothpick around his mouth, moving it from side to side with his tongue. The sunshine made the grass around the building grounds glisten even though dark gray storm clouds were forming to the west. He had enjoyed this view many times, but it was different now. What he thought lay beyond those hills, beyond the horizon, beyond his understanding, was something he couldn't quite comprehend yet.

After two intense days of indoctrination in the ultimate reason for Otter One's existence, Kevin still found the concepts hard to fathom. The need for secrecy was understandable. What if a life continuum does exist? Is reincarnation real? Is seeing the future or reaching into the past possible? All these thoughts raised even bigger questions in his mind.

If there was a way to undo his new knowledge, he would do it. He didn't want to be part of this. He wanted to go back to his old life no matter how complicated it had become. Prison would be safer than this.

Wade was killed right in front of me!

There was no way out, no way to get rid of Solomon's heavy pressure and his wristwatch of death unless he could find the elusive Mr. Sizemore. He didn't want to even think about what would happen if he did find the man.

Kevin's cellphone rang in his pocket. He cringed at the screen but had to answer the call from Solomon Carr.

"Sir?"

"Mister Sharpe, you're going to Memphis. A body has been found."

"I see."

"It's not Sizemore, from what Twig tells me, so you have no immediate health concerns to trouble you. Likely the other Shelby brother. The body is being transported to Otter One for an autopsy."

"Any of the drug found?"

"No, but there was a lab in the basement of the house that I want you to examine. A car will pick you up at eight p.m. tonight. A plane is waiting at Camp David. A man named Dobson will be your contact in Memphis. He has a team posing as DEA agents securing the house."

"At least there's time to pack."

"Pack heavy. I want you in Pine Bluff after Memphis. Shelby got the compound from somewhere. Somebody delivered it to him, wanted him to test it, and I want to know whom."

"Understood."

"I hope you do."

Solomon hung up on Kevin.

And so it begins. A nice, tight leash around the neck.

Kevin plucked the toothpick out of his mouth and flicked it onto the floor, even though a trashcan was close by. He contemplated returning to the buffet for another cheeseburger but thought better of it. There were files to review in his new office, covering Sizemore's trail across the Midwest before he could head back to his apartment and pack.

Kevin caught a glimpse of Becky's lemon-yellow dress as she swirled into the doorway of the cafeteria. She saw him in the corner and swished her way over with her hands held behind her back.

"Been looking for you," Becky said.

"That's nice to hear for once."

Her expression made it clear this wasn't a purely social call.

"I'm sorry about Doctor Kearns. I liked him. I know he was your friend, and he was fond of you."

"Thank you. Pretty terrible."

"He seemed, well, you just don't expect a massive heart attack would take him. And at a convention in Chicago, too."

"I didn't expect it, either."

"Are you taking over for him?"

"I don't know. Not up to me. You'll probably find out before I do."

Becky brought out a piece of paper from behind her back and showed it to Kevin.

"What's this?"

"Just a message for you, a rather odd one. Hertz wants you to call them. That's the number. Sounds like you left something in your rental car."

"Nothing odd about that," Kevin said.

"Well, they said the package from the car was safe and sound and also that the five-minute rule had been broken. What's that supposed to mean?"

Kevin tried not to react to the news.

"Hmmm--not sure, but I'll find out. Thanks."

He took the piece of paper from Becky's hand and studied the phone number while holding back a smile. Becky waited for a moment before she frowned and spun away and disappeared out into the sea of cubicles. Kevin pocketed the note.

Erin is safe!

72

DAY 143 – Bowling Green, KY

Matt wrote out his final thoughts about Day 142 in his notebook as Bob the cat sat on the dinette table and looked out the window of the RV. He closed the notebook and studied the Niagara Falls picture on the cover for a moment before pushing it aside. He joined Bob in looking out over the big Walgreens parking lot across from the campus of Western Kentucky University. He petted Bob on the back.

"They'll be back soon. Any time now."

Matt wondered what was keeping them, too. Nikki and Donna had ventured off to the school's library to find any information online about Kevin Sharpe before they pushed on to Washington to search him out.

He returned to his notebook while Bob maintained an anxious vigil. A few final thoughts came to mind to record covering the last few days. He was still sore from Travis's beating, and the shoulder was plenty stiff. At least they had found a quiet place to park for a few days behind an old barn on an abandoned farm. The rural location had kept the nightmares to a minimum and allowed him to get some relatively decent rest. Nikki and Donna had needed a break too, after all that had happened.

Matt groaned as he slid out of the booth seat and walked up to the front of the motorhome. He snagged a folding map from the dashboard. He returned to the dinette and unfolded a map of Kentucky and Tennessee. A route to Washington using back roads had to be planned.

Bob suddenly popped up to all fours and held his tail high. Matt looked out the window and saw Nikki and Donna running across the parking lot carrying sheets of paper, their faces tight with worry.

Nikki jumped through the door first and made a beeline for Matt's kitchen drawer full of cash. She jerked it open and pulled out wads of bills, tossing them on the open map.

"What's all this?" Matt asked.

"They know! They know about you and Nikki!" Donna gasped from behind.

"She needs cash to find Kevin's sister! She can't leave a trail!" Nikki yelled.

"Tell me!"

Nikki handed Matt the sheets of paper and plopped onto the booth seat across from him. She started smoothing out the wadded-up bills and made a stack. Matt looked over a printed article from the *Washington Post*.

"That's him. The man I saw," Matt said.

"Says he was fired from the FBI last year for dating a spy," Nikki said. "We also found a news video of his sister standing up for him, saying her brother didn't know the woman was a spy. Lives in Columbus, Ohio. Donna is going to go find her so we can contact Kevin."

Matt was confused.

"He's an FBI agent right now, I mean I saw him. He had a partner with him in Cincy. The man there said he was meeting a federal agent."

"I'm sure the sister will know," Donna said.

"We figured to use Father Frank to communicate. It's all worked out," Nikki added.

Matt looked at the next sheet of paper. He quickly understood why Nikki was wound up like a top.

"Got it all worked out, eh?"

The police in Evansville had found a dead man in Jill's crime-scene apartment. The prime suspects were Matt Sizemore, aka Alex Trotter, and a Nicole Cook. Worst of all, authorities from New Mexico to Iowa and now Indiana had just asked the federal authorities for help.

"You guys have to hide somewhere," Donna said.

"I can't disappear," Matt said. "I don't have much time. Sharpe can help me. I can feel it."

"We have to hide! Let Donna find him," Nikki implored.

Matt stood up and surveyed the motorhome.

"Bringing in the feds changes things. We'll need new identities, and maybe a new rig."

"How do we--"

Matt cut Nikki off.

"I can handle identities. I have a way to do that. You two can chase the sister if you want, but I'm going to

Washington while there's still time. Sharpe is there, and I'll find him."

Matt took the map off the table and slowly walked up to the front of the motorhome. Nikki stared at his back with her hands on her hips.

"Jesus! You really think I'm not going with you?"

Nikki turned to Donna and handed her the cash. She hugged her tight and whispered in her ear.

"Father Frank, remember. Use one of those prepaid cellphones."

"Yes, honey. Take care of him, and be careful."

Donna rubbed her eyes before stepping out of the motorhome. Nikki closed the door, picked Bob up off the table, and put him up on the bunk above the cab. Matt started to work his way into the driver's seat. Nikki grabbed him around the waist.

"No, you don't. You're over there. I'm driving."

Nikki directed Matt into the passenger seat. He settled in and opened the map on his lap. Nikki sat down, turned the key, and the engine sputtered to life. Matt looked over the article from the *Washington Post* and studied Kevin Sharpe's face.

"Before we go, there are some ground rules," Nikki said.

Matt turned towards her. She was smiling.

"One. There will be *zero* complaints about my driving. Two. You're gonna eat what I tell you to eat. Number three. You're taking a shower first chance we get, and number four, don't question my loyalty."

Proclivity

Nikki leaned over the center console and planted a kiss on Matt's lips that lingered long enough for him to forget his issue with Rule Number One.

About the Author

Born in the Chicago area, Kris Kaiser currently writes from his home in Northern California. Tired of reading and watching suspense stories that bounce around the globe, he decided to write one set in interesting, little-known areas of his native Midwest.